Shamini [...] nd two children. S[...] began [...] worked at an international law [...] extensively around Asia for her work, before resigning to be a stay-at-home mum, writer, part-time lecturer and environmental activist.

Shamini also writes children's books with cultural and environ-al themes, including *Ten* and *The Seeds of Time*, as well as the a series of children's books.

Visit Shamini online:
www.shaminiflint.com
www.facebook.com/ShaminiFlintAuthor
www.twitter.com/ShaminiFlint

Praise for Shamini Flint:

[...]s impossible not to warm to Inspector Singh. We should cherish him'

Daily Mail

'An unconventional new crime hero who has the potential to be as compelling (and successful) as McCall Smith's Precious Ramotswe'

Daily Record

'It's impossible not to warm to the portly, sweating, dishevelled, wheezing Inspector Singh from the start of this delightful novel'

The Guardian

'Flint has a clear authorial voice and stands out from the crowd in the originality of this novel'

Reviewing the Evidence

Inspector Singh Investigates: A Frightfully English Execution

Shamini Flint

piatkus

PIATKUS

First published in Great Britain as a paperback original in 2016 by Piatkus

13 5 7 9 10 8 6 4 2

Copyright © 2016 by Shamini Flint

A CIP catalogue record for this book
is available from the British Library.

ISBN 978-0-349-40272-7

Typeset in Caslon by M Rules

Printed and bound in Great Britain by
Clays Ltd, St Ives plc

Papers used by Piatkus are from well-managed forests
and other responsible sources.

MIX
Paper from
responsible sources
FSC® C104740

Piatkus
An imprint of
Little, Brown Book Group
Carmelite House
50 Victoria Embankment
London EC4Y 0DZ

An Hachette UK Company
www.hachette.co.uk

www.piatkus.co.uk

'It is a far, far better thing that I do, than I have ever done; it is a far, far better rest that I go to than I have ever known.'

Charles Dickens, *A Tale of Two Cities*

PROLOGUE

'We know what we've got to do, right, lads?'

The three men around the wobbly Ikea dining table were pumped on adrenaline. They fidgeted on their three-legged stools like children after too much chocolate. Especially Ahmad. For good reason too as it was his house, his family that was asleep upstairs.

Their leader, Hassan, leaned against a wall, arms folded, the calmest among them because he had the most experience. He studied his men, his troops. There was a sameness about them. Not in their physical appearance although all three were dressed in black leather jackets and cargo pants; one was tall, good-looking, unshaven, another short, portly, gap-toothed and the third nondescript to the point of anonymity. It was their absorption in the moment, the expression on their faces and the tension across the shoulders, which created a likeness.

'How long does it have to be?' asked Ahmad.

'Two minutes.'

'Isn't that a bit short for a *Wasiya*? And the lighting in here isn't great either.'

'What does that matter? There's not much chance of a sequel to a martyrdom video, is there?'

This drew laughter from two of them and a sheepish grin from the speaker. 'Awright then, I just want it to be good. So that the family's proud of what I done.'

'They will be proud. You need have no doubt about that.'

The men wolfed down the rest of their takeaway from the Indian down the road, wiping the remnants of vindaloo with naan.

There was something valedictory about this meal because it was their last one together.

'And you're sure we have everything we need?' asked Ahmad.

'Of course.'

'Even the explosives?'

'Courtesy of the Americans,' explained Hassan. 'Their Iraqi lackeys fled so fast, they left enough ordnance to last a generation.'

'That's brilliant, man!'

Revenge with a dollop of irony was better than just revenge. Hassan allowed them a few seconds of merriment and then raised a finger.

'C'mon, let's get to work.'

On his instructions, they pushed the table against a wall. The stools were arranged in a row facing the sink. The leader produced the regulation black flag and with some difficulty, because the tape would not adhere to the wallpaper, they stuck it up as a backdrop. And then all three changed into the robes he had prepared while he went to check that the doors were

2

locked and the curtains tightly drawn. Small errors undermined big plans and Hassan was known for being meticulous, and therefore successful.

Solemnity descended.

Hassan arranged them on the stools, tall to short and then changed his mind and placed the tallest in the middle, stopped to contemplate his handiwork, and decided it would work well enough. He retrieved his iPad from the rucksack on the table. It was the latest model; funds were not a problem these days. Not with ransom payments, donations from Saudis and Qatari sheiks and oil and weapons sales on the black market. The only difficulty was getting the cash out of the Middle East and into the financial centres, freshly laundered and smelling sweet.

'All right you know what to do, left to right. Make sure you introduce yourself, they must know that the enemy is everywhere, that no one is safe from brother, neighbour, friend. And don't worry if you get it wrong, we can do it again or I can edit out any mistakes.'

'What happens if we abort?'

'Why would we do that?'

'I dunno, but shit happens, right.'

'Not when I'm in charge.'

This statement of confidence seemed to soothe Ahmad for a moment but then his head popped up again. 'If something goes wrong, this kind of thing is just evidence.'

'What is your point?' Hassan's heavy brows were lowered.

'Look, I'm in, right. I'm ready. But I don't want to be picked up one cold January morning when I ain't even done nothing yet just because of some video.'

3

The other two were watching Hassan, eyes glinting like creatures of the forest.

'I will keep the tape – it will not be released until our plans have been executed.'

'You swear it?'

'I swear it on the Holy Book.'

They all nodded; backs straightened, eyes shone, they were ready.

He held up the iPad and nodded to Ahmad to go first.

'Know without doubt that the Muslims who die due to your attacks will be in paradise. But the infidels we kill . . .'

The front door was kicked down. The men leaped to their feet as one. Hassan made a dash for the back exit but it was too late. Heavily armed men burst in, fanned out, guns trained on them with the precision of the highly trained and the highly motivated.

'Put your hands where I can see them,' barked the leader. 'You're all under arrest.'

Upstairs, a child began to cry.

Despite the presence of the armed response team, Hassan's anger was directed at his fellow conspirators.

'We have been betrayed. Which of you has let down our cause?'

Only Ahmad's eyes dropped.

CHAPTER 1

Shaheed Muhammad waited outside the kindergarten in Finsbury Park for his daughter. It was around the corner from the station and he could hear the trains rumble past. It was almost four, the end of the school day. There was a lot of laughter from within, that high-pitched, uncontrolled delight that children exhibit over small things. No doubt one of them had fallen over his feet or snorted orange juice up his nose. A teacher cajoled them to identify their lunch boxes.

'Adrian, I'm quite sure that is not yours.'

'But I like this one better.'

'It belongs to Harry.'

'But I want it.'

'We can't just take things that don't belong to us.'

Shaheed grimaced. Wasn't the correct lesson the exact opposite in this capitalist feeding frenzy masquerading as society?

A brisk breeze caused a pink plastic bag to swirl on the

quiet street and he watched it dance. A few other parents drifted up. Mostly mothers.

His Bollywood good looks: square jaw, straight nose, high cheekbones, melting brown eyes, immediately attracted a few of the women.

'Mr Shaheed, you're so helpful with Emma.' The speaker was a frumpy creature with a chubby, blond son.

'I do what I can.'

Regina, the mother of his child, his beautiful four-year-old girl, had gone back to work when Emma was not yet a year old.

'There's no rush,' he'd said. 'She needs you at home.'

'Now don't go all Indian sub-continent on me,' she said, giving him a hug.

'Women these days don't have to give up their life for a child,' she added when she sensed his hesitation.

'Isn't our life this child now?'

'I'd drive her nuts if I was at home all the time.'

Shaheed had been cajoled into agreeing that she couldn't be expected to give up her job. He stepped in, did his best for the child. He attended concerts when Regina was stuck at work, picked Emma up at nursery when his wife was running late, made himself dinner and hers too. Listened to the floorboards creak as she went straight to the spare room 'so as not to wake you', she'd say in the morning, dropping a kiss on his tousled hair as she rushed back out to work – 'Please be a dear and drop Emma at school? I have an early meeting.'

'I think you should speak to them, explain that you're … not home enough.'

'Don't be silly. I'd be out on my ear!'

6

Shaheed bit his tongue so often it had become an alternative food source.

It galled him to admit it but his mother had been right. No good came of marrying outside one's kind. They had sent him to London to wed within the community but instead he found Regina.

He cast his mind back to the conversation he'd had with his mother earlier that day. Thanks to Skype, he could see their airy Lahore home, the old furniture, everything going to seed now that his father was dead and his mother losing her strength.

'Are you not the man in this household of yours?'

'It's the twenty-first century – there's nothing wrong with helping out with the child.'

'With the child, with the housework, with the cooking – is that how I brought you up? To be a slave to a woman?'

They spoke in Urdu.

'They are all the same, the young women in that country. They have no respect for tradition, for family.'

Over his mother's shoulder he could see the row of china figurines, farmers and milkmaids, pink-cheeked and plump. He didn't have to be there to know that she would be using the fireplace to store old newspapers. He grimaced. He'd read the Urdu headlines online just before calling home. More drones. Dead civilians, dead children.

'And is this the sort of example you want for Emma?'

His mother rose to her feet with difficulty, leaning on her cane, *salwar kameez* stretched across her broad hips. She hobbled over to the dining table, picked up a plate of sweetmeats and took one, holding it up to show him.

'You are so thin, Shaheed. You must eat.'

Since he'd been a child, she would temper her criticism, show her affection, with food; a samosa or something sweet – 'Sweet desserts for a sweet boy.'

He did his best to teach Emma the ways of his home in Lahore, said to her sometimes, 'Sweet desserts for a sweet girl.'

'Then I can't eat any nasty vegetables, can I?'

'What do you mean?'

'Because I'm not a "nasty girl", am I?'

Was that sharp wit inherited from her mother?

Shaheed was dragged back to the present as the brightly painted blue front door opened and tiny tots streamed down the path.

He spotted Emma and his heart turned over. She was so beautiful. The long silky hair tied into two plaits with a fringe that brushed her eyebrows. The big brown eyes framed with dark lashes, the button nose and pink cheeks. Her sturdy form was dressed in a polka dot red dress, white leggings and a red jacket buttoned neatly down the front.

'You're picking up Emma today, Mr Shaheed?'

'Yes, her mother was held up.'

'That's all right then, it was good of you to step in.'

'I do what I can.'

He took a step forward. 'Emma?'

She flung herself into his arms and he tickled her vigorously, her shrieks drawing smiles from the other adults.

'Where's Mamma?' she asked breathlessly.

'She's busy . . .'

'She's always busy.'

'. . . so I've come to get you today.'

*

'London?'

'Yes, you can learn policing methods from English bobbies.'

This almost sounded appealing to Inspector Singh. Maybe the British police would lend him one of those big helmets to perch on top of his turban. Or he'd buy himself a deerstalker and a pipe. But not that furry egg-hat the fellows outside Buckingham Palace wore – he had some dignity.

'It's a Commonwealth task force on policing in a multi-racial, multi-religious context,' continued his superior.

Singh's face fell. 'Let me guess, you told them I was an expert?'

'Our senior man with a delicate touch . . .'

Delicate touch? He, who stepped on toes so often?

'They're sending us an expert on terrorist infiltration of in-country communities,' he continued. He clearly felt it was an exchange in which he came off the better. One overweight, opinionated policeman in exchange for Scotland Yard's best.

His subordinate pulled a face. Inspector Singh of the Singapore police had no gripe with a policeman's lot when he was demonstrating yet again that he was Singapore's finest investigator with the best solve rate on the force, a statistic that kept him in employment despite the hearty antipathy of his superiors. What he disliked was being sent on irrelevant matters to faraway countries with poor food, poor heating and strict smoking laws.

'Why me?' he asked, unable to keep the plaintive note out of his voice.

'It's not just you – policemen from other Commonwealth countries will be present too.'

'But we have nothing in common with them.'

9

'Nonsense, we share a common language, institutions and heritage.'

'Despots, extremists and bureaucrats.'

'I hope you plan to keep that opinion to yourself.'

Singh stuck out his bottom lip. 'I'm surprised they can spare their experts,' he said. The arrest of four men, caught in the midst of making suicide videos, the London Underground their target again, had been in the news for days.

'Maybe they've caught all their terrorists . . .'

Singh, familiar with the hydra-like ability of terrorist organisations to grow new heads to plan and limbs to execute those plans, shook his head.

' . . . and so they can help us catch ours.'

'Tell me the truth – why am I being punished?' he asked.

'If you must know, because of that diplomatic kerfuffle you caused in China.'

'I identified a murderer!'

'You undermined the authority of the Communist Party.'

'Isn't that a good thing?'

'The Beijing authorities don't like to lose face.'

It was a trait that the Chinese immigrants had brought with them to Singapore – at least as far as the higher echelons of the police department were concerned.

Chen slipped a file across the table and Singh flicked through it, licking his thumb to give him the right amount of adhesiveness to turn the pages of the shiny document. 'Apparently, "We are to maximise the use of cultural intelligence, utilise faith organisations in policing communities and share best practices to place the public at the heart of better decision making and policing."'

'Worthy goals,' said Chen.

Singh snorted. 'You know this sort of thing is for paper-pushers, not real cops.'

'Someone like me?'

'Exactly,' agreed Singh, self-preservation cast to the four winds in his desperate desire to avoid the trip.

'Most policemen would jump at the chance,' pointed out Chen.

'Most policemen *can* jump,' retorted the corpulent copper, folding his hands over his ballooning stomach like a resting Buddha.

Chen remained unmoved so Singh played his last card.

'Aren't you concerned I'll cause a diplomatic incident in England?'

'Of course not – *they* have real policemen who combine investigative ability with observance of the rules and regulations. You might be able to cause a stir in the Far East but not in the home of modern policing.'

Who would have thought that Superintendent Chen was a closet Anglophile?

'There you'll be a tiny fish—' Chen held up thumb and forefinger an inch apart to indicate just how minuscule Singh in Piscean form would be '—in an enormous pond.'

Martin Bradley helped an old woman into a seat on the train. The creature's hand felt like a small bag of dry bones. Did age have to be quite so awful? Martin arranged her shopping bags at her feet and wondered again whether it was possible to atone for a big sin by doing lots of small good things.

If there was a hierarchy of good deeds, helping an old

woman find a seat on a train must be right at the bottom. Still, he could only seize the opportunities available. Ever since *it* had happened, he'd been on the lookout for good deeds. He always thought of the incident as 'it', sometimes in capitals, 'IT', or with exclamation points, 'IT!!' He'd done time for IT, of course, and some would say that was sufficient redress to society but Martin didn't think so.

He'd quite like to do a big good deed, save a family from drowning, or a child, or a dog. He'd even taken a weekend trip to Brighton and walked along the pier, hoping for the chance to be a hero, but everyone had been remarkably careful and sober and it had turned out to be a waste of time. Mind you, even a big good deed might not be sufficient restitution. But it would be better than nothing and a lot better than giving up his seat on a train and seeing some youth mouth 'wanker' at him for being such a sucker.

His reflection shimmered against the big glass panes of the train. Nondescript. Mousy hair, glasses (but without frames, which he hoped made them look invisible or at the very least chic). He couldn't see his eyes but he knew they were brown. Not hazel or chocolate or anything like that. Just brown. Puppy eyes, his one and only previous girlfriend had called them. Could he still refer to her as a girlfriend after everything that had happened? He'd smiled but hadn't been sure it was a compliment. Were men supposed to look like puppies? Not real men. The train turned a corner and he disappeared for a few moments before solidifying in the glass once more. Medium height. Light trench coat that looked like a flasher mac. Note to self: bin coat.

The train came to a juddering halt and the lights went out.

There were a few muffled exclamations and one shriek but on the whole the British stiff upper lip kicked in and there was a silence thick with resignation. Martin wondered if it was a terrorist attack. There might be hope of restitution in such an event. He could break the windows before they all suffocated. Or provide first aid to a victim. Perhaps he would have the opportunity to fling himself on a suicide bomber, absorb the explosion, save dozens and get an obituary in *The Times*.

Except, of course, he didn't want to die. Not now, when he had found true love. Indeed, that was probably the greatest irony of his present existence, the conviction that he was living on borrowed time just when he'd developed this almost melodramatic desire to live.

The train began to reverse slowly. He looked around for the suicide bomber who might require a heroic effort from him – he knew the drill: spot the sweaty, swarthy (but you couldn't make it obvious in case people thought you were racially stereotyping), young male; backpack on lap, held tight. No such individual was visible, which was a relief really.

The train drew into a station, the one they had just passed, Victoria. 'This train terminates at Victoria. All change to the train on Platform Four.'

All change? If only life were that simple.

Bottom line, Hanif hadn't expected the place to be such a dump. Which just showed how naïve he was really. The background of the recruitment videos had the same dusty lack of features, bullet-ridden cement structures, dirt tracks and scrubby outskirts. It was not like they lied to the recruits or anything. But of course one focused on the training and the martial arts, the camaraderie and the sacrifice, not the dust that got up the nose and down the throat and into the eyes. Not the faces of the hungry children, not the soldiers of Assad screaming for mercy, not the women on their hands and knees begging that their lives be spared, that their children's lives be spared, that their menfolk – husbands and brothers and fathers – be spared.

They weren't spared, of course.

It wasn't what he'd expected when he left with a rucksack, as much cash as he could muster and a note to his mother that he'd gone to do the right thing. He regretted that he couldn't be clearer than that but there were eyes and ears of the enemy everywhere – trying to stop the youth from doing their duty by their people, painting them as the enemy while planes rained down death on innocents throughout the lands that belonged to his brothers. His real brothers, not the sons of his parents, who might as well be infidels for all their awareness or concern about the suffering of their people.

He'd taken a British Airways flight to Turkey; there was something amusing about being able to fly Economy Class to jihad, passport in hand and a rucksack with minimal possessions. From Turkey he'd slipped over the Syrian border at night where he'd been met as promised and shipped to a camp in the back of a pickup truck with a whole bunch of other Western recruits with soft hands.

At first, everything had gone to plan. He'd made friends, turned out to be adept at tactics and caught a glimpse of their red-haired leader about whom so many rumours abounded. It was said that he'd killed six men in a fight once, disarmed every one of them with his bare hands and torn their heads from their shoulders with brute force. Hanif assumed the stories were apocryphal; he was a martyr, not an idiot. But brothers from as far away as Sweden and Canada lapped up these tales of battle prowess, repeating them in whispers over campfires, their bright beards and pale faces catching the light of the fire and demonstrating to one and all that this was a global war against the crusaders.

He'd been spotted soon enough as someone with potential. Perhaps it was because he maintained his composure in battle, perhaps it was his adaptation to the harsh surroundings – he never complained out loud about the dust and the rocks and the bone-chilling cold. His biggest coup was capturing a massive cache of American weapons that the Iraqi soldiers abandoned on their flight from Mosul. To be frank, it was as easy as taking candy from a baby.

He was glad that he was too valuable to be risked in those convoys who rode through villages far from the cities to attack infidels, whether Christians or idol-worshippers, sawing off their heads when they refused to convert. Hanif was not convinced that conversion under duress was valid in the eyes of God.

He'd raised his doubts round the campfire. 'But there is no telling whether they mean it, right?'

A Malaysian, who had taken the name Ibn Anfal, loosely translated into 'the spoils of war', said, 'Allah will know what is in their hearts.'

And then the Americans came, not on foot, but raining death from the sky with their drones and their F-16s.

The Islamic State took severe losses and the red-haired leader's face was grave – but also triumphant.

'The enemies of our people see the threat posed by a just army,' he explained. 'And so they come with their bombs and their missiles, giving us only the added victory of martyrdom.'

'But we have also lost Mosul,' said Hanif, who was now sufficiently senior – partly because of the decimation of the ranks in recent days – that he could occasionally speak his mind. 'And many soldiers.'

'For every martyr, more flock to the cause.'

This was true enough – the most recent was an influx of Turkish fighters, looking forward to being joined in battle with their old enemy, the Kurds. More score settling than jihad, but still useful.

'The armies of Allah will rise up and defeat the Americans,' continued Ibn Anfal, his eyes lighting up in his dust-caked face as if he was privy to a vision of victory. There were shouts of 'Allahu Akbar' and a waving of guns in the air. A few idiots fired off rounds into the sky, as if they had ammunition to spare.

'The armies of Allah will only defeat the Americans if we can get our hands on more surface to air missiles,' said Hanif, the party pooper. 'Otherwise, they will eventually wear us down and limit our capacity to engage or expand our territory.'

'That is true, brother, and the Americans and their lap dogs must be taught a lesson not to interfere with the establishment of our Islamic caliphate.'

Hanif had learned to read the other man's moods – manic, quiet, exultant. He recognised this one too. 'You have a plan, I think?'

'I have a plan.'

16

'Am I a part of it?'

'Insha Allah, you are the point of the sword.'

Mrs Singh, when he had brought the news home of his impending London trip, had been enthusiastic. 'You can go to Harrods!'

'Why would I do that?'

'It's what everyone does!'

'There's a Harrods at Changi Airport.'

She shrugged bony shoulders and caused her gaudy caftan to flutter like a pennant in the wind to indicate what she thought of franchise outlets in faraway destinations. 'It's not the same.'

His wife continued to slap dishes of food down in front of him while ticking off further points in favour of a London trip. 'Selfridges, Oxford Street, Buckingham Palace, Prince George.'

'Is the Prince George a pub?'

'He's the heir to the throne.'

'I thought he was called Prince Charles.'

'That's the son.'

'Prince William?'

'That's the grandson, I'm talking about the Queen's great-grandson.'

'He's not the heir then, is he?'

'He will be when the rest die.'

Singh was not convinced. If the Royal Family had one abiding trait, it appeared to be a reluctance to meet their Maker. This George fellow would need to learn some patience or start bumping off the competition.

'All hail, Macbeth, thou shalt be king hereafter!'

'What are you talking about?'

'Nothing, nothing,' he said hastily. 'Anyway, I don't expect I will have much opportunity to consort with future kings.'

'And there's Big Ben and Kew Gardens and Piccadilly Circus.'

Why was his wife a walking *A–Z* on London? As far as he was aware she had only been once, on a short package tour with her sisters. She'd come back with dishcloths featuring London landmarks and a snow globe containing a London bobby. She still gave it a vigorous shake from time to time as if she wished her policeman husband was within.

'Have you been to England since your student days?' she asked.

The inspector shook his head decisively.

In the distant past, when he'd been thin and unmarried, he'd spent a year at University College London before dropping out to join the Singapore police force. It was an act that had led to the untimely demise of his own father – the ingratitude of his only son breaking his heart. Either that or a penchant for cottage cheese curries, whisky and gambling.

Singh felt both annoyance and regret when he thought of his father. Singh Sr had been the ultimate Anglophile. The British were the best; their benevolent hand had provided Singapore and Malaysia with the finest example of good governance. In his opinion, the haste to independence had been a mistake – 'biting the hand that feeds' he'd said bitterly at the time.

Singh ladled a large helping of rice and chicken curry on his plate and followed it up with a spoonful of *saag*. Unless things had changed a lot, he'd soon be eating fish and vinegar-covered chips out of the *News of the World*. He needed to enjoy his lunch while he could.

'And of course you must go to Southall.'

'Why? What's there?'

'We have many relations there; I will send them some gifts.'

'There is no way I'm going to South or North or any sort of Hall bearing presents for members of your family.' This impending trip was assuming nightmarish dimensions.

'Maybe it's better,' she agreed.

He stared at her; his eyebrows raised liked curious caterpillars in conversation with one another. Why this unexpected retreat?

'If you go near them, one of them will surely be killed.'

'What's that supposed to mean?'

'Death follows you around ...'

'I'm a murder cop!' he protested. 'I follow death around, not the reverse.'

'After what happened in India, my relatives all say to me, "Please keep your husband away."'

She was referring to their trip to a family wedding that, he had to admit, hadn't ended 'happily ever after'.

'They're worried that you'll accuse them of murder.'

'If I'd known that's what it would take to avoid your friends and relations, I'd have done it years ago,' said Singh.

'I have an even better idea.'

'And what's that?'

'You don't have to visit them – I will.'

'What do you mean?' he asked although he already guessed, already dreaded her answer.

'I will come with you to London.'

CHAPTER 2

Cold cases.

The mark of Cain for a policeman, indicating a failure to achieve the one and only goal of policing – the apprehension of the person responsible for the crime. The right person, mind you, the guilty party. The inspector from Singapore didn't subscribe to the practice, when confronted with a cold trail, of 'rounding up the usual suspects'.

Inspector Singh was slumped in a high-back chair, stomach wedged against a vast cherry mahogany table. The table was the centrepiece to a high-ceilinged conference room at Marlborough House, home of the Commonwealth Secretariat. He was not a man usually given to karmic contemplations but he could not help but wonder what he had done to deserve such a fate as this. Perhaps he'd been an earthworm of a particularly dastardly nature and this had led to his rebirth as a long-suffering inspector of police. Not that he minded being a policeman – there were many criminals languishing in the bowels of the Singapore prison system who had Inspector Singh to thank for their food and board. Armed robbers, terrorists, wife beaters – they'd all crossed his path and paid the price. But his favourite type of crime, from an investigative rather than an artistic point of view, was murder.

And yet, here he was, the file of an unsolved murder before him, and he was miserable.

The reason?

His task was not to solve the crime.

'This case has been selected as it has attributes that are relevant to the issues being addressed, namely, policing amongst minority groups, policing in communities that have a historical distrust for the police and policing where the ... er, cultural framework of the investigation might not be considered the norm in wider society.' The young woman who spoke, Regina de Klerk, had hair like spun gold, a face so pale as to be almost translucent and blue eyes the same shade as the autumn sky outside. As she straightened the papers on the table in front of her, her silk sleeve drew up slightly and he noticed fresh bruising on her wrist.

'Surely the best solution is to actually catch the murderer?'

'We are here to explore whether the investigation might have had more success if it had engaged with the wider community and submit a paper with recommendations to the conference.'

Was there a special school that taught bureaucrats to speak double Dutch?

The inspector looked down at the smiling face on the cover of the file he'd just been handed. A murder unsolved meant both a victim unavenged and a murderer at large. A person free to kill again, secure in the knowledge that he or she had the wherewithal to escape undetected, notwithstanding the best efforts of the police.

Singh had not left many unresolved cases in his wake over decades of policing – the advantage of policing on an island so small 'that one could run, but couldn't hide'. But now he had a case colder than an ice chip.

She was beautiful, the dead girl. Long dark hair, bright eyes. Fatima Daud, twenty-four years old, five feet tall, a hundred and ten pounds – a tiny thing, not much bigger than a child – bludgeoned to death in an empty house five years before. No one had ever been charged with her murder.

'All the information you need is in the file and you will work with a police officer seconded to this conference by the Metropolitan Police,' she continued. 'Detective Inspector Carmen will be with you shortly.'

'I think it's a waste of time,' insisted Singh.

'Why is that?'

The policeman had to admire her calm manner in dealing with rebellious policemen. He wondered about the bruising on her wrist. Boyfriend troubles? Husband troubles? How did independent young women find themselves in abusive domestic situations? Maybe it was the eternal optimism of the female of the species, the belief that men could change, would change, if exposed to enough feminine suffering.

Had this Fatima Daud also thought that she could change a man for the better?

'Murder investigations are about only one thing,' he growled, 'and that is finding the perpetrator. All this community hand holding is a waste of time.'

'I'm not sure I agree, Inspector Singh. After all, a failure to engage can sometimes mean that evidence is lost, eyewitnesses don't come forward, people are more likely to protect the perpetrator ...'

Did her general appearance of smart competence mean that the episode of violence had not affected her deeply or was she just putting on a brave face? He'd seen the former before but the latter was more common. He'd also been called in to view the bodies of dead lovers when that brittle self-control shattered.

'I think that the public should be expected to do the right thing.'

'You paint a picture of a policing Utopia.'

'Low crime doesn't mean no crime,' he muttered, cornered into quoting Singapore police department slogans.

She continued as if he hadn't spoken – had she been taking lessons from his wife? 'The purpose of the exercise is to better comprehend the role of race relations in policing.' She smiled, even teeth except for the front two that overlapped slightly. 'We thought that conference attendees would find the exercise more stimulating if we looked into an actual case, the unsolved and tragic murder of a young woman.'

'I only know one way to work a case,' said the policeman, folding his arms across his belly.

'And what way is that, Inspector Singh?'

'To solve the murder, what else? To find out who killed Fatima Daud five years ago.'

Hanif took the Heathrow Express to Paddington and then decided that a black cab was in order. He needed time to prepare himself for a return to the family's whitewashed, run-down Edwardian home, four bedrooms, an overgrown garden with drooping roses and tufty grass, the musty indoor smell of overheating, curry and cigarettes.

He joined the taxi queue and paused to take in the hustle and bustle of London, people gathering at pubs in the dusk, the sounds of laughter and the odd shout, the smell of chips and stale pizza, sirens in the distance, always in London, sirens in the distance.

Ask not for whom the bell tolls.

This was his London, all right. And for a fleeting moment he was glad to be back, before he remembered why he had flung his things in a bag and rushed to the airport. 'Insha Allah, you will be the point of the sword.'

A taxi pulled up and he got in, wedging his bag against the fold-down seat in front of him. The cab smelled of cigarette smoke under the heavy cover of a dashboard deodorant. Hanif didn't care; a bit of passive smoke was the least of his problems. Besides, the smell reminded him of home. Not in a 'good, welcoming' sort of way but in a 'preparing him for the inevitable' sort of way, which was even better.

The journey went quicker than he expected. Half an hour felt like five minutes. A discovery. There was a fold in space that sped time up when hurtling towards some cosmic disaster. He should have been a physicist, not a freedom fighter.

The black cab drew up, and the driver, who'd been unusually silent for a London cabbie, said, 'We're here, guv.'

'Home sweet home,' said Hanif, reaching for his wallet.

'Where you back from?'

'Here and there.'

24

'It's great to travel, isn't it,' enthused the man. 'My missus and I save up every year and go somewhere. Thailand's our next stop.'

Sex tourists and beaches? But he said, 'That's great.'

'Funny thing is, wherever I go, each place is so different, but people are just the same,' philosopher taxi driver continued. 'I mean, we're all the same under the skin, aren't we?'

A picture of flesh and bones strewn across battlefields flashed into the other man's mind. 'You're right, we are,' he said.

Hanif watched as the vehicle drew away, black and shiny, like a beetle, lit from within, the cabbie with the proverbial heart of gold inside. It was a lesson, only Allah knew for sure what was in the hearts of men.

He rang the doorbell and heard the chimes within. He pulled his jacket closer; the evening had turned chilly. That typical autumn plunge in temperature the minute the sun went to bed.

At last, however, the key turned in the lock.

'So you're back.'

His older brother, Fauzi, was the titular head of the family now that their father was dead.

'Yes.'

'The prodigal son.'

'And also your much beloved younger brother,' replied Hanif, dropping his heavy rucksack at his feet.

'Tired of playing soldiers?'

'I have played my part in a just war.'

'Bunch of idiots running around the desert imagining they are doing God's will.'

Hanif smiled suddenly. 'You are right, brother, that many of the martyrs were subject to natural selection.'

At this hint of the old Hanif – the one with the sense of humour, the one who kept the peace between his older and younger brother, the one who had tried to make peace between Fatima and his father – Fauzi flung the door open and enveloped him in a bear hug.

'Welcome home,' he said and there were tears running down both their cheeks.

The attack that had killed Fatima Daud was as vicious as anything Singh had come across in his long career as a policeman.

'I guess you've seen more of this level of violence than I have,' said Regina. The fine spray of freckles across her nose and cheeks stood out against her pale face. She must have been through the file before but had not yet become hardened to the contents. She swallowed rapidly a few times as if she was choking – true horror provoked a physical, not just emotional, response. Singh had seen the same in rookie cops.

The inspector pushed his coffee away. 'You never come to terms with the death of the young,' he replied.

'And in such a way ...'

'She died from blunt trauma to the head,' stated the policeman, 'no more than a couple of hours before the body was discovered.'

'She was discovered by a cleaner who'd been employed by the real estate agency appointed to sell the premises,' continued Regina, making a visible effort to pull herself together. 'Fatima Daud worked as an estate agent.'

Singh noted that she did not refer to the case files. Regina de Klerk had done her homework on this cold case. 'And was lured to the house by the murderer posing as a potential buyer.'

Singh steepled his fingers and rested his elbows on the table. 'Too easy, really.'

'There's testimony from the agency of the call – it was taken by the boss, Raj – but nothing useful about the caller except that the voice was muffled.'

'Man or woman?' asked Singh.

'Woman. She identified herself as one Mrs Hamid looking for a home for her family of four.'

The inspector's brow furrowed but he made no comment.

Instead, he read the summary of the autopsy report. 'Significant amounts of blood were found at the scene, all belonging to the victim. A hammer was recovered at the entrance and many of the injuries had a circular or semicircular pattern that matched the weapon in question. No fingerprints – either the killer wore gloves or it was wiped clean. Autopsy findings revealed blunt trauma to the head with numerous abrasions, contusions and lacerations. There were also fractured ribs and bruising. No traces of alcohol or any other prohibited substances were found in the bloodstream of the deceased.'

Singh sighed. He doubted any autopsy on him would be negative for alcohol.

He turned the page.

'What is it?' asked Regina.

His tongue felt thick in his mouth. He pushed the file across the table and tapped the salient bit with an index finger.

'I know,' she said. 'That is the worst bit.'

Singh read the passage again – both hands of the victim

had been neatly severed at the wrists with a sharp cutting blade that was not found at the scene.

'Ever seen this kind of thing before?' she asked.

'No,' said Singh. 'In Singapore we have a few murderers and some perverts, usually in government, but hardly ever both at the same time.'

'There must have been a reason ...'

Two eyebrows almost disappeared under the rim of Singh's turban.

'I don't mean a reason that would mean anything to you or me,' added Regina hastily.

'A souvenir hunter? Or to cover any evidence affecting the hands.' Singh was pleased that he had regained the capacity to reason. He didn't want Regina to think that Singapore officers were soft.

'What evidence?'

'DNA under the fingernails?'

Regina blanched but did not speak.

'Or a religious thing.'

'What?'

'Hudud – the Sharia legal system that punishes certain offences with the ... amputation of hands.'

'Offences?'

'Theft, robbery, that kind of thing. But not for petty theft and usually just one hand for a first offence.'

'She *was* Muslim.'

'But even if this was some bizarre implementation of a different system of law, the punishment is *not* usually accompanied by a bludgeoning.'

Regina nodded. She looked relieved, a bit of colour back in

her cheeks. Did she find the idea of a religious killer worse than a mere murderer? To Singh, there was no difference. The victim was dead either way.

'Premeditated . . .' he continued.

'Why?' she asked.

'Because the murderer lured her there and had his murder weapons to hand.'

The inspector trained his turban on the file. 'And brutal, with particular damage to the head and face.'

His mind conjured up a picture of the dead girl with the round-headed hammer wounds. He closed the file, looked at the photo on the front, tried to wipe the bloodied image from his mind. This was almost worse than the body in the flesh. There was no way to walk away from his imagination.

'Your conclusion?' asked Regina.

'I doubt she was a victim selected at random by someone who had a bad experience with an estate agent once.'

'I guess you're right,' replied Regina.

'No forensic evidence so a murderous frenzy and then the sangfroid to cover his tracks.' Singh's skin had a greyish hue too.

He noted that there had been no sexual assault and the victim was still a virgin. How common was that in England generally and how common amongst the Pakistani diaspora in particular?

'I still don't see what this has to do with community policing and race relations,' grumbled Singh.

'There's a note,' said Regina.

Singh read it reluctantly; he had a bad feeling about this case.

'A review of the file by the Major Crime Division of the Metropolitan Police looking into cold cases concluded that there was a closing of the ranks of family and friends. There is a suspicion that information was withheld that might have led to a more satisfactory conclusion. There were concerns expressed by the panel of reviewers that no attempt was made to engage directly with the community. Further, no police personnel from ethnic minorities were involved in a senior role in the investigation. This may have led to a reluctance to share vital information with the police during the course of the investigation.

'So what am I supposed to do – visit the nearest and dearest and ask them what information they withheld just because the Met didn't send someone from an "ethnic minority" along to talk to them five years ago?'

'It's not an investigation, more of an analysis of what went wrong, and an apology.'

'I don't apologise.'

'Well, perhaps Detective Inspector Anna Carmen, who will be accompanying you, might be more conciliatory.'

'They're wasting a DI's time on this? Have all the criminals been caught in this country?'

'You're an inspector too,' pointed out Regina.

'Yes, but my superiors hate me.'

Regina shrugged. 'Well, I'm sure it will become clear why DI Carmen was picked for this project soon enough. She's on her way here.'

Martin Bradley walked home. It took him half an hour. His feet hurt; leather shoes were not meant for walking any great distance, only for looking smart at office meetings. He carried his coat over one arm and loosened his tie, striped like all his ties – Regina said he was like an extra from *The Office* but he didn't know what that meant. He looked exactly what he was, a desk jockey making his way home to a microwave-ready meal bought from a Tesco Express. A life that would end in dull, unremarked upon death and then clods of earth or cremation.

Martin had decided on cremation as the environmentally friendly option; there was no need to use up good land to house his worm buffet. But recently he'd read that cremation was too energy intensive and, after all, worms needed to eat too. It was all part of the great cycle of life. He knew that because he'd seen *The Lion King* at the Lyceum. He'd felt fairly self-conscious sitting in the cheap seats, almost as high as the rafters, watching men in silly costumes sing. Did grown men who were not American really enjoy this sort of thing? It had all been part of his self-improvement programme. He'd gone about his task diligently – attended evening forums sponsored by the *New Statesman*, signed up for an Open University course on Philosophy, went for those cruises that weren't just a holiday but brought along an expert to inform guests (except that the archaeology guy on the Egypt trip had drunk himself into a stupor, suffered a heart attack and been medivac-ed out).

And then the best thing that had ever happened to him happened.

Regina.

Divine machinations at their most egregious.

He wished Regina had agreed to spend the evening with him. Not at his horrible little studio flat, of course.

But she'd said, 'I've got loads of paperwork to do this evening.'

'I can help,' he'd insisted.

'Of course you can,' she said. 'But there's no reason for you to ruin your evening like I'm about to mine.'

And then she'd turned and walked away. He followed her with his eyes, admiring the colour of the shirt, some silky material in ochre and the smart tweed jacket with leather elbows, faux masculine, over it. But he was definitely not a fan of the knee-high, tan leather boots on block heels. It lent her inches she didn't need, rendering her taller than him. He knew he shouldn't care about such things, proper modern men didn't, but he couldn't help it. He wanted to be envied when in the company of Regina, not mocked.

No one knew about their relationship at the office.

If it had been up to him, he'd have shouted it from the rooftops. He couldn't help but wonder whether she was ashamed of him, or at the very least embarrassed by him. She was his senior in the place, of course, but that didn't really mean much in this day and age. He was quite happy to be the quiet man behind the successful woman, maybe even stay at home with the kids someday. Not just Emma. He hadn't met Emma, the time wasn't right yet. There was no getting around the fact that Regina was still married and matters would have to be dealt with delicately.

Martin let himself into his tiny flat and wrinkled his nose. The smell of hot oil from the chippie two shops down pervaded the room. It didn't matter that he kept the tiny place spotless, vacuuming three times a week and wiping surfaces every day.

He flung his stuff on the two-seater sofa that faced a small cathode ray television. Its antenna hung hopefully out of the window as if it was looking for life on another planet, not just *Big Brother* reruns. The pantry – the space couldn't be described as a kitchen – was just a tiled alcove off the main room. Martin opened the small fridge, which was decorated with magnets from his travels: a pyramid, the Leaning Tower of Pisa, the Empire State Building. His travels or a series of clichés? he wondered. Why hadn't he done something a little more interesting like white-water rafting or a safari? Or would that just have been a different type of cliché?

He took the frozen dish at the top of the neat stack and stuck it in the microwave. Chicken tandoori with some basmati rice. Perhaps he should plan a trip to see the Taj Mahal. Regina might like that. And then he remembered that Regina's husband came from those parts and a black cloud descended, suffocating his good humour. Even the child, as much as he intended to love her as if she were his own, bore the unmistakable stamp of foreign-ness, the dusky skin and dark hair.

What was the use of having the love of a beautiful woman if her husband stood in the way of their happiness?

And what was he, Martin Bradley, going to do about it?

Inspector Singh returned the beady-eyed glare of Sir Shridath Ramphal – not in person fortunately, but his representation in art. The full-length portrait in a gilt frame was unfazed by Singh's hostility. The same could also be said for the other person in the room, Detective Inspector Anna Carmen.

Chasing after murderers in his shiny, white sneakers was Singh's fourth preferred pastime – after long lunches, cold beer and afternoon naps. Unless, that is, it was a cold case in a foreign country where perfectly competent coppers had failed to find a solution. The inspector acknowledged to himself briefly that the 'chasing after' was largely figurative. His was a mostly cerebral approach to police work. A picture popped in his head of his wife, his doctor and his boss, Superintendent Chen. All three, side by side, glared at him like a modern incarnation of the three furies. He could read their minds.

Cerebral approach? Of course he adopted a cerebral approach. How could he possibly chase down criminals when getting out of a chair provoked panting and a shortness of breath?

But here, in the matter of the murder of Fatima Daud, he was not tasked with catching a killer, but with writing a discussion paper on policing within tight-knit communities. If Fatima Daud was hanging around in purgatory, unable to go to her final rest until justice was served, she'd have a long wait.

He scowled at the woman, DI Carmen. So what if she was petite yet tough, looked good in a trouser suit and had thoughtful grey eyes? She was still wasting her time and his time.

'I say again, I only investigate murders.'

'I must emphasise once more that the purpose of this exercise—'

'I don't exercise!'

'—is to identify flaws during the investigative process and make recommendations for improvements.'

'All right – you want a flaw? I'll give you a flaw. The murderer of Fatima Daud is still out there, probably having a cigarette and congratulating himself on escaping the long arm of the law.'

'Inspector Singh, we don't have either the jurisdiction or the expertise to reopen a murder investigation.'

Her thin lips, highlighted in some sort of colourless gloss, were pursed into invisibility. The rigid cast of her square jaw suggested that her patience was wearing thin. Singh had already written her off as a paper-pusher, a stickler for rules, without the imagination to be a proper detective. Why else would she have been assigned to this thankless task? But her body language, the precision in her choice of words, and the hardening of the slate eyes all suggested a tougher cookie than that. Maybe she'd annoyed her bosses as well.

'So how do you intend that we go about this project then?'

His attempt to be conciliatory was met with a small nod.

'The plan is to re-interview relevant people: family, witnesses, anyone strongly connected with the original investigation.'

'About the crime?'

'About whether they feel that the investigation was carried out in a manner that gave them confidence in the process.'

'What if they refuse to talk to us?'

She shrugged. 'We're still the police.'

'Can we visit the crime scene?'

'I cannot see how that would serve any purpose.'

'If we are not entirely familiar with the case, how will we convince the family that we are serious about addressing their grievances?'

35

She nodded her head slowly, not so much agreeing as considering the possibility he might have a point.

'It is the respectful thing to do,' he continued.

DI Carmen shrugged and tucked an escaping strand of hair, a shade of blonde so light it might have been white, behind her ear. 'No skin off my nose.'

'In which case,' said Singh, using the table edge to hoist himself to his feet, 'I think that should be our first port of call!'

'Our schedule commences tomorrow morning at eleven with a visit to the victim's family,' said Carmen, slipping typed sheets out of a clear file and handing a copy to Singh.

'Aren't they going to be surprised when we turn up at their doorstep after five years?'

'We gave them notice of our project.'

'You told them it was about this community policing nonsense?'

'Of course.'

She passed him a letter addressed to the family dated almost two weeks earlier and he read, '... policing shortcomings, appreciate cooperation, looking at unexplored avenues, blah, blah, blah.'

'They'll think that you've found new evidence and this is just a ruse to keep them in the dark.'

'Nothing I can do about that,' she said. She rose to her feet. 'I'll see you tomorrow.'

'What am I supposed to do in the meantime?'

'Take in the London sights?' suggested Carmen, only a slight curl of her lip betraying her disdain for overweight policemen from the tropics on pseudo-work trips to the United Kingdom.

'Big Ben? The London Eye?' she continued.

'You sound exactly like my wife,' said Singh, his tone making it quite clear that the statement was not intended as a compliment.

She had a hand on the door when he asked, 'So how did you end up with this assignment?'

She didn't pretend to misunderstand him.

'I guess that's one more mystery you won't be solving on this trip, Inspector Singh.'

Hanif woke up every night screaming – nightmares of severed limbs and dead eyes, of small cocoons of white cloth containing children for hasty burial. He was bathed in cold sweat mingled with tears, both salty on the tongue.

It frightened his mother and caused his brothers to look at him in the morning with suspicion, but he didn't tell them anything; they wouldn't understand. Maybe if Fatima were still around, it would be different.

But she wasn't and that was it.

Allah was truly great but he didn't bring back the dead or provide an explanation for the deaths of innocents.

His whole family pretended that he'd never been away. It was as if he'd overslept for six months in his small room, come downstairs for breakfast and not been missed in the interim. He knew it was their way of coping – and also of keeping him safe from prying eyes – but he didn't like it. It showed no respect for what he had done, no interest in his experiences and no kindness and empathy to help him adapt to civilian life.

Only his mother, fading in and out of the present as her

dementia took over, acknowledged changes in him and these were trivial and superficial.

'You are so thin,' she said to him three times a day. Sometimes, 'Your sunburn is fading.'

And she would prepare his meals carefully and press sweet desserts into his hands, not understanding his lack of appetite, the way he picked at his food. How to explain that rich food made him sick to the stomach after the hard rationing in Syria without upsetting her, confusing her, telling her too much?

Hanif stretched and sat up, pushed himself back and leaned against the cold wall. He'd given up on the bed, his own since childhood, but now too soft. He slept on the floor and then made his bed before his mother came in to tidy the room so that no one would ask him difficult questions. Not that anyone seemed inclined to do so.

It had been two weeks since he'd arrived home, burned as brown as weathered teak, eyes surrounded in fine lines from squinting against the sun, arms and legs scratched from hiding in trenches and from the bed bugs that crawled out of his dirty clothes to feast on his flesh.

He'd put out feelers, tried to pick up where he had left off, but there was wariness, a lack of trust that dismayed him. Hanif knew that he would have to persevere, earn their confidence, and all this while saying little, doing little that might attract the attention of the authorities or those who would tell the security services of his recent exploits. British radicals returning from Syria to fashion their own version of Enoch Powell's rivers of blood was the talk of the town.

When he went down for breakfast, Fauzi and Ibrahim were

still at the table. This was a shame because Hanif usually made it a point to come down only after his brothers had cleared out. He had nothing in common with them except blood and loss and he found it hard to be in their presence. When his older brother went on the attack, he knew they had waited for him.

'You need to go back to work,' said Fauzi.

He said it like it was advice but Hanif knew it was an order.

'Perhaps he should recover his health first,' said their mother, looking from one to the other. 'He is very thin.'

'He's fine,' was the curt response. 'There will be raised eyebrows in the community if he remains indolent. And we do not want any trouble.'

Hanif knew what he meant. There were plenty of Muslims, indeed the vast majority of British Muslims, who would be happy to turn him over to the authorities if they got wind of his recent activities. The arrest of the would-be terrorists in Bradford meant that many of their friends, neighbours, co-workers – and brothers? – were walking on eggshells.

'But what type of job can he get,' said Ibrahim in his languid tone, making mischief as was his wont. 'After all, he has such an unusual skills set.'

'He can help you at the restaurant,' snapped Fauzi, referring to the family business, Khan's, established by their father and now under the day-to-day control of the youngest brother.

'That's not necessary,' said Ibrahim, sitting up a little straighter to ward off this unexpected suggestion.

'You are able to run the place into the ground yourself? I'm sure of it but I think we should see if Hanif has developed any transferable skills on his recent ... errmm ... holiday.'

The middle son felt the rage wash over him, so intense that he wanted to tip the dining table over, smash things, attack his brothers. Instead, he took a deep breath, counted to ten in his head, and pictured an empty place, just red dirt and a few rocks and the vault of heaven above. He could have laughed out loud at the irony of them thinking he had learned nothing in his battles against the infidels in Syria; he'd learned that most important life lesson, how to keep his thoughts to himself.

'Well, Hanif?' demanded Fauzi.

'It shall be as you wish, brother,' he replied.

The house was empty and had been empty for some time.

Debbie Tailor sneezed once and then again. Her spirits sank rapidly until they reached the bottom of her sensible shoes. She was the kind of girl who liked high heels with a bit of bling but there was no way she could wear that sort of footwear on the job. She'd really needed a sale so the boss had taken pity on her and sent her to have a look at an old run-down two-storey property, but, sadly, this place was not the end of any rainbow, there would be no pot of commissions hidden within. She flicked on a light switch and an overhead bulb flashed and then went dark. It must have shorted.

The estate agent walked forwards slowly – it was not dark, just gloomy – until she reached the end of the corridor and felt for another light switch against a wall. This one came on and stayed on, but, looking at the stained wallpaper and noticing for the first time that the rough carpet was brown – who actually chose a brown carpet? – Debbie was not convinced this was any real improvement.

She flung open a couple of doors but didn't enter the rooms. She'd heard scurrying feet in the first one and there was no way she was going in there to be attacked by feral rats or something equally unpleasant. Debbie read a lot of science fiction and was reasonably convinced that either through the machinations of a mad scientist or the accumulation of toxic garbage, new and dangerous creatures were being bred beneath these old houses.

Ten more feet and she stepped into the hall. This room, large and with a certain shabby dignity, improved her spirits.

'Perfect for entertaining,' she rehearsed in her head, preparing to impress any dowdy housewife with aspirations to be Delia Smith. There were curtains against the far wall that might obscure a back garden or even an entrance to a conservatory. That would make the property infinitely more sellable despite its questionable location two roads down from the last decent address in Bayswater.

Debbie drew the curtains gingerly and found herself face to face with overgrown shrubbery. Despite the mess, there were splashes of colour. Newly enthused, she rattled the window handle; fresh air and natural light would go a long way towards making this place more habitable – and sellable. She managed, after a struggle, to fling it open and then took a quick step back, trying not to gag. What a bloody stink. Something dead. A rat. Maybe even a cat. Fishing a hankie out of her purse, she held it to her nose and peered out, trying to get a sense of the size and layout of the garden. The stench was overwhelming.

There was nothing more she could do here. She'd have to tell the owner that if he wanted the place sold for a decent price, he'd have to stump up to make it slightly more 'family home' and slightly less 'house of horrors'.

Debbie scanned the garden one last time.

And saw it.

She opened her mouth to scream, but instead she choked and gagged, stumbled backwards, caught a sensible shoe on the frayed edge of a carpet, lost her balance and fell.

And then the screams came . . .

CHAPTER 3

The inspector stepped out of Marlborough House and took a deep breath, filling his lungs with the sharpness of cold air – so different from the humidity that clogged the breathing pipes in Singapore. The chill was invigorating and the late autumn leaves were incandescent in the evening sun. The windows on the west side of the square building – red brick and grey stone – glowed gold as they caught the last of the afternoon sun in a cloudless, watery blue sky.

It was a shame that DI Carmen had vetoed his plan to visit the murder scene immediately, insisting that they reconvene the following morning. On the other hand, it meant that he was done for the day. He could ferret out an Indian restaurant and read Fatima's file.

Out of the corner of his eye, Singh saw Regina de Klerk making her way with a brisk step. St James's Park Station was her probable destination and he was less likely to get lost if he stayed on her tail. He followed her past old townhouses that had been converted into flats. The buildings, with their red brick and stone cornices, were so ancient, soot-stained and worn that he half expected to see horses and carriages instead of cars. It was amazing to wander through streets essentially unchanged for hundreds of years. In Singapore, anything that smacked of history or a more gracious era was an excuse to call in the bulldozers. Singh was almost reconciled enough to start his own collection of souvenir tea towels.

His first impression of London, courtesy of Heathrow Airport, had been less positive.

'And what is the purpose of your visit?' the immigration official demanded. No smile, no nod, just a glare from a Sikh man at least twenty years his junior, turban and facial hair both raven black.

'Attending a conference at the Commonwealth Secretariat.'

'What is the subject of the conference?'

'Policing.'

'You're a *police*man?'

'You're an immigration official?'

Luckily, this last comment was not uttered aloud. Singh still had moments where self-preservation trumped sarcasm although as he grew older and more set in his ways, these instances were on the ebb. Besides, his wife was waiting behind the yellow line a few yards away and she would not thank him if he were arrested.

Taking a deep breath, he said, 'Yes, I'm a policeman.'

A long look at the passport as if it were a novel with a particularly tawdry ending.

'From Singapore?'

Singh didn't respond. It was, after all, self-evident – the name was emblazoned on the thick, scuffed, red document.

'Do you have anything to prove that you're here for a . . . a policing conference?'

It had taken a lot of paperwork to convince border control to let him in by which time Singh had lost all fondness for his Sikh brother. He disliked people who went hunting for a better life in foreign countries and then tried to pull the draw-bridge up after themselves.

Mrs Singh had been more sanguine.

'You see how well *our* people are doing in this country,' she said to him at the luggage carousel.

'What do you mean?'

'Even working in immigration.'

'He's just a glorified security guard.'

'Like you?'

The appearance of their suitcase allowed him to ignore this sally with feigned dignity.

'In *England*, they trust the Sikhs to manage their borders,' she continued.

'In *Singapore*, they trust the Sikhs to hunt for their murderers.'

She pointed at their second bag with a bony forefinger.

'They should let our people control immigration in Singapore as well.'

'Why?'

'Stop all these mail order brides coming in.'

'I'd welcome them,' said the policeman and then swivelled the trolley towards the exit with some haste.

But now, his opinion of London had gone up a notch.

In the distance, he saw that Regina de Klerk had reached a wrought iron gate with a crest on the top. She was taking a short cut through St James's Park. It seemed like a fine idea and he entered the gates after her with energy, his step almost reaching a trot. This brisk walking might cause him to lose weight. Perhaps, he would return to Singapore a svelte fellow such as Mrs Singh had not seen since their wedding day.

Singh paused on a bridge to catch his breath. He leaned over the railings and stared down at the waters and his swirling image, one hand on his chest as he felt the furious thumping from unaccustomed exercise.

Was there an argument, he wondered, that his wife was slowly and intentionally killing him? Not with obscure, slow-acting poisons but with cottage cheese curries and buttery *naan*?

'What was the murder weapon?'

'A hot curry, M'lud.'

The Old Bailey would never have seen a case like it.

He set off again at a more sedate pace. A signboard indicated that St James's Park Station was four minutes away. Four minutes as walked by whom? Not podgy policemen from Singapore wheezing their way forward.

A squirrel regarded him with a suspicious eye, two paws clutching an acorn with the same firm grip Singh might have used on a beer glass.

'Inspector Singh!'

The hunter had become the hunted.

'Ms de Klerk, what a surprise.'

'Call me Regina. I was just sat on a park bench when I spotted you and thought I'd check if you were lost.'

'Not at all, I was merely ... errm ... immersing myself in nature.'

'Are you headed to the station?' she asked. 'Shall we go together?'

The company of a beautiful woman, and one who was still alive, made a change. They fell into step.

He wondered again about the bruising around her wrist.

'Your thoughts on our cold case?' she asked.

'Women sometimes get on the wrong side of a man and it doesn't end well.'

'So you think it was a man? And that she knew him?'

'Stranger danger is stranger than the danger.'

'There must have been signs surely – if she knew the ... killer? That sort of thing doesn't happen out of the blue ...'

'Probably,' said Singh, turban bobbing up and down in agreement. 'In my experience, the problem is identifying the signs for what they are.'

'What do you mean?'

'Violence – starts small ... and escalates.'

He stopped and turned to face her, voice deeper, serious. 'A slap, a shove, a bruised wrist ...'

'Why don't you just come right out and tell me what you're talking about?'

'That I saw the bruising on your wrist earlier.'

'And therefore I'm going to end up like Fatima Daud?'

Singh didn't miss the rising anger in her voice. He wasn't Singapore's finest for nothing.

'Therefore ... you should consider any assault on your person, however minor, a warning sign.'

She surprised him by breaking into a warm chuckle. 'If

that's your usual conversational style, Inspector Singh, I'd be surprised if you weren't offered violence regularly.'

'A policeman's lot is not a happy one,' he said.

'Speaking of unhappy police officers, I asked around about DI Carmen.'

'And?'

'And she's a good cop – on the fast track to promotion – they're lining her up for big things.'

'The fast track runs through a five-year-old unsolved case?' What was the slow track then? Solving the Ripper murders?

'I gather she has to do some minority outreach to round out her CV.'

'Your criminals must be dancing for joy.'

'You don't reach out to minorities in Singapore?'

'Only if I need to slap a pair of cuffs on them ...'

'I don't see why we had to come here,' Raj grumbled. 'Are you trying to demonstrate that I pay you too much?'

Jimmy Kendrick looked around appreciatively. He loved the fine gold work, delicate lamps, freestanding vases and orchids. The clientele at the Savoy appeared to consist of Americans with European sensibilities and Europeans with American money. The new rich – the Arabs and Russians and Chinese – were not here. They no doubt felt excluded, like Raj did, by the faint air of old money and snobbery. He doubted that guests of the Savoy objected to ill-gotten gains, but they wanted the lucre to be laundered through a few generations before being used to pay for a drink at the American Bar.

'You pay me what I am worth,' he said.

'All right, prove it then. Do we have a problem or are you going to make it all go away?'

Kendrick smiled and adjusted his tie – Ermenegildo Zegna, Windsor knot – with one hand. In his experience, you could always spot a rich man from the pronouns they used.

We have a problem. *I* have all the money. *You* might have to solve *our* little difficulty.

Mind you, all that money was wasted on Raj, wearing a thin cotton shirt through which his singlet was visible and black horn-rimmed glasses that Kendrick hadn't realised were still manufactured. He looked completely out of place at the 125-year-old hotel tucked in from The Strand. What was the use of accumulating money if you didn't use it to buy beautiful things? He and his client would never understand each other, but that didn't matter too much to Kendrick as long as money continued to change hands between them.

'Well?'

'I assume we've learned from the mistakes of our youth?' Kendrick asked, grabbing a handful of cashews.

'Of course.'

'Then I don't see why any of this should affect us.'

The lawyer was dressed with precision, from the matching tie and handkerchief in his breast pocket, the shirt, blue with white collar and cuffs, the sapphire cufflinks and the handmade leather shoes, polished to such a high reflectivity that the wicked stepmother might have demanded of them, who was the fairest of them all. It did not disguise the fact that he had grown large; a taste for rich food and red wine had added fleshy pounds to the muscular base and he'd started to sag in various places. Man breasts. How did one fix man breasts?

'They're going to press charges. You know they've been after me for years.'

'They've been after you but they're *charging* the minions.'

'Bloody fools couldn't follow simple instructions.'

'Not all employees are of the same quality, that's why we're here and those two idiots are going to jail.'

'You can't get them off? I don't want to be tainted by association.'

'If only they could all afford such refined sensibilities. I'll do my best – it's possible. In any event, none of it will touch you.'

'I have a new organisation to pick up the slack caused by this current difficulty.'

'Already? Very impressive.' He meant it as well.

Raj shrugged. 'We all have clients to please.'

Jimmy Kendrick poured them both some tea from the silver teapot, waved over an Aryan-looking waiter, requested a slice of lemon, stared at the gleaming chandelier for a moment and then asked, 'Is there anything else bothering you?'

'Why do you ask?'

'You didn't ask to see me to talk about a matter as trivial as some employees with competency issues.'

Raj nodded. He reached into his pocket and pulled out a letter; handed it over with the care of someone handling a venomous snake.

Kendrick read it and then looked up. 'So?'

'So why are they reopening the investigation after all this while?'

'They're not – it's some sort of outreach-to-the-community rubbish, it says so right here on their pretty letterhead.'

'That must be a lie.'

'You think your tax money is ever used for anything worth-while?'

'Fatima was like a daughter to me. But that doesn't mean I want to go through the whole thing again. It was a very difficult time for me—'

Kendrick put up a hand. 'I know perfectly well why you don't want the whole think raked up again. It was a difficult time for all of us.'

'I blame the family,' said Raj.

'They certainly had antiquated notions,' agreed the other man.

'So I have nothing to worry about? You are quite sure?'

'Nothing except the waste of your tax dollars.'

By the time Detective Chief Inspector James Harris arrived, the house outside Bayswater was festooned in yellow tape, patrol cars were double parked along the street and uniformed officers were keeping a large crowd at bay, their efforts video-ed and photographed for posterity. He spared a moment to hope that the uniforms were managing their tempers and their manners. Otherwise, the recording would go viral and the police, already held in low esteem by the population, would sink further in their estimation.

The PC ushered him past – did she recognise him or did he reek of cop? – and he stepped into the house, wrinkling his nose as he did so. He knew it was his imagination on over-time, but he could smell death.

A DS from his manor was waiting for him and she said, 'A young woman. She hasn't been dead long.'

Harris scowled at his junior. 'So suddenly you're the pathologist?'

'I just meant . . . '

'We don't do guesswork at crime scenes.'

'OK, boss.'

Should he have been kinder? On reflection, he couldn't be bothered.

'Who found the body?'

'An estate agent coming to look over the house before putting it on the market.'

Did that ring a bell? Harris wasn't sure. Two decades of policing, ten of them in CID, with alcohol to blunt the images of man's cruelty to man, his memory wasn't what it used to be.

'Are we sure it's murder?'

'I doubt it is possible to beat oneself to death.'

Harris scowled. 'Was she interfered with?'

'We'll have to wait for the pathologist's report before we can make a determination, sir.'

The young woman was a quick study.

Harris put on the full body suit required to avoid compromising a crime scene and walked into the hall. This time the smell was real. The room was brightly lit with lamps and so was the garden. Everyone outside was in white overalls; it could have been a scene from a science fiction film.

The senior detective looked down at the corpse. He understood why his deputy had said the woman was young. Despite the mess that had previously been her face, the short skirt without stockings and lush hair, rich and brown, suggested youth.

'Anything for me?' he asked the pathologist.

'Of course not.'

'All right then.'

His lack of curiosity was sufficient to rouse the other man into further communication, a tactic that had worked for Harris before.

'Off the record, she's not been dead that long. Rigor has been and gone. Decomposition has set in but is not advanced. Some small animal damage . . .'

Harris winced.

'Cause of death?'

'I'll give you the formal answer to that question when I've completed the post-mortem.'

'The informal answer?'

'She was viciously beaten by a really sick bastard.'

'Don't see it as a domestic, why come here to beat up your wife or girlfriend?' Harris mused out loud, not looking for feedback, perusing the overgrown garden in disgust. Who had so much money that they could let a prime piece of London property fall into such a state?

'Definitely not a domestic, or at least a very odd one if it is.'

The medical man's tone caught Harris's attention. 'Why do you say that?'

He showed him.

'You're home early!' exclaimed Shaheed.

'There's no need to be sarcastic.'

'I wasn't. I just . . .'

'I took a cab home,' said Regina.

53

Why did she snap at her husband like that? Was it because she was trying to get some distance between them?

Because of what she knew?

Or was it just the symptom of a marriage that was not in the best of health – her long hours, his recent unemployment, all leading to tension on the home front?

Regina looked around the tiny flat, feeling a residue of the pride that came of having worked hard to create this snug environment, perfect for a young couple, perfect for a child. It hadn't been easy and it hadn't been cheap. And now she was considering throwing it all away. Which made her so many types of fool. But she had to know. She wasn't one of those women who could just believe the best in their men, unthinking loyalty was not her way.

'I couldn't face rush hour on the Tube,' she said, extending an olive branch.

'That's good,' he answered. 'You deserve to treat yourself once in a while. You work too hard.'

'Yes . . .'

Emma bounded into the room, drawn by the sound of her mother's voice.

'Mum, you're home!' she screeched, leaping into her mother's arms.

At least she didn't have to suspect her daughter of caustic undertones.

'You can help me with my bath and put me to bed.'

'That's why I'm home,' said Regina, hugging the little girl tight, relishing her unique child smell – milk, perspiration and baby shampoo. She wished she could bottle it and take it to work. She would have said it aloud except that Shaheed would have pointed out that it was her choice to leave the child and go to work in the first place.

Right now, it was a relief for Regina to walk out the door in the morning with a place to go, a place of respite, of distraction, and maybe – if she played her cards right – a place that offered a solution.

'Do you need dinner?' he asked.

'I'm fine,' she replied, trying to sound normal. 'I had a late lunch.'

'I had a cheese dog for dinner,' said Emma, pointing to the ketchup stains on her blouse. 'At the park.'

'We went to Hyde Park,' said Shaheed.

Why did he feel that she needed an explanation? Emma was his too, and whatever else might come between them, she knew he loved his daughter with his whole heart. Which made it almost impossible to believe him capable of any kind of wrongdoing. But that was naïve, and she knew it. Was a small lie about a big thing worse than a big lie about a small thing? Or were they both equal evidence of a lack of trustworthiness?

Shaheed sat down on the sofa, perched on the edge as if he might need to flee. Maybe he did feel that way, thought Regina. After all, she did.

To distract herself, she walked to the window and drew the curtains, letting in a shaft of evening light. She stared out, watching people on the street. Why did everyone seem so happy? Was it just distance that created that impression? Were any of them trapped too? Did one of them have a bruised wrist? And was it a precursor to further violence?

According to that scraggly policeman from Singapore,

death or flight were her only options. She smiled a little at this – she suspected that the faintly comic figure was a serial exaggerator.

A figure across the road caught her eye. He was standing next to a green recycling bin, glasses reflecting the last rays of the sun.

'That's strange.'

'What is?'

'Someone from work.'

She had been under the impression that he lived south of the river.

Regina shrugged and turned away from the window. What did it matter? Her problems were contained within this one-bedroom flat in Kilburn, nowhere else.

'Interesting day at the office,' she said, flinging herself on the sofa and letting Emma clamber up beside her. How was it that small children fitted so well, finding a way of snuggling that maximised contact, brought such warmth?

'How so?' he asked, sitting across from her.

'Scotland Yard is working with Commonwealth countries to look into community policing in London.'

'What does that mean?'

'You know the sort of thing – whether the police are engaging with minorities, respecting different cultures.'

'Instead of shooting them dead unarmed?'

She knew he was referring to Mark Duggan, an unarmed black man shot dead by the police. He'd been so outraged at the time.

'They have a lot of experience of that type of thing in Asia and South Africa,' she continued.

'I guess so.'

'We're examining cold cases – where the police cocked up.'

'Oh?'

'My guy – a Sikh fellow from Singapore – is looking into a case involving some poor Pakistani woman killed a few years ago.'

She sensed his sudden heightened awareness even though he hadn't moved a muscle.

'Fatima Daud, her name was. Must have been just after you came to this country.'

He didn't say anything, could not have said anything with his mouth clamped so tight that a thin white line followed the contours of his lips.

Regina's hand went to her bruised wrist, an automatic gesture. Was she really so afraid of this man whom she had once loved with her whole heart and soul?

'Fatima Daud?' he asked.

'That's the one.'

'Never heard of her,' he said.

'Well, you can't wait tables.'

'Why not?' asked Hanif.

'Because you look like a bloody terrorist, that's why not.'

'Is it better to look like a homosexual?'

Ibrahim's laughter was a sharp bark as he glanced down at the button-down, freshly ironed shirt, the dark jeans and Italian leather shoes. 'Is that what I look like to you? Better than the pyjamas you wear all day.'

He was referring to Hanif's baggy trousers with drawstrings and a long top in the same heavy cotton.

'Our father would despair of you too,' added Ibrahim.

Their old man had been a dapper, grey-haired individual given to wearing three-piece suits and a watch on a chain. They used to say in the neighbourhood that he was the living embodiment of Jinnah.

'I have no desire to ape Western customs.'

'It's not aping, it's assimilating, you fool,' snapped Ibrahim.

'Anyway, despite the suits, our father was still loyal to the old ways.'

'If you mean he was a misogynistic fool over Fatima, then you're quite right.'

Hanif bit his lip. His sister's death was still an open wound, even after five years. 'Father did what he thought was right.'

'She's dead because of him.'

'He wanted what was best for her, that's all.'

'To marry her off to some goatherd from the motherland?'

'The fellow was a computer scientist.'

'Whatever.'

'I remember when you too showed the correct respect towards Islam and our culture,' said Hanif.

'I was a teenager, brother. It was a phase; I grew out of it. I get more girls this way, you know, you should try it.'

'You mock what you don't understand.'

'And what is it I don't understand, Hanif? Enlighten me.'

'The drones that kill our brothers in Pakistan. The cluster bombs that rip children apart in Palestine.'

'You parrot the nonsense spewed by jihadi websites,' snapped Ibrahim. 'And simplify complicated issues.'

'What is complicated about dead babies?'

'It is the response that is complicated, brother, not the crime.'

Both had come to a standstill, standing by the side of the road, yelling at each other like children.

'We have an obligation under the Quran to fight injustice.'

'But only a long-bearded cretin like yourself thinks that means lying face down in the dirt in Syria, cowering from the Americans.'

'If you are so smart, why does Fauzi say that the restaurant is losing money?'

'It is difficult.'

'At the time our father died, the place was very successful.'

'There is more competition now. Other restaurants – competing with us on price, quality of food.' He glanced sideways at his brother. 'And there has been a drop in visitors to Southall.'

'What do you mean?'

'Muslim establishments are not the most popular. What do you expect, after the beheadings that involved British Muslims?'

'I heard about that,' said Hanif.

'I hope that is all.'

'What's that supposed to mean?'

Ibrahim turned to face his brother, toe to toe, shaved chin to unshaven chin. 'I think you know.'

The brothers glared at each other like strangers in a car park. Hanif was the first to look away but Ibrahim grabbed his arm, forcing him to turn back.

'Do you understand me, Hanif?'

'The problem is that you don't understand *me*.'

'Anyway, although I have not yet informed our brother, the situation with the restaurant has improved.'

'What do you mean?'

'For the last couple of months, sales and profits have gone up dramatically. Our worries are over.'

'Is that really so? God is great,' said Hanif and he meant it.

'God? If you don't mind, I'm going to keep the credit to myself.'

Despite having arrived with his wife a few days earlier, Inspector Singh was pleased and relieved that he had seen her only briefly in the evenings. This evening was no different. He was sitting on the edge of the bed – too soft and covered in a duvet with frilly edges – turning the pages of his cold case file when the door opened and Mrs Singh made an entrance, wielding shopping bags like an Olympic weightlifter.

'You're back,' she said.

'The evidence backs up your assertion,' he agreed.

'I've been out all day. My feet are swollen.'

'I'm not surprised – you seem to have covered every shop in London.'

He read the names on the bags: Harrods, Selfridges, Fortnum & Mason. Only the best for his wife apparently.

'Souvenirs.'

If souvenir hunting was his wife's only holiday activity, shouldn't the souvenirs be figurines of Sikh women carrying paper bags?

'For whom?'

'Your family.'

By which she meant *her* family. He was not Winnie-the-Pooh's friend, Rabbit, with all of the friends and relations.

She sat down on the bed next to him and kicked off her shoes. Sensible walking shoes, he noted. And she was wearing trousers. Trousers! He'd never seen her wear those before. Had she bought them in a street market in Singapore? Had they been specially tailored for her on Arab Street? It would seem she was wearing the pants in the family. It had really only been a matter of time.

'What are you doing?'

'Working on a murder.'

'Here?'

'Cold case.'

'What's it about?'

Her attention had been caught by the picture of the girl on the cover of the file. Mrs Singh's interest in murders was limited to those cases where the victim was female and from the Indian sub-continent. As far as she was concerned, the rest of the world pretty much had it coming, if not for conduct in this lifetime, then on some general karmic principle.

'Fatima Daud. Beaten to death.'

'When?'

'Five years ago.'

Where would she be now if she was alive? Married, two children, a good job? A young life cut short was a tragedy for the ages. From the downward twist to Mrs Singh's mouth, he knew she thought the same.

'Why?'

'Don't know. It was a very violent attack. Personal.' He didn't tell her about the hands, couldn't bring himself to do it.

'Who did it?' she demanded, kneading her low back with bony fingers.

'If they knew that, it wouldn't be a cold case.'

'Rubbish. The police always know.'

Was she right? It was true that the cops often had an eye on a likely lad. And, sometimes, that gut instinct was not backed up by sufficient proof so it never came to trial. Did he have any insights on Fatima's death now that he'd skimmed through the file? Right now, he patted his tummy ruefully, he was much more gut than instinct.

'Sometimes the police don't know.' It was galling to make such an admission to his wife.

'If the police don't know, definitely the family will know something.'

From the précis of interviews, the parents had been taciturn, siblings broken-hearted, friends shocked. There had been no boyfriend, no lover, none interviewed anyway.

Singh squinted down at the beautiful girl smiling at him. Was that likely?

With that uncanny ability she had of putting his thoughts into words, Mrs Singh said, 'She's so beautiful. Definitely the boyfriend did it. Jealous type.'

'There wasn't one, just some talk of arranging something with a boy from Pakistan.'

A thin eyebrow, plucked and shaped into a look of perpetual mild surprise, was raised. 'Maybe it was one of those men sleeping on cardboard boxes.'

There was never a shortage of suspects when Mrs Singh was on the case and now her ire was directed at London's homeless.

'I don't think this was a stranger.'

'Their hair and clothes are so filthy.'

Was she suggesting that the unwashed were more likely to be murderous?

'I guess it's difficult to have regular showers if you're homeless.'

'They're not *really* homeless.'

'Method actors practising for a role?'

'In this country, if you have no job, they give you money, can you believe it? So nobody has to be homeless.'

'Social security is not that uncommon in developed countries.'

'They give you money for *free!*'

'I'm not sure that's the right way to look at it.'

'No wonder no one works if you get paid anyway.'

Singh opened his mouth and shut it. He might as well argue with the government of Singapore, as his wife. Both of them were convinced that the dole was a slippery slope to indolence, drugs and a desire to express oneself in art or ironic editorial pieces about the nanny state.

'I bet you wouldn't work if someone gave *you* money.'

That was an interesting question. Would he, Inspector Singh of the Singapore police, bother to maintain gainful employment if he could live on the benevolence of the state?

He opted for firm denial. 'Nonsense. I love my job. I don't do it for the money.'

'Definitely you don't do it for the *money*.' His income without regular promotions to the higher ranks was a source of annoyance to his wife.

'Anyway, how can you love your job? You only hang around with killers and corpses.'

'Not for the conversation . . .'

'At least when you're in London, you should do some London things.'

'When in Rome?'

'Why are you talking about Rome?'

'Like shopping?' He'd rather pilot a fighter jet in a war zone.

'Like going to a musical.'

'I don't approve of men wearing make-up or singing.'

'What about Madame Tussaud's?'

'Waxworks? Isn't living in Singapore enough?'

'They have Hitler and Michael Jackson.'

'I'd go if they had me.'

'No need for a waxwork, you'll soon be pickled in beer.'

That was a little bit too close to home.

'I'm investigating a murder in the fine tradition of Sherlock Holmes and Miss Marple. What more do you want?'

She walked back towards him, holding a hot cup of tea. She handed it to him – a dutiful wife in actions, a termagant in conversation. Her eyes moistened as she stared at the photo of the dead girl.

'I looked just like that when I was young.'

Singh had no recollection of such a thing. Perhaps it was just as well. As far as he was concerned, Mrs Singh had arrived in her present form, wiry and opinionated, from the womb.

'If we had a daughter, maybe she would have been just like this girl.'

'Maybe.'

'Do you ever regret that we didn't have children?'

It was the first time in her life she had ever asked him that question.

'No,' he said firmly. How to regret such a thing when in his job he saw what happened to the children of others?

He knew she was waiting for him to ask her the same question but he didn't dare articulate it, didn't want to know her answer, didn't want to discover a lifetime of regret.

Mrs Singh touched the photo, Fatima's cheek, almost a caress.

'Maybe it *is* better if you find her killer ... instead of wasting your time sightseeing.'

The policeman looked down at her foldout map and spotted the correct inspiration for his London sojourn.

An Inspector Calls was showing at the Garrick Theatre. Let others spectate, he would investigate.

The dead woman was called Cynthia Cole. She was twenty-eight, a hairdresser, unmarried, an only child, engaged to a young man who worked as a car mechanic. She'd been trying to save up money for the kind of wedding she saw on television. Her father had been carried off with a heart attack the previous year.

'She wanted it all, see?' her tearful mother told Harris, clutching at a handkerchief with two fists. 'A white wedding and a really beautiful gown like that Kate wore and bridesmaids in matching dresses, six of them she had in mind.'

'And you were keen on the same thing?' he asked the young man he'd nicknamed Bob the Builder in his own mind but who was actually called Nick.

'I didn't mind.' He was red-faced and tongue-tied, holding back tears.

'Weren't you worried when she disappeared?'

'Of course we was.' It was the mother again. Had the daughter been as garrulous? 'Especially when she wasn't picking up her phone.' Harris had a flash of imagination, the phone ringing next to the corpse.

'But you didn't go to the police?'

Nick stared down at his feet, but the mother stepped into the breach again. 'Well, we thought maybe she got cold feet about the wedding on account that she and Nick had a big quarrel just before she left.'

If she knew that she was elevating the man who would have been her son-in-law to chief suspect, she gave no sign.

'A quarrel?' asked Harris, turning his attention to the red-eyed young man.

'Because of me not liking it that she'd sometimes flirt with my mates at the pub. It wasn't right when we was going to get married.'

'When and where did you have your quarrel?'

'Right here in this living room,' said the mum. 'And I could see why Nick was so mad. She always was a bit flighty, our Cynthia. 'Twas her dad's fault, always spoiling her.'

'And when did she leave?'

'The next morning. She woke up early, said she was going to stay with a friend, took a bag of clothes and left without any breakfast.'

'And this was six days ago?'

'Yes.'

'Did she say why?'

'She said she wanted to think things over, that she was fed up with Nick here always being on her case about who she saw, what she did.'

The mum spoke with a clarity that suggested an accurate account of events.

'And what did you do when she left?'

'I called him, Nick, right away, didn't I?'

'And what did you do?' asked Harris, turning to the boyfriend, cast by the mother in the role of jealous lover, looking more like a long streak of piss to the policeman.

'What could he do?' demanded Cynthia's mother.

'Perhaps you should let Bob ... errm, Nick here answer the question.' Had he almost referred to the suspect as Bob the Builder to his face?

'I didn't do nothing. It had only been a couple of days, innit?'

'*You* didn't call?'

'She never picked up when she was mad, didn't matter how many times I tried. It was her way, you know?'

This Cynthia had been a right piece of work, thought Harris, but if that were an excuse for murder, the planet wouldn't be overpopulated.

'Besides, it wasn't the first time she'd got mad at me. My Cynthia had a hot temper. I knew she'd come back, right?' continued Nick. 'We was going to be married.'

And on this note, the realisation that Cynthia wasn't coming back finally hit home because he sat down on the sofa and buried his face in his hands.

CHAPTER 4

The following morning, after some difficulty with a folding map and a toilet that required loose change, Singh found himself on the slow train to Southall. Singh took a seat and stared out of the window at a landscape of scattered trees and squat buildings. He put the case out of his mind and allowed himself to be hypnotised by the slats on the parallel track until the violent rush of a train passing in the opposite direction dragged him to the present. Just in time, as the sonorous voice announced that the next station was Southall.

Singh, once the train was stationary, clambered out and stared at the signboard that read 'Southall'. It also read 'Southall' in Urdu in green lettering underneath. You wouldn't get any of this political correctness in Singapore where the government had stamped out dialects in favour of Mandarin – in order to better communicate with the mainland Chinese. Unfortunately, the mainland Chinese had mostly learned to speak English. The best laid plans of men and authoritarian governments.

A car tooted and he looked up to see DI Carmen waving to him. As they rolled down the high street, he had to remind himself he was in London. The passers-by either hailed from the Indian sub-continent or were whites dressed in tie-dye T-shirts. The shops consisted of restaurants selling Indian food, saree shops and travel bureaus offering to bring one's nearest and dearest over from Pakistan.

DI Carmen, obedient to the dulcet tones of the car's GPS – did that device make society as a whole more obedient to instructions? – pulled up on a dilapidated street. A few scrawny plants grew along the pavements and most of the houses could have used a lick of paint. The front porches were so truncated that larger cars protruded on to the walkway like tumours.

She led the way to number fifty-two and he noted that she wore another trouser suit, this time in dark blue with a mandarin collar. She definitely didn't look like someone whose career fast track had taken a detour to a parking lot.

Carmen rang the doorbell. Singh waited for ten seconds – his patience threshold – and was about to press the buzzer again when he heard the snap of tight bolts.

A young woman, swaddled from head to toe in black except for two beautiful almond eyes, peered at him suspiciously from behind a chain.

'Yes?'

'I'm here about Fatima Daud.' Singh took the lead. It seemed prudent to demonstrate to DI Carmen that he was never the sidekick.

'Who are you?'

'My name is Inspector Singh and this is Detective Inspector Carmen.'

'Police?'

'Yes.'

'What do you want?'

'We're just here to ask a few questions.'

To his consternation, she slammed the door shut in his face.

'I thought you wrote to them,' he whispered.

'I did, and called – spoke to a man though.'

He was on the verge of sticking a stubby forefinger on the doorbell when the door was flung open once more, this time by a man with a black beard down to his chest dressed smartly in a suit. He stood aside by way of invitation and the inspector marched forward to find himself in a long dark corridor that smelled of stale curry. In cold climates the smell of spices got into the carpets and the curtains. Singh didn't mind. It was a better option than eating salads and cold sandwiches.

'This way,' said the man and led them into the room. It was neat, musty and cold. Singh smiled. In his younger days, his own home had a room earmarked for visitors, decorated with a few prized possessions and with all the life of a funeral parlour.

'I'm Inspector Singh and this is Detective Carmen.'

'Dr Fauzi. Fatima was my sister.'

As they shook hands, other members of the family put in an appearance. Mrs Fauzi sidled in. An old woman – Fatima's mother? – swaddled in shawls like a newborn, collapsed into an armchair. Her rheumy eyes wandered around the room.

There was no sign of her father. Dead, Singh assumed. From what he had seen of the residents of Southall so far, he would guess diabetes or a stroke. The dietary habits of the sub-continent had been lovingly preserved by the diaspora.

'My wife and mother,' said the doctor. 'You are here about my sister Fatima?'

'Yes.'

'To reopen the investigation? You have new leads?'

Singh considered lying, caught Carmen's eye and eschewed it. 'We wish to find out whether you would like to provide any feedback about the conduct of the investigation.'

'Now? After five years?'

'The police are reviewing cold cases.'

Fauzi laughed, but the underlying bitterness was painful to the ear. 'My sister, my beautiful sister, a cold case? To us, it is as if she left yesterday.'

'I'm sorry.'

'It does happen, despite the best efforts of the police,' said Carmen.

'Best efforts?'

'You don't agree?' asked Singh.

The doctor opened his mouth and then closed it again as firmly as a rabbit trap in the forest.

'What is it?'

'As your colleague says, it does happen.'

'You were going to say something else.'

'What could I possibly say about an institution as fine and upstanding as the British police?' The doctor stroked his beard as if it were a pet cat.

'What about your family? Do they share your views?'

71

Singh turned to look at the wife and the mother. There were shrugs all round, a closing of ranks. Was this what the reviewer had meant when he said that not enough had been done to break through the family's natural defensiveness?

'Looking back, there's nothing you would have done differently?'

Fauzi looked surprised. 'Of course there is!'

'And what's that?'

'I would never have let my sister take that job with the property agent.'

This was met with a corroborative nod from his wife although Singh noted that her almond eyes were glistening. Had she been close to Fatima?

The old woman said something in Urdu and Singh looked at Fauzi for a translation.

He was embarrassed, you could tell from the sudden fidgets.

'What is it?'

'She says that Fatima will be down shortly and bring some cakes.'

Understanding and sympathy dawned.

'My mother ... she drifts in and out,' he continued. 'At moments like this, I think it is God's way of protecting her.'

'Did Fatima have any other close family?' asked Singh.

'Our father died shortly after. He had a stroke.'

'Siblings?'

'She has two brothers apart from me.'

'And they're not at home?'

'Some of us have to work for a living, *Mr* Singh.'

Mister? Work for a living? Singh had a good mind to pin the murder on him.

'I informed them of your belated interest in Fatima's case, of course, when the letter came from the police.'

'Thank you for your help,' said DI Carmen. She rose to her feet and they all rose with her like some quietly choreographed dance.

Except Singh.

'What about a boyfriend?' he said, prompted by his wife's voice in his head.

'What are you asking?'

'Did Fatima have a boyfriend, a fiancé? Such a beautiful young thing.'

DI Carmen was glaring daggers at him but he ignored her with the practised air of a man who'd been married to Mrs Singh for uncountable decades.

'Of course not,' snapped the doctor.

'But surely she must have been very popular with the opposite sex?'

The old woman spoke to her son in Urdu once more. Perhaps she was having a lucid moment.

'Does your mother have something to share with us?'

'She was reminding me that Fatima was betrothed when she died. What I meant was that she would not have a boyfriend *outside* the family's wishes.'

'Oh? Who was the fiancé?' asked Singh.

'A young man from Pakistan.'

'So he was in the country at the time of her death?'

'No. They had not met yet,' he said.

'What? How could she be engaged to him if they had not met?' demanded DI Carmen.

'It was an arranged marriage that had the blessings of both families.'

'I'm familiar with the concept of arranged marriages,' snapped Carmen.

'What about Fatima?' asked Singh, cutting in before Carmen got them both thrown out for a lack of sensitivity to other cultures. He preferred to be thrown out for a lack of sensitivity to other people. 'Was she happy about it?'

'Of course,' he said. 'Why wouldn't she be?'

'A young woman growing up in Britain with her whole life ahead of her . . . she might not have understood the old way of doing things.'

'Fatima was a very traditional girl.'

Dr Fauzi's wife dropped her gaze to the floor.

'Anyway, she didn't run away from home because she didn't want to get married, she was murdered in cold blood, robbed of her life, her future . . . ' His voice cracked. He had loved his sister dearly, that much was evident.

Singh didn't put much stock in that. In his experience, people killed those they loved more often than those they despised, disliked or hated.

'And her killer is still on the loose,' continued Fauzi. 'No thanks to the police.'

'What about the . . . *hands*?' Singh whispered the last word, stealing a glance at Fatima's mother but she was lost in her own world again.

'Who comprehends the motivations of a killer?'

'You have no other explanation?'

'Are you – like the police of five years ago – trying to suggest that the family chopped her hands off in some sort of Muslim ritual?'

'It is a prescribed punishment for certain transgressions.'

'And if she had been crucified, would you now suspect all Jews? If she'd been shot, would you round up Americans? If you wonder why you struggle to earn the trust of minority communities, I think you have your answer, right there.'

White feet look blue after death. Black feet look grey. Cynthia Cole was no different. Her feet, protruding from the end of the green sheet, a label with her name and a number tied to an ankle, were bloodless.

'So when did she die and how was she killed?'

'Give me a moment – I think I left my magic wand back at the office.'

Despite his antipathy, the pathologist drew back the sheet almost respectfully, revealing the dead girl. The wounds showed up clearly against the cleaned, bare body and Harris felt his stomach turn.

'Most of the wounds are punctures; I've counted seventeen in all. She bled a fair bit so quite a few were pre-mortem, but I'm equally certain that the killer didn't stop after she was dead. Based on the depth of wound and level of bruising, I'd say this one to the throat—' he pointed and Harris swallowed his bile and looked closer '—or this one that pierced the sternum and reached her heart are most likely to have been the proximate cause of death.'

'Was she . . . ?' Harris was getting squeamish in his old age, unable to face down his job despite decades of practice.

Retirement beckoned. And then he'd sit at home alone and remember cases like this one.

'Raped? There were no signs of violence but she definitely had intercourse recently.'

'DNA?'

'Must have used a condom.'

'What about these other marks on the body?' Harris pointed at rough surface wounds on the arms and legs.

'The amount of wildlife in an English garden would shock you.'

At this rate, one of his few hobbies, tending to the boxed herbs outside the kitchen window in his small bachelor flat, would have to be abandoned.

'When was she killed?'

'Difficult to be precise. I'd say three to five days ago approximately.'

'She left home for the last time five days ago.'

'In which case she met her killer very soon after.'

Bob the Builder? Harris pictured the lanky sobbing fiancé and then ran his eye over the wounds. It was hard to imagine him being capable of such viciousness.

'The weapon was probably some type of screwdriver, heavy, large handle. No sign of it at the crime scene. The killer was probably right-handed, taller than her. A few of the wounds have a downward slant, the rest are more or less level.'

Harris realised what the pathologist was driving at. Some of the wounds had been inflicted when Cynthia was on the ground.

'You see these?' continued the pathologist, pointing at marks along both forearms.

'Defensive wounds?'

'Yes,' agreed the other man, looking pleased at the policeman's perceptiveness.

They both stared down at the truncated wrists.

'So why the hands?'

'Why don't you ask the killer when you find him?'

'Anything else?'

'I've swabbed everything and anything and sent the bits and bobs to the lab. The killer might have "missed a spot", as my mum used to say.'

'He?'

'That's supposition, of course.' He looked down at the body. 'Although a reasonable one.'

'What about the clothes?'

'Soaked in her blood. I found a couple of strands of hair – short, blonde – on her jacket, I've sent that in too.'

'Anything else?'

'A handkerchief in her pocket with some blood on it.'

'That's not news, is it?'

'But this was folded over with the dry bloodstain on the inside.'

'The lab has it?'

The medical man took off his blue mask and was human again, a father, a husband, a man who had one of the most unpleasant jobs in the world but who did it with diligence and delicacy, trying to right some of the wrongs that had been done to the murder victims who ended up on his steel table.

'Yes, but this isn't *CSI Miami*. I suggest that you look for her murderer the old-fashioned way.' Noting Harris's expression – inward-looking, contemplative – he said, 'What's up?'

'Something about this whole thing ... it's ringing a bell.'

They walked down the corridor. In the room they'd vacated, a shrill argument broke out in Urdu. Singh wished he understood what they were saying. It might have a bearing on the case.

Stepping out into the afternoon sun felt like an escape. Singh drew a deep breath; the crisp air was refreshing after the overheated house. The door behind them shut firmly, just short of a slam.

'Sorry,' he said. 'I guess that wasn't very tactful.'

DI Carmen's concerns lay elsewhere. 'Did you hear what they said?' she demanded.

'Which bit?'

'An arranged marriage to someone she'd never met!'

'I thought you said you were familiar with arranged marriages ...'

'I am – but to import a stranger from Pakistan?'

Singh sniffed his sleeve; the smell of curry had adhered. 'I doubt it's that uncommon. Even now.'

This small part of England seemed trapped in a time warp. Amazing that he'd been able to take a train to get here, he would have expected to need a Tardis.

'Poor woman.'

'That was not the worst outrage of Fatima Daud's brief life.'

DI Carmen's curt nod indicated her acknowledgement of his point.

'Was there anything in the file about this fiancé?' she asked.

'Just a mention that they were looking into the possibility of arranging a marriage,' said Singh. 'So it looks like the family was not entirely forthcoming during the initial investigation.'

'He wasn't in the country. I guess it isn't relevant.'

'There is no such thing as irrelevant information pertaining to the victim in a murder investigation,' he responded sharply, reaching for his packet of smokes.

She didn't answer, merely got in the driver's side and turned the key.

'What about the other two brothers?' asked Singh.

'What about them?'

'We need to talk to them.'

'No we don't.'

'How do we solve a murder without talking to all the family members?'

'We don't. However, we get a sense of the family's response to the policing environment during the murder investigation by talking to a select few.'

Singh glared at her. She must be one of those who wrote policing manuals. All PC rubbish about safety, and not endangering the public, and lines of communication and yes, race relations and community relations, but nothing about catching the bad guys. No wonder she was on the fast track. It was the same in Singapore. How else to explain the fact that Superintendent Chen was his boss and not the reverse?

'Besides, I think you've done enough damage,' she continued, impervious to his irritation.

'Where to now?' he asked.

'The agency where she worked.' Carmen engaged the gear with both efficiency and aggression. 'It's not far.'

In a few moments, they were cruising down the high street, passing supermarkets with vegetables and fruits piled high on the pavements outside.

She drew up along a double yellow line.

'You're parking here?'

'No, I'm dropping you. I'll find a space and join you.'

Singh made his way to the estate agent's. It was called Raj Real Estate and had been established in 1972. The window was filled with neat white cards containing photos of houses, interiors and exteriors. From what he could see, most of the properties were in the neighbourhood, which made sense. Glancing at the prices, the policeman noted that he was in the market for nothing fancier than a studio flat directly above a hairdresser's.

Singh pushed the door open and was greeted with an insincere smile from the girl behind the front desk who had, from the paraphernalia on the counter, been attempting to paint her nails black.

'Can I help you, sir?'

She was about the same age as Fatima would have been if she were still alive. Would she have been working here five years ago? He doubted it. He looked around. The three other desks in the cramped space were empty. Perhaps the agents were out showing places.

'Sara,' he said, reading her nametag.

'Without an "h",' she said.

She was very beautiful. Natural gifts – rich auburn hair, translucent skin, fine eyes the colour of a stormy sky – had been enhanced with expensive clothes and a deft touch with light make-up. What in the world was she doing working in a real estate agency?

'I'd like to speak to someone who's been here for a while?' he asked. 'Is there a Raj of Raj Real Estate?'

'Mr Raj does not deal directly with clients, sir.' She looked him up and down with the air of someone who doubted that any property he wished to buy or sell would be of sufficient value to interest the firm. 'Perhaps you could tell me if you're buying or selling?'

'My name is Inspector Singh. I'm here about the murder of Fatima Daud.'

'OMG! Really? That was the most shocking thing in the world. She was my best friend, you know. My husband doesn't even want me to work here. But I said, lightning doesn't strike twice does it, love?'

'So you were employed here then?'

'Yes, I was an intern just like Fatima. But I don't show houses any more. Jimmy won't allow it.'

Singh assumed the protective Jimmy was the aforementioned husband.

'We still talk about it all the time.'

'Who is "we"?'

'The staff, the agents – especially the women.'

'Why the women?'

'Well, it could happen to any of us! Sometimes, I swear I don't dare leave my house!'

'That must make it difficult to remain in employment.'

If she recognised the sarcasm, she didn't show it. This wasn't the brightest bulb in the firmament.

'She was killed while showing a house, can you believe it?'

Two doors opened at once. The front door heralded the arrival of Detective Inspector Carmen. A door to a back office revealed a thin face with receding hair carefully combed over a walnut pate.

'You are looking for a property, sir?' asked the new arrival.

'I'm looking for a murderer,' replied Singh.

'I beg your pardon?'

'I called earlier,' said Carmen. 'We're here as part of a review of the case of Fatima Daud?'

'Why didn't you say so?'

'I did,' muttered Singh.

The girl giggled and then clasped a hand over her mouth, maybe recognising for the first time that her excitement was macabre, especially for someone claiming to be Fatima's best friend. Singh would have liked to continue the conversation with this gossipy receptionist but Carmen was looking decidedly impatient.

'Come in to my office. I am Mr Raj. Fatima was like a daughter to me.'

Singh followed Mr Raj into his inner sanctum, but not before Sara without an 'h' had slipped him her name card, smudging the polished nails in the process, with the words 'Call me! I can help!!!!' scrawled on it.

'Something is going down, I know it, I feel it. Soon. Very soon.'

'But you don't know what it is?' The policeman was scruffier than his informant but neither of them would have made the front cover of *GQ*.

'No, I've been sniffing around, putting myself out there. But if I ask, show too much interest, I will draw attention to myself.'

'You must know something? The target? The trains again? Newspaper offices like in France?'

'Something different. They're excited, I don't know why.'

'That's all we need, excited bloody terrorists.'

The sarcasm wasn't lost on the first man. 'If I push, I will lose the trust.'

'If you don't know anything, I don't see the point of this trust you claim to have gained. Nobody is telling you anything.'

The informant shrugged. 'You never know when or where you might hear something, be approached by someone – it just takes one loose tongue and a sharp ear. But it takes time.'

'But, according to you, we don't have time!'

The men glared at each other, impotent to do anything, lashing out, supposedly on the same side, hating each other with a passion.

'Who do you suspect is involved?' asked the detective. He was unshaven, tired. A good disguise but also a true reflection of his state. These were difficult times. Chatter on websites, threats on the streets, potential jihadists everywhere, too much for one man or an entire police force to bear. He was terrified of missing something. Of being wrong. Of being responsible. Of being out of time.

The security forces had picked up those four jihadists as they recorded suicide videos, but that had been more by luck than judgement. Cold feet by one of them and then a desperate attempt to buy himself clemency with the authorities by shopping his fellow would-be killers. But it was like a game of whack-a-mole – one attack thwarted, one cell captured, another and another appearing.

'Names?' he asked again.

'None so far. There are any amount of possibilities unfortunately. You know that as well as I do, better. Every community has its angry young men, its returning jihadis, the whole country is a time bomb.'

'But there must be a planner in there somewhere – it can't just be wannabe suicide bombers with shit for brains. I don't lose sleep over them.'

'I don't know.'

'What about your family?'

'What about them?'

'Just asking.'

'Well, don't.'

'I don't need facts or evidence. Just give me a handle.' The undercover detective cracked his knuckles as if to suggest that he would find a way of getting the information from anyone identified.

The informant was unimpressed. He knew the system with its courts and Human Rights Act and recorded interviews. The British police did not beat information out of prisoners on home soil – only if they managed to get suspects picked up abroad in which case they had no qualms about outsourcing the violence to less particular security forces.

'Even if I could give you a name these guys won't talk.'

'But at least they'll be out of circulation.'

'For how long? Thirty days, give or take? And then what?'

'And then I don't know! But if you're telling me an attack

84

is imminent but you don't know by whom, when or where, what do you expect me to do? Sit here and wait?'

They were both standing so this was a misnomer – side by side along a line of porcelain urinals, a strangely private place to have a brief conversation without attracting attention. The place was damp and stank, graffiti scrawled on the walls, substances on the floor that would keep a forensic chemist occupied for weeks.

'Aren't you picking up anything? Surely you have other sources? Electronic surveillance?'

All the silver bullets of the movie industry. These bloody terrorists – even a turncoat like his informant – overestimated the power of the police, the government. All things considered, it was just as well. Or there might be more of them out there, trying their hand at mass killings.

'What about money?'

'What about it?'

'These guys must be getting funding from somewhere for whatever they're planning.'

'There's no shortage of financial backers of jihad,' said the informant.

'But they still need to get the money into the country – any ideas on that?'

'Do I look like an accountant?'

The detective zipped his pants. 'We need you to come through – you have to get me something, anything.'

'I'm doing my best.'

Was he looking for sympathy? He'd come to the wrong place. There were no prizes for best effort in this class.

'Save it for the widows and orphans.'

CHAPTER 5

'She was like a daughter to me,' Raj said again when they were seated facing him across a desk with such a polished surface that Singh could see his shimmering reflection in the wood. The neatness of the desk contrasted with the clutter in the tiny office, files piled high on the floor, a coat stand draped in jackets and scarfs.

'How long had she been working for you before she was killed?'

'About six months. Only part-time, mind you. She attended a walk-in interview and I hired her on the spot.'

'Part-time? What was she doing the rest of the time?'

'Studying for an accounting degree. At the Open University.'

'An ambitious girl?'

'Yes, yes. In fact, she used to help me with the firm's accounts. A girl like that, I knew I wouldn't keep her long.' Perhaps recognising that his words were unfortunate, Mr Raj had a quick gulp from the mug of tea in front of him.

'No American will pour coffee in this mug. Ever!' Singh read on the side. Souvenirs from the Iraq War turned up in the most curious of places.

'And was it your practice to send young girls to show houses on their own?'

'We have a rule that our female agents be accompanied by one other person when meeting a client for the first time.'

'But?'

'But I was short of staff.'

'And so you sent her to her death?'

Silence greeted this statement. DI Carmen's narrowed eyes suggested to Singh that she thought he'd overstepped the mark.

'How did you decide on Fatima?'

'She was our best agent. Could sell snow to an Eskimo.'

'And this property required your best agent?'

'The asking price was on the high side, that's all. It was a lovely place.' He added regretfully, 'Impossible to sell afterwards, of course.'

'So what's the system for a sale?'

'We have numerous property listings on our website and window plus a lot more on file.'

'And if someone is interested in a particular property?'

'They might call – our number is listed next to each property description – or walk in and ask for further details or a viewing.'

'And in this case?'

'Someone called, asked for that property specifically.'

'Whom did they speak to?'

'Errr . . . me.'

'According to the record, a Mrs Hamid wished to see the property?'

'Yes, another reason why I allowed Fatima to go on her own – because it was a viewing by a woman.'

'Or a man pretending to be a woman?'

'Nonsense. I would not have been fooled by such a masquerade.'

'Or an accomplice arranging the encounter?'

'I suppose that's possible,' he said, the words almost inaudible. 'I had no reason to suspect anything at the time.'

'There were no red flags?'

At this question, Raj looked up and made eye contact, an honest man with nothing to hide or a man who knew how an honest man with nothing to hide would be expected to behave. 'No, nothing at all.'

'So what happened?'

'She went along a bit before the time – my rule is that the customer should never be kept waiting.' His chest puffed up a little at this, a man who liked to think that he ran a tight ship.

'If it had been a man waiting for her at the property, instead of this Mrs Hamid, would she have gone in with him?'

'I don't know. Probably … he might have said he was the husband, or that Mrs Hamid would be along in a minute. I don't know! The point is that she must have gone in because she was killed indoors, right?'

Singh pursed his lips, tried to imagine the girl, meeting a stranger, going in with him. Surely, her radar, as a single young woman, finely tuned by society, would have seen the potential for danger?

As if sensing Singh's doubts, Raj continued, 'On the other hand, she might already have entered the premises. She was very diligent so she'd have gone in to switch on the lights, make sure that there were no dead rats lying on the kitchen floor, that sort of thing.'

There was more to this house-selling business than met the eye, decided Singh. He was fortunate that he'd lived in the same house for thirty years, every element perfect for his comfort except when Mrs Singh rearranged, spring-cleaned or furniture-shopped.

'I need to see the house,' said Singh, more to himself than to Mr Raj or DI Carmen.

'Err . . . it is not on our books any more,' said Mr Raj.

Singh couldn't blame the owner.

'It's been unoccupied since the murder,' interjected DI Carmen. 'I checked yesterday.'

'Such a shame,' said Raj. 'A beautiful property – rarely find that kind of value on the market. But people are superstitious, you know?'

So much for Fatima being like a daughter to him – his thought had turned from murder to mortgages soon enough.

'Mr Raj, is there anything concerning the investigation – I know it's more than five years ago – which you would like to bring to our attention?' asked Carmen.

'Like what?'

'Anything you feel might have been done differently . . . better? Any complaints you might have had but didn't air at the time?'

Singh almost laughed out loud. If anyone reopened his old

cases and asked the parties involved if they had any complaints, their responses would fill a book. By definition a cold case was a failure. The only person happy at the lack of resolution would be the murderer.

'Why do you ask me that now? What's the use?'

'We're conducting a review,' she said.

'Since you ask—' his voice became querulous '—I thought the police were very unpleasant to me at the time.'

'In what way?'

'They seemed to think that I had caused her death by letting her go to the house on her own. As if it's the same thing, sending a girl to show a house to a *woman* and beating her to death.'

Beads of perspiration had popped up along Mr Raj's upper lip and a nervous pink tongue popped out of his mouth like an eel and licked the salt and water away.

'As I told them at the time and I'm telling you now, I had nothing to do with it, all right? Nothing.'

His men were going house to house around Bayswater. So far, they had nothing. No one had seen the victim enter the empty house. No one had seen her on the street, or on the next street. Her blown-up picture, smiling, recent, provided by the mother – 'she'd got a passport recently, you know, for the honeymoon' – was met with indifference, curiosity, concern, but a big blank as far as information was concerned.

Cynthia didn't own a car – 'what would she want with a car when she hasn't even got a licence' – so she hadn't driven herself, but there was nothing to rule out the possibility that she'd taken a taxi, got a lift or even ridden to the place with her would-be killer. A quiet residential area, there were no CCTV cameras on the street. Harris asked for the film from Bayswater Station and the surrounding bus stops.

Enormous amounts of forensic samples had been collected: fingerprints, fibres, mysterious substances scraped up from the house, from the garden, from the body. Harris hated this aspect of policing, waiting for a scientific miracle, for some DNA sample to match that of a person with a history of violence and no alibi. There was no humanity in it, asking a computer to provide a name. On the other hand, it saved a lot of hours and impressed jurors. Harris, scratching his thinning, ash-grey hair, couldn't think of a single case that he'd brought to trial where the jury hadn't convicted in the presence of some damning piece of forensic material. It was the telly. It gave people a misguided idea of the reliability of such evidence. The phone, battery dead, found in her bag, was being analysed as well. And might prove more useful than the make-up, a few ten pound notes in a purse, loose coins, keys which he'd verified came from her mother's house as well as one stand-alone Yale key attached to a rabbit's foot that allowed entry to Bob the Builder's bedsit.

But despite this hive of activity, initiated on his instructions, Harris remained inactive, thoughtful. Bottom line, he wasn't convinced by any of their lines of inquiry. He sat in his car and waited.

His phone rang and he reached into the distended pockets of his jacket until he found the old-fashioned Nokia.

'But what if you need to check something on the Internet, sir?' one of the younger men had the temerity to ask him once.

'Then I call you and tell you to do it.' That had shut the bugger up.

'Boss?'

'Yep.'

'I put your request through the system.'

'And?' Harris didn't fathom the system known as HOLMES, but he did know that an attempt had been made to computerise records that allowed key words searches to be made into past cases. No longer was the process of drawing connections dependent on the memory of old cops or the diligence of young ones. Now the oracle didn't need food or sleep, didn't suffer from amnesia or stress. But the quality of the result still depended on the quality of the input. And so he had asked this young techie to hunt through the records, given him the words to use, the clues to seek, the timeframe to try.

'And we have a hit.'

'When and where?'

'Five years ago – a young woman, Fatima Daud, killed in an abandoned house. She was an estate agent.'

'Who was in charge of the investigation?' demanded Harris.

'Ronald Anderson, sir. He's retired now.'

Harris squinted. He thought he remembered Anderson, worked out of Southampton Row towards the end of his career. A decent chap, old school. Perhaps lacking that spark of imagination that led to conclusions when the evidence was less than crystal.

'Get me the files.'

'There's something you should know about that, sir.'

*

Singh stood outside Raj Real Estate and waved his goodbyes to DI Carmen. He had insisted that they put their efforts on hold for the day – 'I'm sure you have better things to attend to than cold cases,' he'd said.

She'd looked at him with suspicion and he'd beamed at her like an avuncular stranger.

'I thought I might get myself some Indian food,' he'd said confidingly when she appeared to hesitate. 'And then meet my wife, do a bit of shopping.'

'All right. We can reconvene tomorrow.'

'Can you do me a favour in the meantime?'

'Depends on what it is.'

'Check his background.' The inspector had indicated the agency with the point of his turban. 'See whether Raj has got a record – for anything.'

'Why?'

'I didn't like him.'

She'd squinted at Singh, arms akimbo – maybe policing wasn't personal in the UK, decisions not made on the basis of the likes and dislikes of individual coppers.

'All right,' she'd said at last. 'But no getting into mischief, you hear me?'

Had she suspected that he might branch out on his own, investigate a few leads without her? What a nasty suspicious, albeit accurate, mind. He'd have to be wary of this woman.

Singh reached for his cigarettes, trying to decide what to do next. Call the number the receptionist had given him? Track down the other brothers of Fatima? Be true to his word and stop for a snack?

To his disgust, the tatty cigarette packet was empty except

for a few dried bits of tobacco but a newsagent at the end of the road promised salvation.

He stood in line, trying not to fidget, admiring the fact that there were more Sikhs gathered here than he had ever seen in one place before. He hoped that none of them objected to his buying fags. That would be embarrassing – like bumping into his wife in public.

'Yes?'

'Cigarettes, please,' he whispered.

'What?'

'Cigarettes,' said Singh a little louder.

'What brand?'

'Er . . . Marlboro.'

'Sikhs are not allowed to smoke!'

He'd known the woman was a troublemaker from the moment he set eyes on her.

'It's for a friend.'

'I don't believe you.'

There were nods of agreement from some of the other shoppers. Were they going to form a lynch mob?

'I need a newspaper too,' he said loudly, determined to shift his purchases to less controversial items. His audience muttered amongst themselves behind his back. 'And maybe I shouldn't encourage my friend to smoke.' He handed back the packet. The crowd dispersed.

'Which newspaper?'

'Do you have a local?'

'The *Southall Gazette*?'

'OK.'

'It's out of stock.'

'Really?'

'Really.'

The teenager behind the counter, skinny, spotty and grubby, was starting to annoy the policeman. Most of the other shoppers had drifted out and so he was alone again. Even the Richelieu of the Sikhs had wandered off, no doubt looking for some other poor fellow to harangue.

'Is there any other newsagent around here?'

'Two streets down.'

'I'll go there.'

'They don't have it either.'

'How do you know?'

'Because my dad owns that shop too.'

So this irritating specimen was the heir to a newsagent's empire while he, Singh, was a lowly policeman waiting for the day he would collect an inadequate pension. Where was the justice in this world?

'Are you quite sure?'

'Yes.' The fellow decided to safeguard his inheritance by unbending slightly. 'What is it you were looking for?'

'Property for sale.'

'Best look in the windows of the agents then ... there's one right across the road over there.'

'I've done that,' said Singh. 'Anyway, pass me that packet again, will you?'

'I thought you didn't want to encourage your friend to smoke?'

'I'll sacrifice myself then,' replied the policeman. The two shared a smile. A smoking Sikh and a recalcitrant teenager, alike in their dislike of busybodies.

'If I want to track down someone in the neighbourhood, how would I do that?' asked Singh, packet safely hidden in his deep coat pockets.

'What are you? A debt collector?'

'I'm looking for some old family friends.'

'But you just happen to have lost their address?'

Singh's fellow feeling with the spotty teenager subsided.

'Who is it you're looking for anyway?'

'Dr Fauzi Daud's family.'

'They're your friends?'

'Why not?'

The youth shrugged. 'They live just down the street – from the direction you came, in fact.'

So this kid was a super spy as well?

'I know where they live but no one's at home. Where do they *work*?'

'How much is it worth to you?'

'I thought you were going to inherit an empire?'

'Yes, but my dad keeps me short in the meantime.'

'Ten pounds?'

'Dr Fauzi works as a GP on Lewis Road.'

'The others?'

'That'll cost you another tenner.'

'This is the most expensive packet of cigarettes I've ever bought,' grumbled Singh, handing over another note.

The youth held it up to the light, then folded it and slipped it into his front pocket.

'Khan's – it's a restaurant on the high street. The younger one, Ibrahim, works there, runs the place; the middle one seems to be at a loose end.'

'How do you know that?'

'He comes here for cigarettes too ... at odd times of day.'

'Between jobs?'

'He's tanned and jumpy and has been away for a while. Only got back a few weeks ago.'

'So?'

'You join the dots, man.'

Singh refused to be drawn. He had no idea what this young man was hinting at but the best way to find out was to hunt the brothers down. He made his escape, looked up and down the street warily and then at his watch. There was no way he dared light up in this suburb of Delhi so there was only one option. Food.

Food would allow him time to think. And he wanted to think about his cold case. The whole thing stank more than a Serangoon Road wet market on a hot afternoon. The policeman was convinced there was more to Fatima's death than an unlucky encounter with a murderer posing as a house buyer, choosing a victim at random. His nose told him this was personal.

Singh approached the nearest food outlet as if he was part of a covert military operation. The inspector was not one to wander into a restaurant and trust to luck that the food was acceptable. He checked for clues. Was the place packed? If yes, quite likely the food was good. But if it was packed with the wrong type of customers, this evidence was flawed. For instance, an Indian restaurant crowded with white folk? The food would not be spicy enough. A tourist joint was not interested in repeat customers so probably got by on décor and on price, rather than on taste. An empty place might have rubbish food, or it could just be slightly pricy or have a bad-tempered proprietor.

Singh stopped in front of the shop next door to the restaurant. It offered solutions for everything from 'hair loss' to 'psoriasis'. Did he want to eat next door to a place that dealt in skin infections?

'Inspector?'

Singh had seen her in the window so he schooled his face into impassivity before he turned.

'Yes.'

Fatima's sister-in-law was still dressed from head to toe in black. And still the almond eyes shone with unshed tears as if they were back in the cold home she shared with what was left of Fatima Daud's family.

'There is something you should know,' she said. 'About Fatima.'

'Cowards die many times before their deaths. The valiant never taste of death but once.'

That might be true, but it didn't take into account how many times a brave man died while screwing up the courage to go forth where no man had gone before. Martin Bradley winced. Had it really come to this? Mixing his Shakespeare and his *Star Trek* while lurking at the main entrance to Marlborough House?

He just wished that Regina would put in an appearance so that he didn't have to suffer these metaphorical deaths. The fact of the matter was that he was terrified of confrontation. His hands were as clammy as dead fish; his heart was thumping an urgent message, 'Run! Hide!'

He saw her, elegant figure with the long blonde hair falling from a middle parting like an old-fashioned model. She was wearing a trench coat. A slim skirt, vertical stripes in black and white, reached to the top of her boots. The collar of a white shirt was visible in flashes, largely obscured by a silk scarf in a vigorous tropical design hanging loose around her neck. He could have spoken to her at the office but this was better, more private. She'd be less defensive, less wary of being overheard.

He waited until she was close, stepped out into her path from behind a rhododendron bush.

She started and then managed a smile.

'Martin, you frightened me. What are you doing here?'

'Waiting for you, of course.'

'Oh? Is something the matter?'

'I think you know there is . . . '

'What do you mean? Something to do with the cold case you helped me with? It's fine, I've passed it to the cops; the Singapore fellow seems keen to get to the bottom of things.'

'It's not that.'

'What is it then?' She glanced at her watch. He took it for a hint that she was in a hurry but he ignored it.

'You know what you have meant to me, you know what we have meant to each other.' The words ran together in his haste to get them out.

'What in the world are you saying?' She was taller than him, looking down at him with those blue eyes, the colour of the sky in a Magritte painting.

'We've had some difficulties, I will be the first to admit it, but we need to work on it, not just walk away. You really mustn't just walk away.'

She was a little afraid now, he could tell. She glanced around, reassured herself that they were in bright daylight near a major public building with a manned security post not that far away. He watched her size him up, decide that, though his behaviour was odd, he wasn't a threat.

'Martin, there's nothing between us.'

'These past few weeks we've worked together, grown together, I know you feel the same way.'

'I'm a married woman, with a child!'

'Emma is as much part of me as you are.'

'How do you know about my daughter? How do you know her name?' She was backing away, small steps a prelude to a dash for safety. 'What's the matter with you?'

'You told me – you told me everything. About Emma. About your husband. Why are you acting this way?'

'I did not tell you anything. You're really sick.'

'I love you. We love each other.'

'I love my husband and daughter. I don't even know you!'

His fear for her, for them, made him strong. He grabbed her arm. 'Stop, Regina. Listen to me! It's your last chance. Believe me, it's your last chance.'

CHAPTER 6

They were attracting curious looks. A short, plump Sikh man and a devout Muslim woman hobnobbing on the street was not a common sight in Southall or anywhere else on the planet.

'Let's go in here,' she said and swept into the shop offering cures for everything.

'Vertigo, sex problems, foot rot,' he read, once inside. Perhaps because no one wanted to admit to such a motley assortment of ails, the premises were empty except for a gnomic figure reading a book behind a counter that was almost lost in the gloom of the interior.

'My name is Mariam,' she said. 'I wish to tell you what I know but it is important that my husband does not find out that I spoke to you,' she explained in a low voice. 'He would not approve.'

Singh nodded energetically as if clandestine meetings with women were a common occurrence in his life.

'Would he object to you meeting me or to the information you wanted to share?'

'Both.'

'Fair enough.'

'It's about Fatima.'

'What about her?'

'There's something you should know, that the police should know.'

'About the fiancé?' It was a guess but seemed good for a flutter.

'She was not keen to marry him.'

'Why?'

'She was quite independent.'

Was there a trace of envy in the voice of this black-clad woman?

'So what's the big deal? If she didn't want to marry him, surely all she had to do was say "no"?'

Her doe eyes widened and pupils expanded until they overwhelmed the almond irises. 'I think you do not understand.'

Actually, Singh suspected he did. He was familiar with arranged marriages – hadn't he had one himself? – but also forced marriages, where the brides were less than willing. 'Tell me.'

'The family – her father, the brothers – insisted that she had to fall in with the family's wishes.'

'What was her reaction?'

'She was obstinate. There were many quarrels in the household. I was only recently married so my opinion was not sought.'

Was it sought now? The image of Dr Fauzi popped into his

mind, well-cut suit and long beard, a man straddling two cultures. Singh doubted he consulted his wife very often.

'What would have been your opinion?'

Her eyes took on a reflective sheen. 'I felt that she should fall in with the family's wishes ... In fact, I told her so.'

'She talked to you?'

'Yes, even though I did not agree with her choices, I understood some of the fear and the doubt she was feeling.'

'Yours was an arranged marriage too?'

'Yes, and I said to Fatima, "You see how happy I am with your brother? The family always knows best in these matters."'

'But now?'

'But now I understand a little bit more of why she fought it.'

The shop owner regarded them through a magnifying glass held to his eye as if it also functioned as a telescope. The woman turned away and grabbed something off the shelf like a determined browser. Singh sensed her fear; she was like a recently captured wild animal.

'Why are you telling me all this?' he asked.

'It is not right that Fatima's death should be unsolved.'

'Why didn't you say anything to the police at the time?'

The look she gave him spoke volumes. 'I did not feel it was my place.'

'But now?'

'Fatima was a good girl. Happy. Kind. She deserves better.'

'But that's not the official family position?'

'My husband would kill me if he knew I was talking to you.'

Now did she mean that literally or figuratively?

'They would say that nothing can bring Fatima back, so what is the point of reopening old wounds, of exposing the family to public censure?'

Singh's gaze locked on an entire shelf of weight loss products, all promising amazing and immediate results. Would they still work if he went straight to the curry house next door after purchasing the products? What would his wife say if she could see him now? Her dull, overweight husband in a strange land, with a strange woman, contemplating shedding some pounds for the first time in a decade – she would definitely suspect the worst.

'I appreciate your telling me this,' said Singh. And he meant it. This woman had risked an ugly domestic situation to play police informant as a matter of conscience. But so far she had not told him anything he couldn't have guessed or that was pertinent to Fatima's murder.

'There's one more thing,' she said, her tongue loosened by his acknowledgement.

'What's that?'

'The husband-to-be, from Pakistan. He *was* in the country when she died. They asked him to come over. They thought it might change Fatima's mind . . . if she met him, to see that he was not the monster of her imagination.'

'And did it change her mind?'

'She refused to see him.'

'Why was she so determined not to marry this young man anyway?'

'Fatima was quite . . . modern.'

Singh wrinkled his nose. In his experience, Asian girls from strict families rebelled by wearing jeans and make-up but tended to fall into line when it came to the big issues. After all, hadn't his wife married him? Unless, of course, there was someone else involved.

'There was someone else?'

She nodded.

'A boyfriend?' he asked.

'Yes,' she answered, an inscrutable look on her face, a mixture, Singh suspected, of disapproval at these wanton ways and envy at the freedom.

'She met him through work. He was a lawyer. She had not known him long but . . . ' She seemed unable to complete the sentence, unable to find a way to express the intensity of young love.

'Did the family know?'

She didn't answer outright. Instead, she said, 'I advised her very strongly to forget him, that it could never work. But she refused. She said she must inform the family.' Her voice was lost and faraway, almost a whisper, an echo from the past. 'I said, you must not tell them. You cannot tell them. But she was stubborn, Fatima. Just like my husband. They are . . . they were so alike but neither of them could see it.'

'So she told them?'

'Yes.' Her eyes shut as if the memory was too painful.

'And they didn't approve?'

'Of course not.'

'Why not? A lawyer – sounds like a catch to me.' Mrs Singh would think so and she was the final arbiter on desirable features in future husbands.

'He was white . . . '

*

Hanif leaned back in the leather office chair that had once belonged to his father. It still smelled of the old man. That combination of hair cream and aftershave had been so unique and yet so ubiquitous until, one day, it was gone. Just like that. Just like Fatima really. The fragility of human existence – he understood it so much better now that he'd seen the consequences of battle, of bullets, of shrapnel. When his sister and then his father had been taken, he'd been devastated by the loss, but also the suddenness of the loss. Now he knew that death was always sudden – even when one sat in a foxhole with a machine gun trained over a ridge, the actual separation of body and spirit could never be anticipated, although, with the right preparation, it could be accepted.

In that moment, in that back office, he could only be grateful that his father was not around to see the mess his younger brother had managed to make of things. The dapper old man with his well-trimmed moustache would not have survived this flood of red ink. The financial deterioration in the business was staggering. In the six months Hanif had been away, the restaurant had gone from comfortably profitable to haemorrhaging money.

There were receipts for overpriced computer equipment that he could not find anywhere in the small office, staff bills were astronomical even though he could only see, through the glass panel in the office door, his brother and one other young man – a minimum wage earner if ever there was one – out in the front. Even though customer receipts had been falling, the food bill had gone up sharply.

'Are you running a soup kitchen out the back?'

Ibrahim, who had just stepped in, slammed the door behind him with real force.

'What is that supposed to mean?'

'That we are paying staff and buying food far in excess of the demands of the restaurant. I was hoping that you had a hitherto unknown charitable inclination that might explain it.'

'You don't know anything about the business. Prices have gone up. You can't get staff any more.'

'I do know all that.'

'Then why are you complaining?'

'We don't have customers to justify the level of expenditure.'

'There's no point having nothing to cook when a big table walks in. If you'd put in the hours I have, you'd realise that.'

Hanif wanted to punch Ibrahim or scream or take the first flight out, back to where he'd made a difference, found brothers despite the absence of blood ties. Instead he took a deep breath.

'Where's all this computer stuff we bought?' He held up the receipts as he spoke, tempted to actually walk over and wave them under his brother's nose in the best Basil Fawlty style.

'It was a bit rubbish so I've sent it back. Should get the new stuff soon.'

Why was his brother unwilling to meet his eyes over something as trivial as tech repairs?

'Anyway, I told you things had turned around.'

Ibrahim walked over to a filing cabinet and retrieved a document. 'These are the figures from the last couple of months.'

Hanif looked down at the fresh numbers with growing puzzlement. 'But this is a remarkable turnaround.'

'Yes, so there's nothing to worry about and you can wipe that gloomy look off your face before you drive away the customers.'

Hanif watched him go without further protest. His first thought, on looking through the accounts, was that Ibrahim had been embezzling money from the restaurant. To what end, he could not begin to guess. An expensive woman? A gambling habit? Blackmail?

But now he was even more confused by the sudden influx of cash. He stared through the glass panel – only a couple of tables were occupied. How in the world had the place done so well in the recent past? What magic had his feckless younger brother worked? Hanif steepled his fingers and rested his chin on them.

Something wasn't right. But what was it?

And, in the greater scheme of things, did it matter?

Later that evening, as Singh recounted the conversation to his wife, he was not surprised that she too thought the boyfriend's 'whiteness' was sufficient grounds to reject him.

'In this day and age?' he asked.

'It was five years ago. Anyway, they're not being racist.'

'Rejecting someone on the grounds of skin colour is not being racist?'

'It's just their way of saying that he is not from the same background or culture, does not have the same values.'

'Why don't they just say that then?' Singh was feeling irritable. He couldn't reach his feet to take off his socks and they smelled of dried fish after a long day tramping around London.

'Would she have listened?'

'Fatima? Maybe not.'

'The children always think they know best. And always they are wrong.'

'But she was an English girl brought up in England – who is to say that she was so different from this lawyer fellow anyway?'

'If she was quite Western in her ways that would have just upset the family more.'

His wife might have a point. Perhaps the marriage to the Pakistani fiancé had been arranged as a last ditch effort to bring Fatima back within the fold.

'There is also the religion.'

This was probably the real sticking point, thought Singh. A devout family might overlook racial divides, but not religious ones. And Muslims, feeling under pressure by the conduct of their co-religionists in other countries, were circling the wagons like never before. He reminded himself that they were discussing events of five years ago, tried to remember the politics of that time. It hadn't been long after the Tube bombings.

'Are they very religious?' asked Mrs Singh.

He pondered the question. The doctor brother. His wife in hijab with just the uncovered window around her eyes, the eyes themselves the proverbial windows to the soul. 'You could say that, I guess. I haven't met two of the brothers yet.'

'Then they killed her to stop her marrying an outsider.'

109

Singh remained silent, wondering whether there was any-thing in what his wife had said. If she was right, which of them? Or was it all of them?

'There's something I didn't tell you,' he said. 'About the murder.'

She looked surprised; he was rarely squeamish.

'Her hands were missing.'

'How is that possible? What do you mean?'

'The hands were removed at the wrist.'

'You mean like an amputation?'

'Yes.'

'That's disgusting.'

He waited for her to leap to conclusions.

'Muslims do that,' she pointed out.

He refused to provide encouragement.

'But it doesn't make sense,' she added slowly.

'Why not?'

'The hand thing is for theft, right? What did she steal? Even if she stole something, why would the family overreact?'

'So theft is *not* as bad as having a boyfriend of another race or religion?'

'Of course not.'

'I still can't believe that the family killed her.' Was that hope speaking? Was he drawing conclusions based on the world as he wanted it to be rather than as it was?

'Then it was the boyfriend.'

'Why?'

'If she refused to marry him ...' Mrs Singh paused for thought. 'It could also have been the Pakistani fiancé for the same reason.'

110

'All plausible scenarios,' said Singh, 'but not much use without some evidence one way or another.'

Mrs Singh tossed her long plait over her shoulder and climbed into bed, pulling the covers up to her throat so that it appeared as if the decapitated head of his wife was determined to have the last word. 'I can only tell you who did it.'

Was this a good time to point out that she'd named every available suspect?

'The rest is your job,' she continued. 'Otherwise, what's the use of having policemen in the first place?'

CHAPTER 7

The house in Holland Park was empty. In the front yard, grass and weeds had lost the competition for space to FOR SALE signs. Every housing agent in London seemed to have staked a claim to sell the place, but, from the grimy windows, flaking paint and general air of decrepitude, none of them was lining up a commission any time soon. Looking more closely, Singh noted that Raj Real Estate was not present amongst the billboards.

'Remind me why we're here again?' demanded Carmen, who was clearly not a morning person.

Singh was also not a morning person. 'You're humouring me.'

'As long as we're agreed that we're still not *investigating* a murder.'

'The sister-in-law tracked me down yesterday.'

'Oh?'

Singh briefed her on the conversation and watched her

wrestle with the knowledge that they had real leads in their cold case.

'So what do you think?' she asked.

'I think you and I could solve Fatima's murder.'

'We have nothing concrete.'

'A mysterious fiancé? A white boyfriend? Angry brothers?'

She didn't answer, instead gingerly inserted a key in the door. Singh took it as a good sign. Her interest was piqued. She just wasn't going to admit it anytime soon.

'Who's the owner of this place?' asked Singh.

'A man by the name of Rodney Carswell.'

'This is a long way from Southall. How come Raj got the original commission?'

'Apparently this Carswell and Raj have other business dealings, so he gave him the property to handle as a bit of a sweetener.'

'This Rodney fellow told you all that?' asked Singh.

'Couldn't shut him up,' she said. 'He's still bitter that this place is unsellable. It sounds like he could use the cash. But even in London, murder – if bloody enough and unsolved – can tank the value of a house.'

Singh glanced around. 'It looks like a nice neighbourhood.'

'Houses are going for around two million.'

The rest of the homes were freshly painted and well preserved. On the other side of the road was a small park with benches, evergreens and narrow winding paths. A group of women in smart coats were standing in a circle, gossiping and rolling prams with large wheels back and forth.

'This house is a blot on the neighbourhood.'

'It's a mews house,' said DI Carmen.

113

'A what?'

'Used to be a stable.'

Singh looked around with newfound respect. What a remarkable place London was that people paid millions to live in accommodation for horses.

'I also checked to see if Raj was in the files for anything,' said Carmen, 'like you asked.'

'And?'

'He's quite the businessman. Raj Real Estate is just a tiny part of his empire. He has a carwash operation, a halal butcher and a trucking business and has been suspected of everything from people smuggling to money laundering at one time or another. But nothing's stuck.'

'I knew he was a crook. You should chuck him in jail.'

'Here in Britain we require evidence before incarceration.'

Singh opened his mouth and then shut it again. Was this the dry wit that these Brits were famous for?

'Shall we go in?' she asked. She pushed the door as she spoke and tried a light switch at the entrance to no avail.

'Electricity is probably turned off,' she said.

The inspector took a lighter out of his pocket and lit the small blue flame. It flickered in the draught, singed his thumb and went out.

Carmen opened her rucksack and produced a large torch. 'No need to set fire to the place.'

Singh stepped over the vast pile of junk mail and into the corridor. It was easy to see that this had once been an attractive residence. As he wandered through, his path lit by the large torch, he noted that the proportions were cosy but sufficient. Even through the caked windows, enough light came in to suggest that in better times it would have been bright and homely.

'She was killed in the hall,' said Singh, largely because he didn't like the quiet of empty houses.

Carmen pushed open one half of a double door. She stepped through without hesitation and Singh was in two minds whether he admired her courage or rued her lack of imagination.

He followed her but stopped just inside the door. There were no chalk marks on the wooden floor, no fingerprint dust on the surfaces, no blood splatter on the walls, nothing to suggest that murder had once been done here. And yet, the hair on Singh's neck stood up and he felt suddenly cold inside his heavy suede coat. Was the ghost of Fatima Daud tethered to this place, waiting for all eternity to show the home to the Mrs Hamid she'd set out to meet?

'According to the crime scene report, she was found in front of the fireplace.'

Singh walked towards the hollow blackened square.

He tried to picture the scene. The young woman, perhaps drawing the killer's attention to the size of the fireplace and painting a picture of delightful family evenings basking in the flickering warmth of a hearth fire, oblivious to danger. Was that possible? Or had she sensed that something was wrong, kept talking, wondered whether she should make a break for it, good manners and a conviction that she was just giving in to silly fears keeping her there, still talking, until the first blow.

Carmen shone the torch across the floor.

Singh averted his eyes. He didn't want to see bloodstains, or imagine them. His companion was made of sterner stuff.

He opened his mouth to say something and then snapped it shut.

Had he just heard a sound – a closing door?

DI Carmen too had grown still. With a quick movement, she switched off the torch.

In the few moments it took Singh's eyes to adjust to the darkness, he heard the floorboards in the corridor squeak.

The door to the hall was open and they both turned towards the entrance. The inspector wished that the British police were not so reluctant to arm their officers. Was it the killer returned to the scene?

Singh's heart was dealing hammer blows to his chest cavity. At this rate, he'd have a heart attack before he had a chance to fight for his life against this intruder.

He took a step forward, determined to confront the person or persons unknown. DI Carmen raised a palm to stop his progress and then put a finger to her lips.

What were the odds it was the killer come back to relive memories?

Singh ignored Carmen's gesticulations and crept forward. He took up a position behind the half-open door, ready to jump the stranger, the murderer. A floorboard creaked again.

Mrs Singh sat with Goody, her cousin twice removed, in a flat above a kebab joint on the aptly named Punjab Lane. She was making the rounds of the relatives, known by name, age, degree of separation and income level, but not personally.

Her husband was the topic of the conversation as was often the case when Mrs Singh was in the company of her relatives. This was a happy subject because the thirty-something creature sitting across from her was unmarried despite the best efforts of her parents, siblings and acquaintances to find her a suitable spouse.

'He was asked to come here by the British police, you know?' she said.

'What for?'

'They needed some help on a case.'

'Which one? That child who disappeared in Wales? That one I'm sure the mother did it. Don't know why the police are hunting everywhere. Just ask her. Or is it the soldier who was killed?'

Mrs Singh was loath to admit that Singh had not been called in on a matter that was still in the headlines.

'Another matter.'

Goody was not as compliant as she should have been for an unmarried daughter with a middling job who was a disappointment to her wider family. 'The police here are very good.'

'Still they need Singh.'

'But did you see that they caught those terrorists already? Thank goodness. Nowadays I don't even get on a train if I see one.'

Mrs Singh knew that her cousin meant 'if I see a person that my prejudices suggest to me might be a terrorist'.

Inspector Singh might have protested this approach, but his wife was not so inclined.

'The problem is all these converts – like the shoe bomber,' she said. 'Much harder to spot.'

'That's true.' Goody's tone was despondent.

Both women paused to consider the vagaries of fate and

117

then the second cousin went on the attack again. 'So why do the police here need him?'

'He has a lot of specialised experience,' retorted Mrs Singh, hoping that she was not going to be required to detail her husband's abilities.

As far as she could tell, he hunted after murderers successfully because he had an uncanny ability to comprehend the minds of the criminal classes. This was not a talent that would raise her in the esteem of her family.

Goody, who was as broad as she was tall, had an upper lip that merited Gillette's best and was dressed in a pink tracksuit that spoke of an inclination to exercise, but not the execution, looked unconvinced.

'It's a case from about five years ago – a young woman was killed. Beaten to death.'

'So? Girls in this country are getting killed all the time.' She said it as if it was a badge of honour. 'They are drunk as often as the men and they stay out till three am, four am, what do they expect? My father would never allow such a thing.'

From this, Mrs Singh deduced that Goody was referring to Caucasian girls.

'This girl was Pakistani Muslim. Her family lives in this area.'

'Oh! You mean Fatima Daud?'

'You *knew* her?'

'*I* didn't know her.' Goody looked offended, as if knowing someone who was subsequently murdered was the height of bad taste.

'But everyone knew about the case. Her family is quite well known. They own Khan's restaurant down the main street. Her father had a stroke afterwards. Who can blame him?'

Mrs Singh nodded sagely. If a relative had the bad luck to be bludgeoned to death, the family could not expect to carry on regardless. As suicide was frowned upon, a stroke or heart attack was the appropriate way out.

'The youngest son is running the restaurant now. But I hear business is not so good.' From her melancholy tone, it was clear that she attributed this misfortune to the same cause – the untimely death of Fatima Daud. 'The mother is gaga.'

'There are other children?'

'Yes, two more sons. The oldest is a doctor. And the middle one – he's been away but no one knows where. He should try and help out. From what I hear, the youngest doesn't know how to run the show.'

This fitted in with Mrs Singh's broader views on the feck-lessness of the younger generation, a position she could hold with complete freedom as she and Inspector Singh had no offspring. 'Children are all the same,' she said.

'I still don't see why your husband has come here for such a matter.'

'We can't expect to understand.'

Goody placed a whole *ladoo* in her mouth and then spoke anyway, spraying crumbs on her ample lap. 'It's true that they never found the murderer.'

'My husband will surely solve the case then.'

'Not that hard,' said Goody, coughing over the fragments of dessert.

'What do you mean?'

'Everyone knows who did it.'

*

119

DCI Harris was not a happy man. His wife had left him for her yoga instructor almost five years before. He was estranged from his only child, a daughter at Sheffield University studying art history or some such rubbish.

The relationship with his wife had foundered on his long working hours, drinking habits and obsessive-compulsive behaviour. His relationship with his daughter had hit the rocks when he'd suggested that some hairy lout living on the dole and reeking of pot was not a suitable companion for a policeman's daughter. That was almost two years ago.

He still kept two pewter-framed pictures of the women who had walked out on him on the mantelpiece of his small flat south of the river. But the frames were tarnished, rather like his memories.

However, his current unhappiness was not due to any incident in his past but his immediate present. He stepped across the threshold, feeling as tentative as when he was a rookie on his first assignment. The fact of the matter was, this case – the death of Cynthia Cole – was turning into a right pickle.

He'd been assigned to the case because he was murder squad. He'd been around and available and willing – after all, he had no reason to rush home. His station, Paddington Green, was busy with those terrorists they'd arrested making suicide videos and who were now locked in the basement somewhere under the extended detention provisions of the terrorism legislation. So a cop with Homicide and Major Crime, at a loose end because he wasn't involved in the terror investigations, had been ripe for the job when a messy murder turned up.

But now, brushing aside a cobweb and stifling a sneeze, he would have given a lot to be away on holiday using some of that leave owing to him. He took another step forward and then decided to emulate the fools who rushed in. After all, he was no angel.

Harris hurried down the corridor, shouting loudly, 'Is anyone in?'

'Who the hell are you?' demanded Singh.

'This is a private residence. You're trespassing.' DI Carmen was standing on the balls of her feet. Singh wasn't sure whether it was a readiness to fight or flee. The former, he suspected. There was something about her stance that suggested martial arts training. A shame he couldn't imitate her. His stance was more old man with bad knees hoping not to be called upon to move quickly.

The newcomer's shadow loomed large against the wall and then snapped across the ceiling as if he'd arrived with the devil's host at his back.

'I could ask you the same thing,' retorted the man, reaching into his jacket pocket.

Singh was about to throw himself in the way of the inevitable bullets when the newcomer produced an identity card.

'DCI Harris,' he said. 'You must be DI Carmen and Inspector Singh.'

Carmen stepped forward, ran the torch in cursory fashion over the identification and said, 'Sorry, sir. We thought it was an intruder.'

'The murderer come back to the scene?'

Singh didn't like the dry tone adopted by the senior police-man. Although, when said out loud, a return visit by the killer did seem absurd. Walking over, he noted that Harris looked like a rugby player gone to seed, a bodyguard reduced to pro-tecting C-list celebrities. They shook hands and the other man had a dry hand and a firm handshake.

It was just as well the British police were not armed. Otherwise, they'd all be dead in a shootout caused by mis-taken identities and itchy trigger fingers.

'So what are you doing here and how do you know who we are?' Singh was pleased that his voice was authoritative. This Harris fellow spoke like someone who was used to being top dog but Singh was no man's poodle.

'Is this where it happened? The murder?'

'Yes, chief. Fatima Daud was killed here five years ago.'

The inspector scowled. DI Carmen had gone over to the enemy quick enough. She was all co-operation and sweetness now, no sign of the surly face that she apparently reserved for him. Why did all women treat him so badly? He didn't pro-voke it, so it must be a symptom of their gender.

Harris surveyed the room and then turned abruptly on his heel. 'This place gives me the creeps. What say you we con-tinue this conversation outside?'

So he too sensed Fatima's unhappy spirit. They followed him meekly until they were once more outside in the sun-shine, standing on the stoop.

'Let's go over there,' said Harris, indicating the park, now empty of women and prams.

Singh marched across the cobblestones without further invitation. He sat down on a park bench and crossed his arms across his potbelly but the two Met officers remained standing. Again, Singh was struck by how large the other man was, broad shoulders, barrel chest, beer gut and a few inches past six foot if one accounted for the hunch. Outside, in the bright light, the suggestion of wear and tear was reinforced. His thinning hair was ash blond mixed with grey, the face a map of fine lines with deeper crevices around the mouth and eyes.

But the blue eyes he turned on Singh were still clear.

'You're on a task force to look into whether improved community relations would have made a difference to various unsuccessful murder investigations.'

'Just the one cold case,' answered Singh. 'Fatima Daud.'

'And your conclusions so far?'

'Everyone has secrets but not all secrets are relevant to the crime.'

'So why were you visiting the crime scene?'

'I find it helps sometimes.'

'Helps find a murderer, but a crime scene is silent on the pernicious subject of race relations.'

Singh, caught red-handed overstepping his remit, didn't feel obliged to respond. He was pretty sure that the Met hadn't sent a senior investigative officer with eyes like chips of blue glass to hunt him down just to administer a dressing down about jurisdictional boundaries.

Singh looked across at the house, dilapidated even from this distance. 'Why are *you* here?' he asked.

'What do your investigative instincts suggest, Inspector Singh of the Singapore police?'

The policeman looked up, expecting irony but finding only genuine curiosity.

'That there's been another murder,' he said. 'My instincts tell me there's been another murder and, for whatever reason, you think it is related to the killing of Fatima Daud.'

'So who did it?' demanded Mrs Singh.

'Did what?'

'Killed Fatima Daud!'

One moment, 'everyone' knew who had done it. Next, this annoying relative of hers – perhaps Singh was right about the futility of tracking down long-lost kin – was adding two sugars to her third cup of tea.

'The younger brother, of course. He has a terrible temper, since he was young. Always getting into trouble at school. Very embarrassing for the family.'

This was not a satisfactory response as far as the police-man's wife was concerned. Having a hot temper was not evidence of a murderous disposition. Otherwise, her husband would be dead and she would be behind bars. Also, there were two younger brothers.

'The lousy-restaurant brother or the recently-came-back-from-somewhere-but-you-don't-know-where brother?'

'Restaurant brother. Ibrahim. He's the youngest.'

'He wouldn't have done the hand thing, though.'

'What hand thing?'

Mrs Singh stared at her cousin. How was it that she, who appeared so up to date on all the elements of the crime, didn't know about the amputation? Unless the information had not been released to the public. Which made sense; it was the kind of sensationalist stuff that would have enticed all the weirdos out of their hidey-holes.

'Fatima's hands were cut off.'

'What?'

'And the killer took them away.'

'That's a Muslim thing right?'

Mrs Singh had an inkling of how annoying her husband must find it when those around him trotted out the obvious.

'No, it's not a Muslim thing,' she snapped. 'It's a murderer-of-Fatima thing.'

'If you want, we can go over there.'

'Where?'

'The restaurant.'

'I'm not hungry.' Honestly, how much could this woman eat? Hadn't she just shovelled all the *ladoo* meant for two down her gullet?

'No. I mean the restaurant belonging to the Daud family. You can see him, the brother who did it.' Goody's eyes sparkled with excitement and her cheeks wobbled in time to her nodding head. She reminded Mrs Singh of those ceramic cats that Chinese shopkeepers kept at the checkout counters to bring them good luck.

'That is a good idea,' said the policeman's wife, after a brief contemplation of her options. 'My husband relies on me to help him with his cases. Quite often,' she added, casting caution to the wind, 'I have to tell him who the killer is, you know?'

'Really?' This time there was no scepticism from the distant cousin.

Mrs Singh was assailed with doubt, a sensation so rare she wondered at first if she was having an allergic reaction. Had her assertion been too emasculating of her husband? There was nothing to be gained in Punjabi circles from undermining the menfolk; they were the source of all status within the community unless one's children were particularly academically gifted. A wife's role was to cook and claim due credit for any successes, but as the power behind the throne, not the monarch.

'Of course he is the best investigator in Singapore, so sometimes he doesn't need my help.'

'But he always needs your cooking!'

Her reputation had preceded her. 'Yes, definitely he cannot survive without my cooking,' she agreed.

They set out together, détente restored. The policeman's wife was pleased by the array of locks and padlocks required to safeguard the premises. 'Lot of crime here?' she asked.

'Oh yes. Houses broken into, electronic items stolen, everyone murdered.'

'Singapore is just the same,' said Mrs Singh.

Her husband and his boss might have protested this statement but Mrs Singh was not interested in lies, damned lies or statistics, only that nebulous feeling of danger that indicated she was only a well-locked door away from being mugged or murdered.

The two women walked briskly – it was so much easier to keep up a fast pace in a cold climate – down Punjab Lane. The policeman's wife wondered whether to take a photo with the road sign and then decided against it. She didn't want to look like a tourist.

'Is Singapore like Southall?' asked Goody.

'Not so many Sikhs in Singapore,' she replied.

They entered Khan's and paused to admire the décor,

which had stolen liberally from the Moghul era and consisted of arches, decorative tiles and walls embedded with coloured glass that shone like jewels.

'Very nice,' said Mrs Singh.

They sat down at a table and were provided two menus and a bottle of water.

'That's him,' whispered Goody.

'Who?'

'The son who runs the place – Ibrahim. The killer.'

He was a handsome fellow. Tall, good skin, clean-shaven, wide smile for a customer.

Goody ordered two samosas and a cup of tea, waited for the waiter to depart and leaned forward conspiratorially. '*They* say he is taking money from the restaurant for his gambling habits.'

Ibrahim did have a dissipated air.

'They say the father died of sorrow because of what happened to Fatima, but others say that he died when he found out about his son's gambling.'

The inspector might have inquired after the identity of the mysterious 'they' who held so many opinions that they were not loath to share, but Mrs Singh understood the way grapevines worked in small communities.

'If you ask me, he looks like a killer.'

The main door opened and a man in a smart suit and long beard walked in.

'The other brother, Dr Fauzi.'

'Doctor of what?'

'My GP,' responded Goody. 'Clinic on Lewis Road.'

The brothers were having a conversation and, from the scowls, it was not amicable.

'I wish I could hear what they're saying,' said Mrs Singh.

'We should have worn disguises,' replied her cousin.

The presence of amateurs was an impediment to a successful investigation. Mrs Singh rose to her feet and said loudly, 'I'm going to the bathroom.'

She hurried towards the doors at the back, which she assumed led to the toilets. The inspector's wife pushed open the one with a picture of a nubile female figure and stepped in quickly. Once within, she closed it except for a crack and stood with her ear to the gap.

'Hanif is a fool, playing soldiers and then screaming in his sleep every night.'

'What we need is a solution.'

She leaned forward to try to hear more – this was getting interesting – what solution? And which brother had said what? A sudden darkening at the crack gave Mrs Singh just enough warning and she leaped back as the door swung open, almost losing her footing. A late grab for the sink saved her blushes.

Mrs Singh washed her hands and then splashed water on her face. She would never admit it to her husband but this business of investigation could be quite stressful at times. It would be worth it, however, if she could present the killer to him on a plate.

'Cynthia Cole, twenty-five years old, was beaten to death in an empty house in Bayswater. She was found the day before yesterday but had been dead for around two days before that.'

'Was she an estate agent – like Fatima?' asked Singh.

'No, a hairdresser at some posh place on Bond Street, but the body was found by an estate agent,' replied Harris.

How often were people killed in empty houses in London? wondered Singh. Was it sufficient to indicate a single murderer was responsible for two deaths or was it a venue of choice for a motley crew of killers?

'Murder weapon?'

'Something along the lines of a screwdriver.'

'It was a hammer the last time,' pointed out the inspector.

He realised that he was instinctively fighting the suggestion that the two cases were related. Was it because he didn't want his cold case to be snatched away from him as part of an active investigation? After all, there would be no room for Singapore's finest if this fellow took over.

'Doesn't sound like enough to be tying the two murders together,' he said. 'Different weapon, five years apart, different parts of London.' He continued, 'Caucasian victim?'

'Yes.'

'Muslim convert?'

'Lapsed Catholic. Why do you ask?'

'Eliminating possibilities,' said Singh.

'Is there any other connection between the victims?' asked Carmen. 'Did they know each other?'

'We're looking into it. Early doors.'

'So what else do you have? There must be something else. Or you wouldn't be here.'

'There's no reason for me to tell you any of this,' pointed out Harris.

'Quite right,' agreed Singh, 'But you're going to anyway.'

'Why do you say that?'

'A gesture of courtesy between two old plodders?'

'I'm not well known for my manners . . .'

Singh warmed to the other man. After all, he was not famed for his courteous nature either.

'A cementing of the bond between the Met and the Singapore police?'

'We have a bond?'

Singh laughed out loud. 'Well, *you* tracked us down to this empty house. You want something from me, and to get it, I'll need to know what you know.'

'What have *you* found out so far about the Fatima Daud killing?'

'Why would I have found out anything? I'm looking into community relations.' He couldn't prevent a snort punctuating the sentence.

'I know your type, Singh. You're like a bull in a china shop. Once you've smashed everything to smithereens, you hunt amongst the shards for clues.'

Singh quite liked the image this conjured up. 'I've found out that there are people who might have wanted Fatima Daud dead.'

'For instance?'

'A boyfriend she wanted to marry against her parents' wishes and a fiancé who'd been shipped in from Pakistan who had the family's blessings but not hers.'

'And we didn't know this before?'

'Apparently not.'

'Also the family – if her intransigence was offending their conservative instincts. And I took a dislike to her ex-boss, Raj of Raj Real Estate.'

'And yet none of these people would have any reason to kill Cynthia Cole,' remarked Harris.

'And so the question is, why are you so certain that the murders are connected?'

Harris turned his face to the sun as if he needed to ward off a sudden chill. 'I think you know,' he said quietly.

The lines on Singh's forehead were etched in precise parallels.

He had known, of course. But he'd just preferred not to say it, think it, in case words gave shape and substance to such foul imaginings. Sometimes, he was as superstitious as his wife.

'The hands?' he asked.

'The lack thereof,' replied Harris.

CHAPTER 8

After Friday prayers, the rituals so soothing to a turbulent soul, Hanif sat with the other men and listened to the imam deliver his sermon. The man was impassioned – and careful. A plea for Palestinian statehood, a reminder of American drone attacks on civilians, but no suggestion that young men should take up arms for the cause.

Afterwards, Hanif found his slippers and fell into conversation with the others. Men from so many backgrounds – Bangladeshi, Pakistani, the West Indies, Lebanese, whites – all united by an adherence to Allah's word.

It felt good to be back at his East London mosque, the one he had always preferred to the sanitised versions closer to his home in Southall. And what was a trek across town to a man who had crossed deserts?

'The imam says much but doesn't say even more,' said a young man, clean-shaven, wearing jeans and a U2 T-shirt under a motorcycle jacket.

'Since the crackdown at Finsbury Park mosque and the deportation of Abu Hamza, the *ustaz* have learned to pick their words,' agreed another.

'Any mosque that is run by Tablighi Jamaat has to be cautious,' said the first young man.

Hanif was surprised. Not many worshippers knew the sects that ran individual mosques, not even one such as Tablighi Jamaat with ties to overseas jihadists as well as domestic terrorists.

'Nowadays, there is no need to use the loudspeakers in the mosque, messages are more effective on the Internet.'

Hanif knew the speaker by reputation, a middle-aged man named Choudary.

'I am too old for these things,' said a man who could have worked part-time as Santa during the Christmas season, such was his girth and snowy beard. 'And this Internet is dangerous when it means we cannot supervise our young, stop them from foolishness.'

'What sort of foolishness?' Spoken by a man in a suit, scratching his reddish beard. Middle management in some retail chain, guessed Hanif. At a guess, stationery and office supplies.

'Like the four they caught in Bradford – how is it that no one in their community, their family, knew what they were up to?'

'Maybe they knew,' said Choudary.

'Then why keep quiet?'

'Because they understood their motives?'

The old man spat, a gob of white froth on the grey cement. 'Morons!'

'I do not like it that we have to watch our words. The imam should speak from the heart,' said the retail manager.

'Where is our freedom of speech?' demanded the young man who had spoken first. 'Does the Magna Carta only apply to Christians?'

'Your spirit does you credit but you should learn to combine it with wisdom,' said the old man.

'What you call wisdom, I call cowardice.'

'Fighting talk for one with soft hands.'

'There are many ways of fighting, old man – not all of it is about waiting for the American drones to send you to Allah in fragments.'

'What do you mean?' asked Hanif.

'Do you attack your enemy's hands or his head?'

'Neither,' said the old man. 'Islam is a religion of peace.'

'What would you do?' asked Choudary.

'Attack the head, man! What else?'

'Whose head? What head? You speak in riddles.' The old man was too irascible for a Christmas job. 'You should try *using* your head.'

Not bad for a parting shot.

'You just wait, old man. And you will see!'

'Talk is easy,' said Hanif. 'If words were bullets, Muslims would have a worldwide Caliphate by now.'

'Some of us are more than talk.'

The youth seemed conscious that he had said too much because he avoided eye contact and his words were spoken in a mumble. The men in the small group were silent so he walked away, hands jammed deep into his pockets.

They watched him climb on a superbike, pull on a helmet

and race away, spitting dust into the face of the holy. The rest dispersed as well, their minds already on the next thing: lunch, work, wives, mistresses, children – Muslims but just the same under the skin as everyone else – until only Hanif and Choudary were standing alone.

'Wannabe jihadists,' growled Choudary. 'Looking for fame and girls, not the glory of Allah.'

'We cannot know what is in his heart.'

'It is what is in his head that makes me nervous.'

'You believe he might go abroad to fight?'

This was met with a sly, knowing glance. 'As others have done, Hanif?'

Hanif knew that among the mosque committee members there would be those who knew of his exploits. It was inevitable, even desirable.

When Hanif did not respond to his question, Choudary continued, 'No, that young man does not have the discipline for such an arduous journey. However, there are many different ways to serve.'

Hanif nodded his agreement. There was nothing much to say to such a self-evident, if banal, truth but he tried anyway. 'And that is my constant desire, to find new ways to serve.'

'To be the point of the sword in this arduous struggle against injustice?'

Much was understood in that moment. 'Exactly,' said Hanif.

'However, that young man has a valid opinion.'

'About what?'

'That the best way to disable an enemy is to attack the head. Do you agree?'

Their eyes met. Hanif still clear eyed, the other man showing the mild opacity of impending cataracts.

'Yes,' said Hanif. 'I do agree.'

'But the situation is almost hopeless,' said the other man. 'The enemy is strong, we are weak.'

'Pretend to be weak, that the enemy may grow arrogant. If sovereign and subject are in accord, put division between them. Attack him where he is unprepared, appear where you are not expected,' said Hanif, paraphrasing Sun Tzu.

'And that is your philosophy?'

'It is my art of war.'

'A heavy instrument, with a sharp cutting blade, was used to remove the hands.'

'Same MO as Fatima Daud.' Singh remembered his shock and disgust when reading that part of the autopsy report. Neither emotion had ebbed in any way. He could taste bile at the back of his throat. 'Was the weapon found at the scene?'

Harris shook his head. 'Neither the screwdriver nor the chopper.' He grimaced. 'Nor the hands for that matter.'

'Was it the exact same blade?'

'The pathologist won't commit, but it's certainly very similar.'

'Post-mortem injury?'

The policeman from the Met nodded.

Fatima's hands had been removed after death. A frenzied attack followed by this cold-blooded dismemberment. It seemed that this killer was a creature of extremes. Singh's bearded chin came to rest on his chest as he leaned back against the park bench.

'It was a neat job,' said Harris.

'Did it require an expert?' asked Singh. 'That wasn't clear from Fatima's autopsy report.'

His thoughts were on the brother, Fauzi, although for the life of him he couldn't think why the doctor would have seen fit to collect such a gruesome souvenir from the body of his sister. Surely, they had family photos?

And who was Cynthia Cole to him?

'According to the pathologist in the Cole case, it required a steady hand and some general knowledge but not a doctor or a nurse or anything like that.'

'So not an expert but someone with nerve . . .'

'Yes, apparently it's quite common in dismemberments for there to be evidence of hesitation in the nature of the wounds. More than one cut, some not deep enough, trial and error. But this killer achieved his aim with a single slash to each wrist.'

'It was such a peculiar feature of Fatima's case.'

'And now – now that we know there are two women?' asked Harris.

'A trophy or souvenir for the killer?'

'So somewhere we have a murderer with a collection of hands at the back of the freezer.'

'As evidence of kills?' said Singh. 'For someone else?'

'I don't even want to think of that.'

Singh recognised this as a figure of speech. He suspected that DCI Harris had thought about nothing else since discovering the similarity between the two killings.

There was something else bothering him. 'You've found only two?' he asked.

'Only two in the system,' said Harris. 'Mind you, this is

such an unusual feature, I doubt anyone would have failed to input it into our computerised records.'

'What made you look in the first place?'

'I had the vaguest feeling that I had heard of something like it – there must have been some gossip across the stations when the first killing occurred.'

Even in the country that had provided the world with Jack the Ripper and the Moors murderers, amputation was worthy of mention.

'Why only two, that's my question?'

'Who's to say it won't escalate now?' It was the first time DI Carmen had spoken in a while and, looking at her pale face, Singh could see that she was afraid.

'There's no reason to assume that there will be more,' insisted Harris.

'The gap of five years ... this killer doesn't have the usual bloodlust I would associate with a multiple murderer.' He spoke like an expert, but, truth be told, Singh didn't have much experience of murders like these. Singapore had its fair share of killers but perverts were not thick on the ground. Not those who acted out their sick fantasies anyway. And, despite his words, Singh had that cold feeling at the nape of his neck that always spoke of a danger not yet fully grasped.

'There's another possibility, of course,' he said, rubbing his neck to exorcise this sudden fear.

'What's that?' asked Harris.

'That this was a copycat killing.'

'I thought of that,' said the London cop. 'But details of the wound were not released to the press at the time of Fatima's death.'

'Why was it kept quiet?'

'I haven't had a chance to speak to the DCI in charge yet. I suspect they didn't want to turn the whole thing into a circus. Put something like this out there and every nutjob in town calls in to say that they did it, or knows someone who dismembers their pets for fun or was making jokes about needing a spare pair of hands.'

'And it doesn't explain the five-year delay either – how someone would get wind of the details of an ice-cold case and then decide to copy it *now*,' agreed Singh.

'What's the plan, sir?' asked DI Carmen.

'First of all, I need to thank you for your involvement in the case of Fatima Daud.'

'But you don't need us any more ...' Singh had been resigned to this outcome from the outset. It didn't mean he liked it. Or that he was going to pretend to like it.

'This not a cold case so much as a hot potato,' agreed Harris. 'We'll have everyone on it, Scotland Yard, every cop shop across town – the maximum resources.'

'I volunteer to join your team, sir.'

Harris hesitated.

'She's got a head start looking into the Fatima murder,' said Singh. 'You'll need her.'

He was rewarded with a quick smile from DI Carmen.

'And time is of the essence,' he continued.

'Why's that?' asked Harris.

'Because I'm certain that your man will kill again ...'

Harris went straight back to the Major Incident Room, taking DI Carmen with him. There'd be paperwork to get

139

her seconded to him from Southwark for the investigation but he wasn't expecting trouble. And that rotund reactionary from Singapore was right; he needed a head start, if he could get one. And any woman who'd reached this woman's rank at her age was definitely a flyer even if she was currently padding out her CV with cold cases about community relations.

He shook hands with the young man who had found the link between the two killings, a young DS with an Adam's apple that looked like it might slice open his throat. The room was packed to the gills. He'd asked for and received more manpower – this was a double killing now. And his task wasn't just to solve the murders but to prevent any others.

Harris stood up and walked to the lectern, waited for silence. He introduced Carmen and told them that she'd be his Deputy SIO on the case, ignoring the surprised glances that he'd brought in someone from outside. She was Met, she was Homicide, she had the job. He waited until they'd internalised the information and then quickly summarised what he knew so far about the murder of Cynthia Cole, the location, the absent murder weapon, her injuries, the results of the house-to-house, the search for eyewitnesses and the weapon, the interviews with workmates and family. Half the group knew this already – they'd started the investigation with him – but the rest, including Carmen, were new and hearing it for the first time. His explanation was brief, bottom line was that they knew squat.

'There was one feature of the murder that was unusual,' he continued, noting that they were all ears, keen for a quick resolution, most of them ready to pin it on Bob the Builder, wondering why he'd assembled such a large team for a straightforward murder by a jealous boyfriend.

'The victim's hands were removed post-mortem and taken from the crime scene.'

The expressions were puzzled at first and then horrified. 'Do you mean ... like an amputation?' It was the shambling figure of DS Chris Branson, the gruff voice honed by a thousand cigarettes.

'Yes.'

'Jesus.' There were mutters of disgust and a WPC grew so pale that the faint freckles on her face stood out like a smattering of mud.

'There's more,' he said. 'We've found another murder from five years ago with the same MO.'

The rush of air from the sudden exhalation of thirty coppers was audible.

'A Fatima Daud of Southall. She was an estate agent killed when she went to show a house. Her hands were also removed post-mortem. DI Carmen here is familiar with that case.' Now they knew why there was an outsider involved.

'Some bloody weirdo is killing young women and collecting their hands?' Again it was Chris Branson, senior in age but junior in rank, overlooked for promotion, able to speak his mind without thought.

'We have no insight into motive right now.'

'He must be off his bloody rocker.'

Harris prevented himself from nodding in agreement with some effort. 'There is no point speculating about the mental health of the perpetrator until we apprehend him.'

'We need to warn the public to be on their guard.'

DI Carmen made the statement out loud that they would have been better off discussing in private. Had he made a mistake recruiting her?

'There are five years between the killings,' said Harris.

'That doesn't mean that he's going to wait another five, guvnor.'

'True,' he said. 'But I'm not sure provoking a city-wide panic is prudent right now.'

'I think women will want to know.'

He met her eyes, addressed Carmen directly. 'Let's give it a couple of days and see where we are.'

The frigid silence in the room was a bunch of coppers all thinking the same thought: *It'll be on your head if he strikes again.*

'Time is of the essence. So let's work together on this and find the killer ASAP.'

Churchill he was not but he could see that they were raring to go. This was the sort of case that one imagined solving when joining the police force. Instead, it was usually murdered gang members, domestic altercations and drug-related deaths, never straightforward good versus evil.

He separated them into teams, gave them all tasks ranging from more house-to-house visits, interviews with friends and family, tracking down anyone with a record of violence who had known either or both women, to going through the sex offenders registry for anyone with a hand-related fetish even though neither woman had been sexually assaulted. When everyone had left the room except him and Carmen, he asked, 'What else can we do?'

'Psychological profile?'

'Good idea. Get on it.'

He leaned forward on the lectern, thinking hard. 'I'm still bothered about the five-year gap,' he said.

'When we can catch the perp, we can ask him why he waited,' she said.

He almost smiled. This woman, neat as a pin and precise in speech, was an unlikely figure to be echoing the dishevelled Sikh from Singapore.

'And we're not looking at the cases individually at all?'

The Singaporean cop had been convinced that he'd unearthed information about the family dynamics of Fatima Daud that might have led to her death. Was it appropriate to ignore that evidence? And what about Bob the Builder, Cynthia Cole's jealous boyfriend?

'We stick to the theory that it's the same killer.'

Harris was dog-tired but his mind was operating at the speed of a runaway train. He knew that he was putting his eggs in one basket, that if he was wrong, they were wasting valuable time.

On the other hand, 'How many killers cum collectors of hands can there be, even in London?' he asked.

Her shoulders sagged. It was a depressing question. 'More than zero, it would seem,' she said. 'More than zero.'

Mrs Singh was on the hunt for a killer.

Or, to be more precise, Mrs Singh had made an appointment to see Dr Fauzi at his clinic on Lewis Road. Now, she sat in the waiting room and leafed through *Equestrian Living*. It was more than a year old but that did not bother the inspector's wife. She did not need her information on horses to be up to date.

Her cousin sat next to her, occasionally fidgeting. The waiting room was crowded, the doctor was popular or the population was sickly. A youth walked in wearing a football shirt, dirty jeans and big boots. He slumped into the tiny space next to her and coughed a few times without the benefit of a handkerchief. Mrs Singh did her best to avoid inhaling for fear of germs. This investigative business was dangerous work. She might catch a cold instead of a criminal.

The clinic was nondescript. Pictures of obese silhouettes, a man and a woman, were taped to the wall. If she imagined a turban and beard on the male figure, he would be the spitting image of Inspector Singh. The woman on the poster was a skinnier version of her cousin.

There were leaflets in a dispenser informing patients of the dangers of measles and mumps. The inspector's wife, a natural hypochondriac, felt her jawline. Did she sense a slight swelling?

'Thank you' cards were affixed to a whiteboard with coloured magnets.

'I wouldn't have made it without you, Dr Fauzi,' she read.

She remembered her conversation with Goody.

'What do you know about Hanif?' she had asked.

'Middle brother. Very holy.'

'What does he do?'

'He's been away. Just got back a couple of weeks ago.'

'How long was he gone?' If it was more than five years, she could strike him off the list.

'Six months.'

'The brothers don't get along,' she'd said, voice lowered to

144

a mysterious whisper. 'Neither of them is happy with Hanif but there is tension between Ibrahim and Fauzi too.'

'I don't get along with my brothers.' Goody prodded the scrapings of samosa on her plate with a damp finger, stopping from time to time to transfer the slim pickings to her tongue. 'Doesn't mean anything, you know?'

'It doesn't mean anything unless one sibling is murdered,' said Mrs Singh tartly. 'Then it means everything.'

'Shall we order something else?'

'No.'

'So what should we do next?'

'I need to talk with the brothers,' said Mrs Singh.

'About the murder?'

'Don't be silly!'

What would she say? *I think you killed your sister to stop her marrying outside the family.* She'd be lucky not to be slapped. Such public humiliation was not to be risked. That was her husband's job.

'Then what for?' asked Goody.

'I'm sure if I meet them face to face, I will be able to tell which one did it.'

'Are you sure?'

'Yes, as all the family knows—' did her cousin get the implication that she too should be aware of this famous feature of Mrs Singh? '—I am a very good judge of character. My sisters won't go to the wet market without me because I always know which seller is honest and not just pretending the fish is fresh when it is three days old.'

'I just look at the eyes.'

'What?'

'The fish. You can tell if it is fresh by looking at the eyes.'

'Sometimes you can't,' insisted Mrs Singh. 'Better to look at the eyes of the fishmonger.'

Goody prudently abandoned the argument. 'I'm not sure about the others, but it should be easy to see Dr Fauzi.'

'How so?'

'Just pretend to be sick.'

At first unwilling to accede to an idea that was not her own, Mrs Singh had seen the wisdom of the plan which was how she came to be waiting at the clinic.

'Next is your turn,' said Goody.

Mrs Singh felt a moment of raw panic. She had omitted one very important part of her preparation. She had failed to decide what ailed her.

The nurse said, 'Mrs Singh? The doctor will see you now.'

Singh watched them leave in an unmarked four door Audi. He hadn't realised the London police went in for luxury cars. Wasn't the government always going on about austerity measures? Maybe austerity only applied to those not feeding at the trough of authority.

'We can drop you wherever you want,' Harris had said, but Singh shook his head and waved them on their way, watching until their car and his cold case were a speck in the distance. The policeman wondered briefly whether he should tell his wife he was off the case. On balance, that didn't seem prudent. She would insist that he accompany her to visit all the numerous relatives she'd unearthed in London and musicals involving men dressed as cats.

The inspector's phone buzzed and he looked down at the

message: 'Where are you? What are you doing? I have new information for you.'

Even if he hadn't known it was his wife, he would have guessed from the text. A demand and mysterious hints at a greater knowledge, Mrs Singh would have been a natural at writing ransom notes.

Another text followed hot on the heels of the previous one. Mrs Singh was capable of monologues in person and by phone. He peered at the screen short-sightedly. 'I know who did it.'

Did what? Was she talking about his cold case?

He took one last look at the house, scene of the murder of Fatima Daud. He silently apologised for abandoning her case. But there was nothing he could do. Her special status as a murder victim was now compromised. She was one of many, one victim in a series of victims. A line that might stretch further into the past than had been recognised, but even worse, might extend into the future.

And there was nothing that Singh could do about it.

He flagged down a black cab and made his way to Trafalgar Square. Not for any reason except that he felt a sudden desire to crane his neck at Nelson. Singh scrambled out of the car, avoided being run over by a large red double decker bus by the skin of his teeth and was borne by a crowd of Korean tourists holding little triangular yellow flags to the base of Nelson's Column. The sun was out, the sky was clear, the whole place looked like a postcard. The London of sooty alleys and banks of fog would have been a more appropriate backdrop to the murders.

The inspector gazed up at a man who had seen so much,

even with just one eye. But the admiral could not have anticipated the horrors that would be visited on London in the twenty-first century.

Singh walked towards Charing Cross Station. A rumble in his stomach warned him that it was time for a snack. He peered into the various coffee outlets and sandwich bars. Pret a Manger, Costa Coffee, Starbucks. Korean fast food, Japanese fast food.

What about Indian fast food?

The inspector crossed the road and wandered down a side lane. To his surprise it led to Covent Garden. The place was bustling with tourists and diners. Various buskers sang for their supper. A grubby fellow was rather good. Apparently 'he'd killed a man just to watch him die'. Perhaps he should tell DCI Harris.

Singh dropped coins into a hat and felt pleased. He was a real Londoner now. He kept walking, passed Covent Garden Station, turned left and saw a sign for Leicester Square. Wasn't that where the Chinese food was? His step quickened. He'd settle for Chinese – he'd developed a taste for it on his otherwise calamitous trip to the mainland.

Singh came upon a levitating golden man and stopped short. He wasn't the only one. Was it a statue? The man, painted head to toe in gold paint, raised an arm and waved at the crowd. A small crowd gathered, debating the physics of the man's levitation. A child burst into tears. Singh's stomach growled. Biology won. He hurried on.

And found an Indian restaurant.

He could have wept with relief. Singh pushed the door open, stepped inside and sneezed. The smell of cardamom, cumin and coriander assaulted his nostrils. It was like being home. The restaurant had vertiginous Escher-style floor tiles and large puppets in traditional Indian garb suspended from the ceiling – it looked like a mass lynching immediately after a family wedding. Singh didn't care. He was escorted to a table, sat down, scanned the menu and ordered a generous selection of dishes.

'Are you expecting someone else, sir?'

'No.'

The food arrived quickly, accompanied by poppadum and pickles. He had a hot chai instead of a beer, a decision that left him feeling like a hero in a Bollywood movie. Half an hour later, Singh was sated and happy.

Sipping his hot masala tea, he considered what he'd been told by Harris. So Fatima Daud's death was one of two. Harris seemed sure, Singh less so. He agreed with Harris that the amputations, so grotesque in conception and execution, suggested a killer in common. There were sufficient similarities between Fatima Daud and Cynthia Cole, both young, attractive women, to have caught the attention of a killer who was working off some grievance against women.

But why five years between the deaths?

Singh wished for a moment that the world was a less cruel place, although such an outcome would do him out of a job. He could live with it. He'd have more time for long lunches, cold beer and perfecting the art of avoiding Mrs Singh.

In the absence of poor Cynthia Cole, he would have thought that there was enough anger, misunderstanding, thwarted authority, young love and general uncontrolled passion to have led directly to Fatima Daud's murder. And he would have been keen to investigate under the ruse of examining community relations.

He paid the bill and stepped out into the evening chill. The newspaper vendor at the entrance to the shop next door was doing a brisk business.

'Read all about it! Read all about it!'

He stepped forward and peered through the crowd. It was difficult to be a short man in a nation of tall people.

'What's the world coming to?'

'I'm not going to leave the house until they catch him.'

'It's just sickening. Must be some immigrant.'

Singh felt a pricking in his thumbs. He found his way to the front and looked at the headline of the *Evening Standard*:

SERIAL KILLER ON THE
LOOSE IN LONDON

CHAPTER 9

Mr and Mrs Singh sat side by side at the bottom of the bed, feet not quite reaching the floor and ate pizza out of a box that he'd purchased from a takeaway across the road. Pepperoni and cheese. He'd made off with a few packets of tomato ketchup having failed to find either chilli sauce or chilli flakes, but it did nothing to improve his meal. His wife ate efficiently and then dusted the sheets for crumbs with open palms.

'I saw Fatima's brother – Dr Fauzi.'

'You did what?'

'I went to his clinic in Southall. At first I told him that I had a cold, but it was a problem because I had no symptoms even though I held a tissue to my nose.'

'He wasn't convinced?'

'And then I had a better idea and said I was depressed.'

'Why?'

'Because I had lost someone close to me – a sister in an accident.'

'And he believed you?'

'Why not?'

Because his wife combined the acting talents of a shop mannequin and the detective instincts of Inspector Clouseau?

'So what did he say?'

'That it was difficult to deal with loss, especially if it was sudden. I should consider counselling. He could give me something to help me sleep in the meantime.'

'And did you look into his eyes and detect a murderer?'

If his sarcasm was audible, she ignored it with a practised air. 'I could not tell so I asked him about Fatima.'

'Are you completely mad?'

'I said that I had heard his sister had died suddenly too so maybe he understood better than other doctors what I was going through. He just looked down and nodded.'

'He didn't throw you out for being an interfering busy-body?'

'No. It's not a secret in the area. Everyone knows. Most people think it was the youngest brother, Ibrahim.'

'Any evidence?'

'He was wild when he was young.'

Singh too had been accused of being 'wild when he was young' but had avoided bumping off his sisters despite much greater provocation. Fatima had merely refused her family's choice of spouse. His own sisters viewed him as ungodly (because he smoked), criminal (because he associated with the felonious underclass) and ungrateful (because he ignored their advice on how to stop being ungodly and criminal).

'We all make mistakes when young,' he said.

'According to Goody, my cousin, this Ibrahim fellow went through a religious phase, a drugs phase and then a girls phase.'

'I'm not sure that would stand up in court as evidence that he killed his sister.'

'Dr Fauzi said Fatima's death was a good example of how people could recover from grief. He felt very sad about his sister, thought about her every day, but he was still able to carry on with life because there were others who needed him.'

'Doesn't sound like a killer to me.'

'I concluded that it is unlikely to be him,' she agreed primly. 'He is a doctor – they don't kill people anyway. It's against their training.'

'First, do no harm?'

'Exactly.'

Was this the time to mention Dr Mengele or Harold Shipman?

'There have been exceptions to that rule,' he said. 'Although, you're right, not in this case.'

'Why not?' Even when he agreed with her she had to question him.

'Because the police just found another body – a young woman killed and her hands removed too.'

'What?'

'The police are sure it's the same person because of the hand thing ... and they're worried he might kill again.'

'You mean a serial killer?' Mrs Singh was as still as those waxworks she so admired.

'I guess so.'

'Poor, poor Fatima.'

'What do you mean? She's no more dead now than she was five years ago.'

'It is hard to believe that her life should have been lost in such a meaningless way.'

Was it more meaningless to be killed by an anonymous madman than a family member or close acquaintance? He could see Mrs Singh's point of view – there was certainly more ill luck in being handpicked from a pool of almost seven billion to be randomly murdered than to have personally managed to provoke someone to such an act.

'And all my work is wasted – seeing Fauzi and visiting the family restaurant.'

'Why were you doing it anyway?' asked her husband, closing the pizza box and trying to cram it into the small bin next to the dresser without success. Everything smelled of cheese. 'Why were you investigating?'

'Stop you making mistakes . . .'

'But I investigate murders all the time and you don't get involved.'

'This was different.'

'Why?'

He gave up on the pizza box and rested it on top of the bin like a lid. He stood up and rubbed the small of his back with a flat palm, watching his wife at the same time. It was so rare that she was at a loss for words.

'I don't know,' she said, at last. 'When I saw Fatima's picture on the file . . . I just thought . . . I just thought . . . that if we had a daughter, she might have looked like that.'

*

Shaheed lay in bed, as awake as a night owl.

His small daughter formed a buffer between his wife and him. From Regina's even breathing, he knew she was asleep, her back to him, Emma wedged up against her. How could she sleep? What did she know? How had she found out?

Fatima Daud.

How hard he'd tried to put that name out of his head.

The girl he was to marry. The girl whose picture had persuaded him – and his parents – that his future was in Britain, wed to that lovely creature who laughed with her eyes. He'd sensed a free spirit; his parents had seen a dutiful daughter. He'd been attracted to the gleam of mischief in her eyes; his parents to the information that her brother was a doctor and that they were a devout family, highly thought of in the community.

And then, hints that all was not well in the Daud family. A Skype call had been cancelled at the last moment.

'She's not very well.'

'We don't mind. I don't mind!'

'She's in bed – doctor's orders. We'll rearrange very soon. Nothing to worry.'

His family had pressed for the marriage to take place as soon as possible.

'There is no reason to wait. Let the young people start their married life together.'

'She's quite busy with her studies. But *definitely* soon.'

When this was relayed to Shaheed, he said, 'Maybe she doesn't want to get married.'

'Nonsense,' said his mother. 'It is all agreed.'

'We don't want to force her.'

'What nonsense you speak. How can we force her when they approached us?'

'I should go to London,' he replied. 'Meet her.'

The grand gesture. Why should it be limited to the movies?

'Maybe she's just nervous – it's understandable,' he added. 'She might think I'm some cowherd from a village.'

His mother looked doubtful.

'Come, Amma! You have always said that no girl could resist my brown eyes. Let us put it to the test.'

She laughed, swayed by her own perfect love for her only son. Who could refuse her beautiful boy? Certainly not this Fatima Daud.

So Shaheed had flown to London.

And nothing had ever been the same again.

'My husband would like to see you, Inspector Singh.'

He hadn't expected to receive a call from the family, least of all from Mariam. It was close to midnight, Singh was shivering under his duvet watching the news, when the phone rang.

'He does?' he asked in a whisper loud enough to wake the dead. His wife grumbled under her breath, turned over so her back was to him and fell silent again. Was the husband going to offer him violence because of his clandestine meeting with the wife?

'What about?' he asked cautiously.

'This ... new development we read about in the newspapers. About Fatima.'

'What about it?'

'He doesn't believe it.'

'The police are quite certain.'

'Will you meet him, hear him out?'

Why not? It was not like his any of his options were appealing. 'Very well,' he said.

But there was no way he was going out at this hour, it was too cold and he had dispensed with his turban that doubled as his security blanket for the night.

'Would he care to join me for breakfast at my hotel?'

'Yes, that would be helpful. Thank you.'

The doctor's wife hung up after he provided the address.

'Who was that?' mumbled his wife.

He told her.

'They don't think it was this serial killer?'

'No.'

She muttered something under her breath, inaudible to her husband, and turned her back to him once more. Singh stared at the television. The sound was off but the ticker tape was running. The trouble with twenty-four-hour TV was that each snippet of information was presented again and again as 'breaking news'. So far he had been told that there was a serial killer on the loose in London – which he already knew – and discovered that most of the newscasters on the BBC were of Indian descent. This filled him with a vague pride but would have led Mrs Singh to climb on the roof to tie an Indian flag to the aerial.

Members of the public expressed fear and loathing – 'He must be a real pervert!' or 'Who would do such a thing?'

Politicians insisted that the killing spree – did two killings make a spree? – was because of cuts to mental health care budgets.

And a terrorism expert insisted that it was a jihadi plot by returning Syrian fighters – 'What's the difference between an amputation and a beheading anyway?'

The policeman was somewhat surprised that two murders, five years apart, should garner so much publicity. He supposed, even in England, a killer of young women who also dismembered them was still news. Especially with the possibility of more killings, the suggestion by some commentators that there had *already* been more, just undiscovered – 'Why would he wait five years?' – and the unusual quiet on the terrorism front.

Singh sighed. The panic and speculation would make the job of investigating the killings extremely difficult. He felt sorry for that big policeman, Harris, and suspected that he'd done Carmen no favours by getting her involved. He switched off the telly and slept, only to descend into a nightmare where Superintendent Chen chased him around London landmarks trying to grab his turban so that he would blend in with the natives.

The inspector woke the next morning when the sun filtered in through thin curtains and irradiated his closed lids in the red of blood. He sat up, stretched, stumbled to the tiny bathroom and looked at his torso, sprinkled in greying hair. He was as stiff as a day-old corpse. He just wasn't used to the cold and it was no use telling him that it was quite warm for autumn. The whole planet was quite warm for autumn – that was global warming – but it was still too cold for a fat man from the tropics.

Singh had a hot shower – more of a hot trickle, these old buildings had no water pressure – and dressed in a pair of clean trousers and white shirt, saving the business of tying his turban for last. A note from his wife informed him that she was already out and about. What a woman, he sighed, with more energy than the Energiser bunny. Where had she gone? More shopping? More relatives? Hopefully she wasn't still hunting murderers.

He slipped out a side door and had a cigarette and then proceeded to breakfast in the tiny dining room with floral wallpaper and pictures of Alice in Wonderland on the wall.

Despite his reservations about the décor, the breakfast was excellent. Sausages bursting at the seam, a vat of baked beans, two fried eggs sunny side up, rashers of bacon, fresh toast and strong coffee. A profoundly satisfying British experience unlike Ferris wheels, murders and cobblestones.

'Seconds, duckie?'

'Er ... yes, please,' agreed Singh, wondering why this wardrobe-shaped woman had referred to him as a fowl.

'I can always tell a man with a good appetite,' she said.

'You're quite the detective,' said Singh, pulling his napkin over his belly.

She giggled and piled on more food. 'My husband was just the same.' Her face fell. 'Until the heart attack.'

Singh reached for his coffee, appetite temporarily curtailed, and saw Dr Fauzi walk in.

He beckoned him over.

'What can I do for you?' he asked, as the medical man turned down breakfast but accepted coffee.

'You said you were looking into Fatima's death.'

'Yes, but I've been taken off the case.'

'Because of these new developments?'

'Yes – it's not a cold case any more.'

The brother paused to sip his coffee – black and without sugar – so Singh did the same except that his was milky and had two heaped teaspoons.

'We do not believe what the police are saying.'

'About what?'

'That Fatima's death was linked to this other woman.'

'There are features in common which strongly suggest that there is a connection. You know what they are.'

'But it could be a copycat or something like that.'

'The unusual aspect of the case was not widely known, not released to the press at the time of your sister's death.'

'This sort of thing – it always leaks.'

It was a fair point, although it didn't explain why it would have inspired the flattery of imitation only five years later.

'Why does it worry you anyway – surely you are pleased that your sister's case is being reopened?' asked Singh.

'I thought that, as a family, we had moved on from what happened to Fatima.'

'But?'

'My mother has been weeping non-stop since you visited, her brain sharpened by despair.'

Singh winced.

'We tell ourselves it is God's will.'

'I'm not sure, despite his reputation, that God moves in ways that are quite as mysterious as that.'

'You are right – we cannot forget she was taken from us by human wickedness.'

Singh eyed the man thoughtfully. It was possible that the latest developments had led to the soul-searching this man described. On the other hand, the inspector's first impression had been of a dogmatic and autocratic man. And his gut instincts were often right, although not because – as his wife had suggested once – his gut had more exercise than his brain.

'None of this explains why you are here to see me.'

'We would like you to investigate – discover who killed Fatima.'

'The police are doing that.'

'They are obsessed with this new angle.'

'I have no authority in this country.'

'But my wife, whom I understand that you met, assures me that you have both a compassion for Fatima and a passion for justice. *Insha* Allah, that will be enough.'

Singh took the bus from Paddington to Kilburn; apparently the two places were not a great distance apart. The brother of Fatima Daud had not actually offered to fund this private investigation he'd solicited. Perhaps he thought that God would provide taxi money as well as useful leads and a suitable resolution. Pending such largesse from above, the inspector stood clinging to a pillar rod as the bus rocked and swayed, packed to the gills with an assortment of people that were so self-consciously unique that he might have stumbled into a movie. There was a Rastafarian in baggy clothes, a mother with triplets and a man whose dedication to bodybuilding had left his arms so far from his body that he would struggle to get change out of his pockets. This was all in contrast to Singapore where the homogenous Chinese majority would be wearing white shirts and dark trousers, dark-rimmed glasses and have their hair cut close and neat.

The bus smelled damp and the gum-stained seats were not appealing. This was why chewing gum was banned in Singapore – to avoid this layer of stickiness on everything. When the bus driver signalled to him, the policeman hopped off with some relief.

He was on another minor high street; they all looked exactly the same to him. Same shops: Sainsbury's, Boots, Starbucks, Oxfam and a few discount shops offering everything under the sun for less than five pounds. Looking around, he could see that the area was poor but becoming gentrified. Some of the people were young and well dressed, but the shufflers in hand-me-downs and thrift shop coats were plentiful too. Poorer areas had larger populations of minorities as well, he'd noticed – London got whiter towards the centre.

The small block of flats was on the main street and he found it without difficulty. He identified the relevant doorbell, noted that there were sixteen residences over four floors, and rang it.

'Yes?'

'Good morning, this is Inspector Singh. I was wondering if I could have a few words.'

'Why? Is there a problem? Has anything happened?'

'We're just making some inquiries.'

'About what?'

'About Fatima Daud.'

There was silence followed by a crackling over the intercom. 'All right, I suppose I should have expected you.'

The door buzzed. Singh gave it a good shove with his elbow, he didn't like touching strange surfaces with his hands.

You never knew what germs were out there these days: Ebola, bird flu, MERS or something truly awful that might cause loss of appetite.

The apartment was a walk-up and Singh was huffing and puffing by the time he reached the second floor. The door of flat number two was ajar and a man was waiting for him. A small child was trying to see between his legs.

'Shaheed Muhammad?'

'Yes.'

'I'm Inspector Singh.'

'From the Met?'

'Actually, no. I'm from Singapore. Fatima's family asked me to look into the matter of her death.'

Shaheed hesitated for a moment, aware perhaps that there was no reason to allow Singh in, but unwilling to look unco-operative. He pushed the door open further and then turned back in – an invitation of sorts that Singh was quick to accept.

He walked into a light and airy front room, lace inner curtains letting in light but not the glare, pastel pictures on the wall, photos above a fake fireplace, a bookshelf and two comfy sofas in mustard with dark brown throw cushions.

'Nice place,' he said and meant it.

'My wife's doing, not mine.'

'And this is your child?'

'Yes, Emma – four going on a terror.'

He gestured with a hand and Singh sank into the sofa. The child was mixed race so Shaheed had looked elsewhere for his second chance at marital bliss.

Shaheed disappeared while Singh and Emma observed each other solemnly.

'That's not a hat,' she said at last.

'No, it's a turban.'

'What does it do?'

'What a hat does. But better.'

Shaheed came back with a glass of water. He shooed the child away to another room and, when she was gone, said, 'I read about the latest developments in the papers.'

'What do you think?'

'It's too weird.' His voice had the cadences of someone from the sub-continent tempered with a layer of North London. It was strangely attractive although Henry Higgins might not have approved.

'You were going to marry Fatima?'

'That was the plan.'

'Tell me the whole story ... '

'Her parents and mine arranged a marriage between us.'

'And you agreed?'

'I was willing. I wanted to get out of Lahore. Plus, they showed me a picture of her and she was so beautiful.'

Singh waited, observing the young man. He looked tired and a little sad, but not nervous or guilty. On the other hand, he wouldn't have let Singh upstairs if he didn't have faith in his own ability to dissemble.

'I came over – the families had agreed that we meet beforehand.'

'Where did you stay?'

'With some rellies in Southall.'

Singh nodded.

'After I arrived, even before I left Pakistan really, I sensed something was wrong. No one was telling me anything. I guess they didn't want me to get cold feet – but the meeting with Fatima kept being postponed. I guessed she wasn't keen and I grew quite concerned.'

He smiled and his face creased like an old shirt. 'By then I already knew I didn't want to return to Pakistan. So I was kind of desperate to see her, sweep her off her feet, you know what I mean?'

'No,' said Singh coldly, 'I don't.'

The young man was taken aback but tried to disguise it by sipping his water.

'So when did you finally meet her?'

'I didn't.'

'What?'

'I was trying to think about what to do – I didn't want an unwilling bride and I feared the pressure her family might be putting on her. But then … she … she, you know, she was killed.'

'And you really never met her?'

'No.'

Singh noted the sideways shift to the right of Shaheed's eyes and remembered that he'd handed the water over with his right hand. It seemed that his answer was constructed, not remembered, and therefore a lie. Not that Singh placed much store by these sorts of neurolinguistic programming assertions.

On the other hand, Shaheed was straightening the drink mats on the coffee table between them. That struck Singh as much more indicative of dishonesty. In his experience, unpractised liars fidgeted. But how was he going to prove it?

'Did you speak to the police at the time of Fatima's death?'

'No, as I hadn't even met her, the families thought there was no point.'

If there was one thing that really annoyed Singh, it was witnesses editing information to provide what they thought was exculpatory and nothing else.

'Do you know why she didn't want to marry you?'

'I'm guessing that she had a boyfriend. Once she died, my family was desperate to put some distance between us and the Daud family.'

'Why?'

'They didn't want to get involved in any scandal. There were a lot of rumours that the family might have been involved.' He added hastily, 'Not that I believed it for a second.'

'So how come you're still in the UK?'

'After ... after – my parents enrolled me in a computing course. I completed it but also met the woman who is now my wife.'

'So everything turned out all right in the end, eh? Even if your fiancée was murdered because she didn't want to marry you.'

'That's not what happened!'

So he didn't like guilt, not even vicarious guilt.

The child ran in again, avoided her father's eye and climbed on the sofa next to Singh.

'My mummy's at work.'

'That's all right, I can chat to your daddy.'

'She's very beautiful, you know.'

'I'm sure she is – just like you.'

The girl giggled. It didn't matter the age, women – except Mrs Singh – just liked compliments.

'Would you like to see a picture of her?'

'There's no need,' said Shaheed.

But the little girl was already pulling a small photo in a frame out of her pink backpack.

Singh took it from her hand, prepared to be gracious – and then his jaw dropped.

'Don't you think she's beautiful?'

'What's going on?' demanded the policeman.

'To be honest, I don't know,' said Shaheed. 'I really don't.'

Singh placed the picture on the coffee table.

It was a recent photo of a woman with a child – this child – in her arms. Both were smiling, the girl at the camera, the woman at the girl. Lovely really.

Except that he knew the woman in the shot.

It was Regina de Klerk.

The woman from the Commonwealth offices who had given him the cold case of Fatima Daud.

CHAPTER 10

'This is your wife?'

'Yes.'

'That's Mummy,' added Emma.

'Your wife is Regina de Klerk?'

'Yes.'

'But she was the one who gave me this case.'

'She works for the Commonwealth Secretariat.'

'Did you put her up to it?'

'I've never told her about Fatima, never even mentioned her name to Regina.'

'It can't be a coincidence.'

Shaheed slumped back in the chair and covered his face with his hands. 'I have been wondering the same thing since she mentioned that a task force was looking into a cold case, that of Fatima Daud.'

'When did she mention it?'

'A couple of days ago.'

'So before it was in the news again.' He tried to get his head around this latest development – that Regina, the beautiful young woman from the Secretariat who was supervising their task force on community policing, was married to a grade-A suspect.

'How did she hurt her wrist?'

'We had an argument; she wanted to leave, take Emma. I grabbed her hand, to try and stop her. I didn't mean to hurt her.'

I didn't mean to hurt her.

The epitaph of many a woman killed in a domestic altercation. He felt like saying, was going to say and had said to the husbands and lovers of dead women before – 'If you don't mean to hurt someone, don't grab them, hit them, punch them.'

Because that always hurts. And sometimes it kills.

He reminded himself that he was not a policeman in this jurisdiction and he was not there on a case of domestic violence. Regina was alive and well.

But she had deceived them both.

They both heard it. A key in the lock, the creak of the door opening. The sound of keys being tossed on a table; a briefcase dropped on the floor. The tension was like a dense fog.

Regina walked in. Her daughter ran to her, hugged her round the legs. For once she did not pause to acknowledge her, pick her up, hug her. Instead, she looked at the two men both staring at her as if she was a spectre, a visitation from another dimension.

'Singh! What are you doing here?'

'Doing your bidding, I would guess.'

She nodded, not disputing his characterisation.

'I'm sorry,' she said. 'I owe you both an apology.'

Raj of Raj Real Estate regularly frequented Khan's. He had done that before he employed Fatima, while he employed her – when he'd received the odd complimentary dish from her father – and recently as well. The only hiatus had been for about a year after her death when he'd been afraid that awkwardness might attach to his presence. Now he sat at his favourite corner table, an array of food dishes in front of him and nibbled on the corner of a cheese naan. Raj enjoyed having a wide selection but he only ever sampled an offering, leaving the rest to the kitchen staff, portable food kitchens or, most likely, the rats. Otherwise, he might be as wide as he was tall, like the woman sitting at the next table. Her broad back, encased in some shiny pink material, filled his whole horizon.

'Enjoying the food?' asked Ibrahim, stopping by the table.

'Always,' replied Raj. 'Why don't you sit down and join me for a few minutes.'

Ibrahim pulled out the chair opposite.

'Business is good?' asked Raj.

'Turned around in the last couple of months.'

This amused both men.

'That is good to know. This establishment has been here for decades and I would hate to see it go under,' said Raj.

'Thanks to you, it won't.'

'I notice that your other brother has been here a lot recently.'

'Fauzi has ordered Hanif to help out at the restaurant instead of wasting his time mooching about the house.'

'Might he cause a problem?' The middle one had always been trouble with his holy ways – quick to question, quick to judge, quick to blame.

'Why should he?'

Raj's eyes narrowed. That was the question, not the answer.

'After all, he should be pleased at what we are doing. Does it not further the causes closest to his heart?' continued Ibrahim, holding up his hands palms forward.

'Amongst other things,' pointed out Raj.

'You don't make omelettes without breaking a few eggs.'

An apt metaphor from a restaurant proprietor, decided Raj, relaxing a little.

'Did you see the latest developments about my sister's death?'

Was he changing the subject? Raj was not a fan of this latest topic either – the death of his employee had been one of the most difficult periods of his life. This family could be trouble, something he needed to remember.

'Yes, I never imagined anything like that – a serial killer.'

'No one did,' said Ibrahim.

'I don't know what the world is coming to,' said the real estate man.

'Fauzi thinks this is a just another red herring, that the truth must be closer to home.'

'The police know best.'

Ibrahim laughed, a genuine guffaw. 'If that were true, we'd all be in trouble.'

'Fair enough,' said Raj. He patted his mouth with the napkin delicately. 'I'll be on my way so perhaps you could arrange for the bill?'

'It is on the house, of course.'

'Are you sure? That is very kind.'

It was their small ritual; he had not paid for his food since they had agreed their mutually beneficial arrangement. He liked to pretend though, it gave him satisfaction when those who owed him favours delivered, even if it was just a small matter like a restaurant bill.

Raj stood up, nodded his head at Ibrahim and walked towards the entrance, feeling content and a mite philosophical. There was just no way of dressing it up.

Sometimes good things happened to bad people.

And, even more often, bad things happened to good people.

'What's going on?' demanded Singh.

Regina walked over to them. She pulled up a chair from the small dining table and dragged it over, sat down so that she was facing them both, equidistant from both men.

'Did you set me up? Why?'

Even though it was Singh who had spoken, she addressed her answer to her husband.

'I was given a set of cold cases by the Met for our various Commonwealth task forces on policing. They left it to me which ones I was going to use and to whom I would give them.'

'Fatima's case was one of them?'

'Yes, it was. I was reading the case files – not the whole thing but just a summary – when I came across your name, Shaheed. At first, I assumed it was just a coincidence. It was just a passing mention – that Fatima had a potential fiancé who was not in the country.'

She paused and hugged her daughter. 'And then I checked the dates, and realised it was just *after* you arrived in the country that she died. I even checked your passport when you weren't home. You arrived at Heathrow three days before she died. Why did you never mention her?'

He could not meet her eyes. 'I came hoping to convince her to marry me. And then she was killed and in such a horrific way. I put it out of my mind as much as I could.'

'But why did you lie to the police about being in the country?'

'It wasn't me – it was the families.'

'So you decided your husband and the father of your child might be a murderer?' Singh's directness caused them both to wince.

'Our marriage was in trouble – it seemed that I didn't know Shaheed any more.' She turned again to her husband. 'You were always so on edge, so jealous.' Her hand went to her wrist.

'And then I discovered that you hadn't mentioned something as important as being engaged to a girl who turned up dead *and* you misled the police about being in the country.'

'I can't believe you thought I was a killer.'

'I didn't really, but I had to be sure.'

'So you selected the case, hoping some light would be shed on Fatima's death?'

She smiled at Singh a little wanly. 'Yes. When I researched the coppers they were sending us, I decided you were the most likely to go off the reservation and truly investigate the matter.'

'I tried,' he said.

She nodded. 'But I heard today about the serial killer – that it was just some madman who killed Fatima and that poor woman last week. It cleared my head. Shaheed, I was stupid to suspect you even for a moment.'

He nodded and smiled, stood up and opened his arms and she didn't hesitate, walking straight into them. 'It's all right – we haven't been ourselves recently.'

'No, we can do better. I know we can.'

Mr Singh left quietly. He was not one for emotional scenes.

They made him uncomfortable.

'Why didn't he pay?'

'What do you mean?'

'That lowlife, Raj, why didn't he pay? I saw it – he left without paying.'

Hanif was enraged, trying to keep it bottled up, trying to keep his voice down. He hated that fellow who had employed Fatima all those years ago.

Employed her? Exploited her good nature, paid her the minimum, worked her long and hard and then sent her to her death.

'Oh! He's a regular so I thought I'd let him have one on the house.'

'We shouldn't even be serving him!'

'Why? Because our sister happened to be working for him when she attracted the attention of some madman who killed her?'

'Because he's scum.'

'Your business acumen does you credit, brother.'

'Is that why we're losing money? Because you don't charge your regulars?'

'I showed you – we're *not* losing money any more. We've been immensely profitable recently.'

An improvement in their fortunes that Hanif could not fathom and which therefore gave him no comfort.

'It won't last if you keep giving away free food. He ordered everything on the menu!'

'Is that what they taught you in Syria. To exaggerate?'

'Shhh! Be quiet. Someone might hear.'

'What? The great martyr is afraid of being found out?'

'There is a time and a place for sacrifice. You are the *only* one in this family who does not know that.'

'I know exactly what is required, and it is not mullahs in pyjamas playing soldiers in the desert.'

Hanif stormed into the inner sanctum, desperate not to be provoked into violence. He sat down in his father's chair and gulped cold tea from a mug. He needed to keep cool, to remember the big picture, what he was fighting for, why he'd come back from Syria, his mission and his instructions. These ridiculous arguments with his brother were a distraction and that was the one thing he couldn't afford. He took his prayer beads out of the drawer, twirled them between his fingers and felt his fury ebb slowly like the tide going out under a crescent moon.

His phone beeped. He looked down. 'All is in readiness for those who have courage and piety.'

He typed back and pressed send. 'God is great.'

*

Mrs Singh stepped out of her favourite haunt, the women's toilet at Khan's in Southall. Ibrahim was watching her from the till but most likely he was admiring her latest cardigan, baby pink with pearl buttons – on sale at Marks and Spencer. Why should he care about a middle-aged Sikh woman who was obliged to use the facilities after a spicy meal?

She rejoined her cousin whose broad back had obscured her presence at the next table where they'd been listening intently to Ibrahim's conversation with a skinny man in a tan suit and comb-over.

'Did you hear anything?' asked Goody.

'That man with Ibrahim just now is called Raj and Fatima used to work for him.'

'Of course, Raj Real Estate. I thought he looked familiar. His agency is on the high street.'

'Hanif was upset that Raj didn't pay for his food.'

'No wonder they don't make money here.'

'That's more or less what Hanif said too.'

'He's not as stupid as he looks then.'

'But it seems this place is doing very well now ...'

Goody looked around at the swathe of empty tables and staff standing idle against the walls. 'Really?'

'Hanif is also puzzled by the turnaround.'

'It's such a shame that one of them is not the killer. All our hard work gone to waste! Who would have thought there was a serial killer here in London?'

Mrs Singh squinted at her. Like her husband and Fatima's family, she remained to be convinced – hence her return to Khan's. Unlike her cousin Goody, she was not influenced by the quality of the samosas.

The policeman's wife contemplated the fact that Hanif had been in Syria, remembering the news that the British government was worried about returnees from the battlefield who might have an animosity towards their homeland. She stared across the dining space. Hanif stepped out of the back office, ignored his brother and made a beeline for the main entrance.

The fellow looked exactly like the sort of person her cousin Goody avoided on public transport.

'Hanif has been in Syria,' she said.

'That's a strange place to choose.'

'I think he must have been one of those fighters.'

'Like a terrorist? Can't be.'

'Why do you say that?'

'Because I know him, right? We went to the same school even though he is younger than me. People you know personally aren't terrorists.'

Mrs Singh did not dispute this because her mind was on other matters.

'I still don't believe it,' she said.

'What don't you believe?'

'That Fatima was killed by some serial killer.'

Goody shuddered with delicious anticipation. 'Can you imagine, it could be any of us, anytime, killed by anyone. I'm surprised I even dared leave the house this morning.'

'You're not listening – I don't think Fatima was a victim of this madman.'

'Why not?'

A good question. Why not? Because she didn't want it to be so? Because she did not want that beautiful girl of an age to be her own daughter to have been so ill fated? After all, as her husband kept pointing out, Fatima was dead either way. She felt tears and blinked hard. What was the matter with her? She, the hard-headed, practical member of the Singh household, was a welter of uncontrolled emotions. She, who had never had a child, suddenly had an inkling of what it was like to lose one.

And worse, she, who'd never had a daughter, now felt that loss as if it was sudden and present, and not a consequence of time and happenstance, a process of decision and indecision over decades.

Did Singh, despite his denials, ever regret not having a son or a daughter?

Did he hunt down murderers so energetically because he understood that every victim was someone's child?

And was it even worth having a child, when the risks to their person were ever present, as had been so clearly demonstrated by the death of Fatima and the other woman, Cynthia Cole?

As if reading her mind, Goody said, 'I don't know who killed these women, but I'm really glad I don't have any children. I tell you, I wouldn't sleep a wink at night if I did.'

'They're always lining up like bloody fools. Wasting everyone's time but what can you do?'

The cab driver was waiting at the pedestrian crossing next to the Abbey Road studio while four youths in bellbottoms tried to recreate the famous Beatles album cover.

'Last week, another lot was trying to get their bloody dogs to cross in a row. Can you believe it? All barking and snapping.'

Seeing Singh's blank face, he said, 'The Beagles, geddit?'

They drove on, squeezing through tight spaces in a way that made Singh feel that he was on an amusement park ride. He was almost relieved when they were caught in traffic a couple of miles down, courtesy of more essential roadworks. No one seemed to be doing any actual work.

'Lord's is that way,' said the cabbie.

Singh peered out of the window, this was more his cup of tea. He should abandon pointless murder investigations and attend a game of cricket instead. It was the perfect day for it. Blue skies, a light wind and distant clouds so the whole thing would be rained off the minute he was comfortable.

'It's only about a hundred yards down that street if you prefer to walk.'

Rather than tell the fellow that he never preferred to walk, the inspector agreed and headed down a narrow lane where the houses were set back from the road and obscured by high walls, thick hedges and ancient trees. It might have been a country lane. Instead, it was just half a mile from a London landmark and a stone's throw from the home of cricket. His wife was right; London really was amazing.

He found the correct number and peered through the iron railings of the main gate. The house was so far in he could only see flashes of red and white between the foliage. The driveway was lined with flowerbeds that were a riot of colour. Petunias, pansies? Not daffodils, because he knew his Wordsworth and anyway it wasn't spring.

How had someone who worked at Raj Real Estate ended up in such a place as this?

A click and a groan indicated that the gates were opening. The inspector set off down the curved driveway. As the house came into view, he was impressed. Creepers covered the walls, the windows glinting like bright eyes in a hirsute face. A paved courtyard featured urns, running water and a small fountain. An outdoor swimming pool ran down the side of the garden. Was it heated or did the residents voluntarily get into cold water in this country?

He was distracted by the front door being flung open.

'Inspector Singh! I've been waiting for you.'

This observation was accompanied by trill of laughter.

'I'm here because you said you might be of help in the murder investigation.'

'Yes, poor, poor Fatima. You know, she was my best friend.'

Again, the laughter which, aside from being singularly inappropriate, had already begun to grate in terms of pitch and volume. Thank God for a taciturn wife.

'I just felt I had to do everything I could to help – you know?'

Why now? Why not five years ago? Instead of questioning her, the policeman followed Sara the receptionist into the house and sat stiffly on furniture that combined fragility with discomfort. A maid in a black uniform with a frilly white pinafore and puffed sleeves – shades of Singapore – brought tea. Like the furniture, the teacup was as fragile as a baby bird. Plus, he couldn't get his fat finger through the handle.

'So you're investigating Fatima's death?' she asked.

'At the request of the family.'

'But I thought it was this serial killer – the one they are calling the Hand Man?'

'For sure,' agreed Singh, 'but the more we know the better to eliminate other possibilities.'

'I understand,' she said, touching the side of her nose lightly. 'You don't want the defence lawyers to draw wool over people's eyes. My husband says that's what they do – and they get the worst people off, would you believe it? In fact, I think that's what he does sometimes too! But he has no choice, of course. It's his job, being a barrister and all.'

Singh nodded gravely. At least she'd stopped laughing. 'So you and Fatima worked together?'

'At Raj Real Estate.'

'And how was that?'

'I thought it was great but Fatima wasn't so keen.'

'Why not?'

'She didn't think much of Raj.'

'He was a difficult boss?'

'Not to Fatima. He was always saying she was like a daughter to him.'

'So she got favourable treatment.'

A pout greeted this suggestion. 'Sometimes. Higher commissions, better properties to sell.'

'That must have been very annoying for you – after all, you did the same amount of work.'

'Exactly – that's what I said to Fatima.'

'She must have been pleased to be taking in a little extra?'

'No way. When she found out, she went straight to Raj and said she didn't want to be treated different from the rest of us.'

'And what was his reaction?'

'They were yelling at each other, my, you could feel the walls tremble! He said she was ungrateful for everything he'd done for her. And she said that he was just a crook.'

'A crook? What was she talking about?'

'I have no idea. She was helping out with the accounts and she told me there was something strange about them – like too much money.' Her brow was knitted in puzzlement. 'I said, how can you have *too much money*?'

Sara suddenly put a hand over her mouth. 'Jimmy always says I don't know when to shut my gob,' she said.

Indeed. 'So when was all this?'

'A couple of days before . . . she died. I'm sure she was just angry. It didn't mean anything. Why would it?'

Why would it? Was the universe not allowed a pattern? Were all events random?

'Otherwise, I guess Fatima would have most likely quit. That would have been a shame,' she continued.

'Why a shame?'

'We didn't just work together, we were best friends!'

'You mentioned it.'

'Two peas in a pod, that's what everyone said.'

'What did you . . . erm, two peas do?'

This time it was a giggle. 'Well, it was five years ago, so we were much younger then.'

One of them had stayed the same age, would stay the same age forever.

'I think I can guess,' he said, trying to crack a smile, it felt like an attempt to cause a fissure in the continental plates. 'Shopping, long lunches.'

'Exactly! Raj used to go bananas when we were late back from our break. He never picked up the phones, you see. Said it wasn't his job. But he hated missing sales.'

'Why did you carry on working there after . . . it happened?'

'I wanted to keep busy, you know? But, between you and

me, it's getting a bit boring down at the agency. I might just give it up.'

She did strike Singh as someone singularly bored with life, looking for a little excitement to brighten the day even if it meant entertaining portly policemen in her home.

'It doesn't seem like you need to work?' Singh glanced around at the opulence as he spoke.

'This is all my husband's. I didn't have anything then – poor as a church mouse, I was, before I married my Jimmy. But he's very successful and he loves beautiful things.'

'I can see that,' said Singh, contemplating this Jimmy and wondering why his name sounded familiar. She tittered at his clumsy gallantry. 'You and Fatima – the pair of you must have had quite a few boyfriends, eh?'

The first missed opportunity to be amused. 'The family had found someone for her to marry – from Pakistan.'

'And she was excited about that?'

'No way.'

'Why?'

'The family was quite conservative – you know, *Muslim*—' her voice dropped to a whisper at the word '—but Fatima was a free spirit.'

'She refused?'

A vigorous nodding caused the carefully coiffured hair to shift to artful dishevelment.

'And how did the family take that?'

'They were very upset – threatened to lock her up, send her to Pakistan, all sorts of things. I thought Fatima was going to do something terrible.'

'What sort of thing?'

'I don't know – run away? She said she'd kill herself if they tried to lock her up.'

But she hadn't. Someone else had stepped in.

'She *tried* to talk to him but it was no use.'

'Her father?'

'No, Shaheed – the fiancé.' She leaned forward confidentially. 'They weren't allowed to meet but I helped set it up.'

'She *met* Shaheed?'

Regina would not react well to this news.

'Yes, I just said that.'

'When?'

A wrinkled nose suggested deep thinking. 'I don't know – just a day or two before . . . before . . . it happened.'

'She called it off?'

'She tried but it was no use. He refused to pull out.'

'Why in the world not?'

'He *said* it was because he was bound by his promise to her family . . .'

'You didn't agree?'

'Fatima said it was because he wanted to stay in Britain.'

'Surely it would have been easier for a girl her age to fall in with her parents' wishes?'

'Well, there was the Jimmy situation too.'

'Your husband?'

Sara without an 'h' blushed faintly. 'He was her boyfriend at the time, you see, but it wasn't that serious.'

'The guy Raj mentioned?'

'Yes.'

'Why do you say it wasn't serious when she risked her family's disapproval to be with him?'

The sound of a door slamming distracted Singh and he swivelled in his seat to see a large man march in. He was wearing a dark suit and dropped a leather case on the carpet.

'Who is this?' he demanded.

The voice reminded Singh of the British period dramas his wife so enjoyed. Here then was the lord of the manor, the owner of the glowing oils on the wall, the alcoves with Chinese vases, the period furniture and the ornamental woman.

'A policeman asking about poor Fatima Daud. I said I might be able to help because we were such good friends at the time.'

'There's no reason for us to answer any questions.'

He was still standing, the legs apart (what are you so proud to show off, Mrs Singh might have asked), the jaw thrust out.

'You're always such a lawyer, darling.'

Singh stood up, held out a hand. 'Inspector Singh,' he said.

The husband showed no inclination to introduce himself or shake the proffered hand so the wife stepped in. 'And this is my gorgeous husband.' She smiled brightly – how much did teeth like that cost?

'Inspector Singh, this is my husband Jimmy Kendrick. We were just talking about you, love.'

'Jimmy Kendrick? *Fatima*'s boyfriend?'

'So what's it to you?'

His wife stepped in. 'I guess when we both lost someone we loved so much, we turned to each other for comfort, you know?'

Singh, feeling the bile rise in his throat, swallowed hard.

*

185

Hanif went to an Internet café on the Broadway, a tiny shopfront tucked in between an ice-cream parlour and an electronics shop. He ignored the lists of services and pricing and discount plans, bought a temporary user ID and went straight to an unoccupied seat against a wall. The place was deserted except for a pimply youth typing with two fingers at the far end – it seemed that fortune did favour the bold. Or maybe fortune favoured those who visited Internet cafés during working hours.

He sat down on the stool on wheels, rolled forward until his knees were tucked under the counter and his body obscured the screen from the inquisitive. He logged on to a Hotmail account that he'd been provided with. The user ID and password had been committed to memory. The Inbox was empty, had never received an email except for the welcome note when the account was first set up. That didn't surprise him. He wasn't expecting anyone to have sent him a message – not when GCHQ and the Americans had spy software that could pick words out of the ether. Instead, he opened the 'Drafts' folder. It was the simplest but cleverest trick, provide the 'log in' details to people who had to share information – and then leave any messages in the 'Drafts' folder so nothing ever actually entered that peculiar domain of binary communication, the World Wide Web.

Hanif read the plans through twice. It was not what he had expected, was sooner than he'd expected. No specific timings and no names yet. That would come when all was ready. He logged off and pushed his chair back. The steps he took in the next few minutes would determine his fate and that of so many others. He thought about Fatima, his beautiful sister.

Really, at the end of the day, it was all about justice. It didn't matter if people came in different sizes and colour, different opinions and attitudes, different degrees of wealth or intelligence as long as society treated them as equal when doling out justice.

It was the reason he had gone to Syria.

It was the reason he had come home.

It was his deepest regret about his sister.

Hanif adjusted his skullcap with both hands. He closed his eyes and called up an image of his sister, alive and smiling encouragement at him.

Let others grasp the scales of justice; he would wield the sword.

CHAPTER 11

Regina felt more optimistic than she'd been for a long time. Imagining that her husband was a killer had felt like that ice bucket challenge she'd done to raise money for charity. She reminded herself that she had never believed it, not deep down in her heart. It was just seeing his name on the file, associated with a death that he'd never mentioned. Her head, that prudent organ of the successful woman at work, had forced her to consider the possibility, however remote, that her husband was a murderer.

She felt mildly guilty for having dragged that policeman from Singapore into her personal problems. It wasn't really in her nature to use people. If she had a chance, she'd buy him a beer, apologise again. She knew his type – if she assured him that she'd passed him the file because of his gargantuan reputation as a catcher of killers, he'd soon forgive and forget.

It was awful to think of a serial killer in London preying on young women, but that had nothing to do with Shaheed.

Shaheed was a good man and a good father. What did it matter if he struggled to hold down a job and occasionally got a bit Asian with her about her career and the appropriate way to bring up the child?

She kissed Shaheed goodbye with more feeling than usual and he responded with a tight hug. Emma was still in bed; her nursery school didn't begin till mid-morning, lucky thing.

'Have a good day,' he said.

'You too.'

As she turned away, she caught a look in his eyes. Was it fear, a widening of his already dark pupils? She didn't stop, didn't turn back. It must have been her imagination. She'd been so much on edge that her body was still in 'fight or flight' mode. She was not going to second guess her husband again.

A pile of tedious paperwork in the office would soon sort it out; remind her that real life wasn't about cops and killers. Thinking of the office reminded her of that nutter, Martin Bradley, and the way he'd accosted her the previous day. Should she mention him to her husband?

On balance, she thought not.

The guy was a kook but harmless. He'd frightened her at the time but he hadn't really offered her any harm.

There was no need to add an element of tension to her conversation with her husband; it would be like a late frost at the first hint of spring flowers.

Mrs Singh was not impressed to see her husband hustled into the Vauxhall Astra with blue and yellow trim and the word 'POLICE' in large lettering down the sides.

'What have you done?' she'd asked him when two large

uniformed men with a certain beefy sameness came for him at breakfast.

'I haven't a clue,' he said.

'The police don't look for you if you haven't *done* anything.'

He might have asked her why 'the police' in the abstract generated such faith while he as an individual, senior in the ranks, was always assumed to be in the wrong. However, he suspected that beefcake one and two had no desire to hang around while he discussed domestic niceties.

'I haven't even told you all the things I discovered yesterday,' she complained.

'About what?'

'About Fatima.'

'That train has left the station.'

'I was on board,' she said and stalked off, leaving him to the tender mercies of the law.

And now, for the first time in his life, he was a civilian at a police station and he wasn't enjoying the experience.

'Am I under arrest?' he demanded.

'Of course not,' said DCI Harris. 'You're just helping the police with their inquiries.'

'Do I need a lawyer?'

'Only if you've done something wrong.'

'Well, I haven't,' insisted Singh.

Not recently, not in this country, and assuming that 'wrong' was limited to the illegal.

'Did you tell the press about the serial killer?'

'Of course not!'

'Do you know how many crank calls we've had since the news broke yesterday in the *Evening Standard*?'

'A lot?'

'It seems that everyone in London knows someone whom they've long suspected to be a callous, immoral killer of young women.'

Singh shifted uncomfortably in his chair. He supposed he should be grateful that he was in an office and not a cell.

'Why did you do it?' demanded Harris. 'Why did you leak the story?'

'I didn't do it. I wouldn't even have known whom to call if I wanted to splash the story in the press.'

'A detective with your reputation would have found a way.'

Singh scowled at the sarcastic tone. It was hard to believe that he'd quite liked this fellow.

'Why do you imagine it was me anyway? Your whole team knows.' Singh wondered whether they'd leaked the information for cash. He'd been reading about the phone hacking scandal enveloping the tabloids and police. It seemed that the cops in Britain weren't above running with the hares while hunting with the hounds.

'The timing,' said Harris. 'Most of them didn't know in time to get it in the evening edition.'

'Surely the papers called you to verify?'

'Yes.'

'So why didn't you tell them not to print?'

'Why would they listen to me?'

Parallel grooves formed across the inspector's forehead. This was not the way of things in Singapore.

'Did you ask them who provided the information?'

'They're not going to reveal their sources.'

Typical of his luck that the fourth estate should be stalwart in the face of the state on that rare occasion when he was *not* part of the state apparatus.

'It's probably for the better anyway – women need to know so they can be on their guard.'

'That's what my number two, your DI Carmen, said.'

Singh had a fair idea where the leak was from now, but he didn't bother to mention it.

'I don't see why you dragged me in anyway. Even if it was me, it's not worth your time right now.'

'The Commissioner thinks the leak made the Met look bad. He's up in arms. If I don't look like I care, I'll find myself issuing traffic tickets in Cornwall.'

'So I'm window dressing?'

'I guess you could say that.'

Harris abandoned his intimidating pose resting against his desk and looming over Singh. He slumped in his chair and ran a hand through his thinning hair.

'Tough day?'

'No leads on Cynthia Cole.'

'I thought this was a surveillance society.'

'So did I, but there's nothing on CCTV, no sign of the weapon, no indication of anyone with a hand fetish, no witnesses, nothing.'

'Except two dead girls.'

'Exactly.'

'Whose killings might not be related?'

The other man smiled although there was no humour in the stretched mouth. 'You're still riding that hobby horse?'

'The brother Fauzi came to see me, he's convinced that Fatima's death has nothing to do with this new case.'

'Despite the hands?'

'My wife met some distant relation in the Southall area – everyone there is familiar with the case.'

Had it really come to this? Was he about to present his wife's musings to the fuzz?

'And the consensus is that the younger brother did it.'

'Really? Why?'

'He's a good-looking young man who is running the family business into the ground.'

'What's that got to do with anything?'

'If you understood the sub-continental mind, you would know that losing money in business is evidence of a disposition capable of the lesser sin of murder.'

'But why would he chop off her hands? His own sister?'

'I'm afraid my wife has not yet provided me with the answer.'

This drew a genuine guffaw. 'You're a good man, Singh, and you mean well, but I think we need to stick with our theory that it was the same murderer.'

'A serial killer?'

'I've been avoiding using that expression.'

'The newspapers have been less reticent.'

Harris had a point, of course. The expression 'serial killer' brought out the worst fears in society, terror of the unknown maniac in their midst, impossible to spot, but carefully selecting his next victim. In any event, did two killings make a series? Singh rapped his knuckles on the other man's wooden desk.

'I've been given forty-eight hours to show results or I'm done,' explained Harris. 'The Commissioner is going to hold a press conference on the hour—' he glanced at the clock on the wall that showed twenty minutes to '—and he wants to say that we're on the verge of a breakthrough.'

Apparently, it didn't matter where one practised the art of policing, there'd be some jobsworth who'd finessed his way to the top without having the first clue how to actually catch a criminal.

'Have you tried to get a profile on the killer?'

'Yep – we're looking for a white man, unmarried, mid-thirties to mid-forties. He's had a bad experience involving women, which might have been minor but blown out of all proportion because he's a fucking whackjob.' He grimaced. 'That last bit is mine.'

'And the hands? What did they say about that?'

'Bugger all that's any use – the usual blah that we came up with all by ourselves yesterday.'

The inspector folded his arms; the room was chilly and windowless. It felt almost subterranean. His phone beeped: 'Hanif has just come back from Syria. Might be a "T".'

What was a 'T'? A terrorist?

'Fatima's brother – Hanif – has just returned from Syria,' said Singh.

'How do you know?'

'Text from my wife.'

Their eyes met.

Unspoken question – was her information credible?

Unspoken answer – how the hell should I know?

Another text. 'And the restaurant is not losing money any more. He has some arrangement with Raj of Raj Real Estate.'

'Date and time of terrorist plot?' asked Harris, with only low level sarcasm.

Singh decided to back his wife's information. It was like putting money on a 1000–1 outsider at the races. 'I think it is worth checking out.'

'All right.' Harris reached for his phone and barked a few orders. Singh gazed at his nails like a young woman after a manicure. Raj and Ibrahim had a financial relationship?

Another text. 'Raj doesn't pay for his meals.'

Curiouser and curiouser.

There was a knock on the door. Carmen marched in. She ignored Singh as if there was a Sikh-shaped hole on the chair rather than a living, breathing example of Singapore's finest.

'Boss, we have him!'

'What?'

'The handkerchief with blood on it that we found in Cynthia Cole's pocket?'

'Yes?'

'We ran it – we have a match.'

Carmen slipped the file across the table and Harris grabbed it with both hands. He opened it and read, 'Martin Bradley, aged thirty-three, male, Caucasian.'

'Served a two-year sentence for attempted rape about six years ago. Was out in ten months for good behaviour. But that's why we have him in the system with all his beautiful tell-all DNA signature.'

Harris was grinning from ear to ear; he'd shed a decade in moments.

'Looks like you have your breakthrough,' said Singh.

'What's the plan, boss?'

'Any idea where this creep is hiding out?'

'We have a previous residential address, down by Elephant and Castle.'

'Place of work?'

'Nothing on record – he was a post-grad student at the LSE when he was convicted of the attempted rape.'

Harris was still flicking pages. 'She was a fellow student apparently. He pleaded not guilty, insisted she consented, had wanted some "rough stuff, that's all" so the case went to trial. About halfway through he gave in, changed his plea. Saved the Old Bailey some time in return for a reduced sentence.'

'So you have everything you were looking for,' said Singh. He ticked them off on stubby fingers. 'White, male, middle-aged, bad experience with women.'

'Anything else in his past?' asked Harris.

'He was picked up and questioned regarding the death of a young woman a couple of years ago, up north in Scotland, but they couldn't find enough to pin it on him so he wasn't charged. Doesn't look like they had much on him anyway. He was seen speaking to her briefly at a party some hours earlier. Because of his record, they hauled him in.'

'How did the girl die?'

'Strangled. No post-mortem mutilation.'

'Different MO,' said Singh.

'Dead is dead,' said Harris. 'Anyway, we'll get him for Cynthia Cole first and worry about the rest of the women he might have killed later.'

DI Carmen belatedly stuck out a hand to Singh. 'Good morning, Inspector, I wasn't expecting to see you here.'

'Good to see you again, DI Carmen,' he said, not getting

up. On balance, he'd rather the woman thought he was rude than let her watch him struggle out of a chair like an upturned beetle.

'I hauled Singh in for the leak to the *Evening Standard*,' said Harris. 'Commissioner's not happy about it and neither am I.'

Singh caught her eye, raised a single eyebrow and provoked a faint blush.

Harris, oblivious to this interchange, said, 'Anyway, that's not relevant now. We need a warrant for this Bradley guy.'

'On its way, sir.'

'We'll go in hard and fast with a small team. No mistakes, no leaks, no accidents, no corpses.'

'Do we tell the Commissioner?' asked Carmen.

Harris shook his head. 'No – we get this perv. And then we gift-wrap him, add some ribbons and hand him over.'

He stood up and shrugged himself into a coat. Singh deeply regretted his status as chief suspect in a leak inquiry rather than chief inspector on a manhunt. Was he really going to miss the denouement?

'So, Singh, you want to come along for a ride? See a bit of policing in the capital of crime.'

The inspector knew it was testosterone and adrenaline doing the talking. From Carmen's face, he could see that it was not a universally popular decision, but he didn't care.

'Yes,' he said. 'Definitely.'

Elephant and Castle. What an odd name for an area. Neither elephants nor castles were in abundance. The grubby streets across the river – and the river felt like a border between the first world and the third world – were more likely to have rats and council housing. Walls were festooned in graffiti of the generally abusive sort rather than in Banksy style. Sitting at the back of the unmarked Audi that Harris had been driving the previous day, Singh was puzzled by the contrasts that London offered.

Good food and bad food. In Singapore, all food was good.

Clean areas and dirty areas. In Singapore, all areas were spotless.

Singapore did have authorised gambling outlets that sold 4D tickets to desperate punters. But here, every second shop was a William Hill or a Ladbrokes. And you could wager on the outcome of any eventuality. If he went in, they were probably providing long odds on the Hand Man being caught within twenty-four hours. He could make a killing.

Harris motioned for his driver to pull over.

'Second-floor flat. Through that door,' he said.

Singh could see a fried chicken outlet and a beautician on either side. The pink-fronted 'Passion for Beauty' shop offered diamond nails, eyebrow threading and hair straightening. The fried chicken shop offered fried chicken.

'Whatever happens, stay back,' said Harris.

Singh nodded. He had no desire to play the hero.

'Are we ready?' he asked Carmen.

She spoke quickly into the radio and then nodded. 'The ARV is parked round the back. They're ready to deploy.'

It was like being in a movie, decided Singh. In all his years of policing, he'd never been in a SWAT-style arrest situation.

'But we're going to do this the old-fashioned way,' said

Harris. 'I'll knock on the door and we'll see if this Martin Bradley comes quietly.'

'And if he doesn't?'

'Then those highly trained, gun-wielding types can take over.'

Two policemen, weapons in hand, pushed open the door and led the way. Harris and Carmen followed and a phalanx of armed police – they looked more like army – fell in behind them.

Singh watched them go and then occupied himself perusing the list of hair and nail treatments that were available to him. He felt a little ridiculous – why would a turbaned man be looking into a hairdresser's window?

Now that the contingent had disappeared upstairs, there was nothing on the street to suggest the imminent arrest of London's most wanted man. The inspector found a cigarette and lit it, inhaling deeply and watching the tip glow red.

A man walked slowly down the street towards him and Singh watched him out of idle curiosity. He was slim, not much taller than Singh himself, a few decades younger, wearing a trench coat with too many buttons and epaulettes – did he think he was in the army? The wail of sirens, the soundtrack of this city, caused him to stiffen and break step slightly. Singh puffed on his cigarette and exhaled through his nose, enjoying the rush of nicotine to his blood. Why was everyone in this town so jumpy?

A London bus drew up twenty yards down the street and a few kids jumped off followed by a woman struggling to unload a double pram. Singh took two steps in her direction to help.

The slight man with mousy hair pushed open the door between the hairdresser's and the fried chicken shop.

Singh stopped in his tracks.

It couldn't be, could it?

Had she seen his fear?

Shaheed stood at the door in his socks, holding it open, listening to the sound of her heels on parquet stairs. He almost expected her to come back, demand an explanation, provoke more lies on his part.

Why was he still too afraid to tell her the whole truth, nothing but the truth?

It was the immigrant mentality, he decided, that sense that the institutions of a society, which the locals looked to for protection, security, services, were not there to serve him.

Not the police, not the Foreign Office, not social security, not even those women at the jobcentre, always telling him to learn new skills, that his computer knowledge was obsolete, an abacus to Apple. He was an outsider, viewed with suspicion, disbelieved if he told the truth, the first to be suspected, the last to be released. His words assumed to be a lie, his actions presumed to be sinister, his motives always questioned.

And how much worse things were in this country for Muslims. Just look at Moazzam Begg. Kidnapped, incarcerated, tortured by his own secret service, finally vindicated and released. But at the first hint of trouble, he was back behind bars. And each time there was an incremental presumption of guilt on the part of the police and the public.

Was that his future too? To be treated like a pariah? Just for being Muslim?

By his wife? By his child someday?

But to say that he loved his child was to expose the inadequacies of language to explain the mysteries of the human heart.

'What are you looking at, Daddy?'

He turned to face his daughter, standing there in her onesie with the non-slip socks, clutching Knuffle Bunny. Her small face was topped by a riot of uncombed curls, making her look strangely vulnerable. He knelt down, enveloped her in a hug. She smelled frowsty and sweet, like day old trifle.

'Just saying goodbye to Mummy,' he replied.

'Has she gone to work?'

'Yes.'

'I'm glad you don't go to work, Daddy.'

'Why is that?'

'So we have more time to play.'

'That's right.'

'Shall we skip school and go to the park today?'

Shaheed picked her up and she rested her head on his shoulder. Still sleepy, still needy. The bouncy, independent girl usually only put in an appearance after breakfast.

He made up his mind. Life was about choices. Priorities. He'd kept his mouth shut before because he'd feared the consequences for himself. Now he feared the consequences for his family.

'Can we, Daddy? Can we skip school?'

Shaheed tried to shut out the small voice in his head that was calling him a coward in no uncertain terms. It was not fear for himself that kept him quiet. It was fear for Regina and this child of his. A man was not a weakling for protecting his kin.

'The park? That's a brilliant idea, honey. Let's do just that.'

Martin Bradley's life as he knew it was thirty seconds from being over. But although humans were the only creatures with an awareness of the future, this did not include an ability to predict it. So Bradley walked home slowly without any sense of impending doom, only a discontent with the immediate present. His head hurt; he'd suffered migraines since he was a child. His plan was to get into bed with an icepack for company, maybe watch some telly, although he despised daytime rubbish. It always made him wonder – not so much about the programming – but about the sorts of people who had the time to watch TV in the morning. Well, today he was just like them. Karma, he supposed.

He noticed a Sikh man looking at him. It was always the bloody foreigners; they'd never been taught it was rude to stare. You'd never catch anyone born and bred in England looking someone over that way. Avoiding eye contact was a national pastime, more popular than cricket.

He reached his door, faded blue, a row of four buttons on the adjoining wall, one call button for each flat. His wasn't working, not that the landlord gave a damn. The little people got nothing in this town unless they were prepared to turn to riots and looting. And that was not Martin's way. The door was ajar, wedged open with a newspaper. Was it for the convenience of some delivery boy or had one of the tenants lost the key?

Martin mounted the narrow stairs wearily. He was forced to place a palm on the wall to maintain his balance. The stairs were wooden and uneven, old without having that attractive patina of antiquity, and he trod carefully so as not to lose his footing in the dim light. A strip of tape along each stair was intended as an anti-slip device but made no difference. Martin Bradley couldn't wait for the day when he would get away from this place, make a fresh start somewhere with the woman he loved, leave his past behind.

He stepped out on to the landing, smiling a little at the thought of a future away from this place, a future with Regina somewhere in the sunshine.

CHAPTER 12

Martin Bradley – or Singh assumed it was him, the nondescript fellow who had pushed the door open a scant minute ago – flew out of the building like all the hordes of hell were chasing him. He looked both ways and then dashed in Singh's direction. The police, three of them in black kit and black helmets, sprinted out after him, guns raised. The fugitive raced down the pavement, his face a mask of terror. Pedestrians scattered in his wake, some yelling in shock when they saw the armed men, a woman turning to cower against the wall, her baby in her arms.

'Stop! Police!' shouted Singh.

The running man didn't hear, chose not to hear, wasn't going to stop in any event.

One of the policemen fell to a knee and raised his gun. Surely he wasn't going to shoot Bradley with so many civilians about? Bullets from that weapon would probably puncture three humans at once.

The escapee was almost level with Singh.

If there was one thing the inspector wasn't, it was an action man. Not for him the galloping after bad guys, gun drawn, shouting. His white sneakers remained pristine because he didn't take them anywhere unsavoury, didn't even step in puddles. He wore a turban, not a cape.

But sometimes duty called.

Singh's right shoulder rammed into the running man's left. The policeman carried a lot of weight and, once he got moving, a decent amount of momentum. Bradley sensed the attack, tried to swerve, change direction, failed. Singh hit him like a charging hippo. He catapulted forward, arms splayed, an amateur diver doing a belly flop, lost his balance on the kerb edge and fell between two parked cars. Singh didn't hesitate. He leapt forward, braced himself for a shot, for a knife, tensing hardly used stomach muscles as if that was going to help deflect a weapon, and flung himself on the fugitive.

As they struggled, the inspector became aware it was a losing battle. Martin Bradley was not powerfully built but he was decades younger. Even as Singh clung on to his right arm, the fellow brought his other fist around and punched the inspector once, twice, three times on the side of his head. Singh relaxed his grip on the wrist. Took another punch to the head and lolled like a street drunk.

Bradley half rolled his body away, managed to get to his knees.

And was confronted with an array of weaponry held in steady hands by men in reflective visors. Robocop and his friends had arrived.

Singh sat up and realised that his involvement had only taken seconds although there'd still been time for a fair bit of his life, wife edited out, to flash before his eyes.

Harris appeared, flushed, decisive. Two policemen hauled the fellow to his feet and one patted him down. All the fight had gone from him and he stood as if the only thing holding him up was the policeman's grip. He was handcuffed without resistance, his face the colour of bleached paper.

Singh scrambled to his feet and received a nod of thanks from Harris.

'What's going on?' asked Bradley.

'Martin Bradley, I am arresting you for the murder of Cynthia Cole and Fatima Daud,' said Harris, his voice clear, cold and carrying. 'You do not have to say anything, but it may harm your defence if you do not mention when questioned something which you later rely on in court. Anything you do say may be given in evidence. Do you understand?'

'There must be some mistake!'

Someone in the small crowd that had gathered recognised the names of the victims.

'Jesus, it's the Hand Man. They've caught the Hand Man!'

Harris was hero of the hour. Singh was bruised and battered and feeling sorry for himself. They were back at Paddington Green station. Singh had been patched up with antiseptic, a sticking plaster and a strong cup of coffee. Now he was sitting alone in Harris's office waiting to be told what to do, hoping to hear the latest on Martin Bradley. The office was as empty as a cell. There was nothing personal, no pictures, no plants and no squeeze balls. Harris was a cop in the traditional mould, destroying any external relationships in pursuit of, not so much a career, as the bad guys.

He, Singh, on the other hand, had a wife who was busy investigating in her own right, if salacious gossip could be described in those terms.

She would not be impressed by his efforts that day. 'That's why they have younger police – who are fit,' she'd say. 'Not someone who wears sports shoes just for show.'

Carmen walked in and smiled, even small teeth – just like his but without the smoker's patina.

'That was quick thinking,' she said. 'We're grateful.'

'He'd never have got away. I didn't need to get involved.'

Singh shifted in his chair and winced. He really hadn't needed to get involved. And, since he had, it was a shame that no one had recorded the incident and turned him into an Internet sensation.

'Possibly you're right,' she answered. 'But one of our armed crew might have shot him. We're not Americans yet but there are more trigger-happy types than there used to be.'

Singh remembered Robocop steadying himself for the shot. She was right, he might have saved the killer's life, not something to highlight in his autobiography.

'What happened upstairs?'

'There was no response at the door of his flat. We kicked it down. He just walked into our midst and turned tail before anyone had a chance to react.'

'I guess his place is being turned over now?'

'With a fine tooth comb – if he has a strand of hair in

207

there, let alone any dismembered hands in the freezer, SOCO will find it.'

'So what's next?'

'Harris is about to start – he sent me to ask if you wanted to watch?'

Singh rose to his feet with alacrity. 'Lead the way.'

She reached the door, had a hand on the knob, when she said, 'I'm sorry you were hauled in about the leak.'

'Because you did it?'

'Are you going to tell anyone?'

The inspector shook his head. 'No, I'm sure you had your reasons.'

'I wanted women to be on guard.'

'Fair enough,' said Singh.

'Fortunately, it's a moot point.'

'But remember – you owe me a favour now.'

'And I'm sure you'll collect, Inspector Singh.' She smiled as she spoke to rob the words of any offence and he was struck again by the change in her since they'd started on their cold case together. This was a woman who might have agreed to tick some boxes to get promoted but she was in her element in the middle of an investigation.

DI Carmen led the way past corridors and office doors. Open doors showed small offices and bigger open-plan ones. The inside of the concrete eyesore was as ugly as the outside, functionality over aesthetics.

'Nice place,' he said.

DI Carmen snorted. 'The prisoner cells are better – piped music and movies.'

'Really?'

'We hold terrorism suspects here – as they're in a bit longer, it was considered cruel to hold them with the bare minimum of facilities.'

Singh supposed the mark of a civilised society was how it treated its less fortunate members. But the contrast between comfortable cells for terrorists and the homeless on the street was ironic.

'We've got those four we picked up in Bradford a few weeks ago locked up in here somewhere too.'

She led him to a small room that was already crowded with observers and he saw through a one-way window that Harris was sitting across from Bradley at a small table.

Bradley looked pensive, his slightness emphasised by the imposing bulk of the DCI.

'He's turned down a lawyer,' said Carmen in a low voice.

'Are you Martin Bradley?'

'Yes. You know that. Why have you arrested me?'

'I told you earlier – for the murder of two women.'

'But that's just unbelievable. Why would I do something like that?' He rocked his chair back and forth as he spoke.

'That's what we wanted to ask you.'

'But I would never hurt anyone.'

'That's not true, is it?'

'What do you mean?'

'You have a conviction for attempted rape a few years back.'

'I was a kid – still in university!'

'And that makes rape all right?'

'Of course not – what I mean is that she was a student like me at the LSE. I was in love with her. We ... we ... she seemed willing and then next thing I knew she was shouting

209

that I'd tried to force her.' The bewilderment at an old hurt could be heard in his voice. 'I would never do that to a woman.'

'And yet you pleaded guilty.'

'I didn't want to but my lawyer . . . my lawyer said I wasn't a very credible witness in my own defence, that I looked like I was lying even when I was honest.'

There was some truth in that. Bradley was twitchy, eyes flitting about the room, knee bouncing.

'He said he could get my sentence down if I gave in. I was so afraid, you see. In the end, I just did what they wanted.'

'But that must have made you furious?'

'Yes, I was mad as hell.'

'Who were you most mad at?'

'I guess Emily . . . her name was Emily . . . why would she accuse me of something that never happened?'

'And you wanted revenge?'

'Against Emily, you mean?'

'Sure.'

'No,' Martin shook his head vigorously. 'I didn't want to go near that bitch again. Anyway, I had no idea where she was . . . I spent eleven months in jail!'

If Bradley had any idea how damning his remarks were, he gave no sign. He was still reliving the history, the perceived injustice of his previous sentence.

Singh was impressed with Harris. The man's tone was even, non-confrontational, betraying no excitement. He himself would have wanted to dance a jig by now. Martin Bradley was cracking like a Ming vase at a construction site.

'Against other women then?'

'What about other women?'

Singh exchanged glances with Carmen. The fellow seemed to have forgotten why he was there.

'Did you want revenge against *other* women?'

'Why would I?'

'Because of what Emily did to you ...'

'Yeah, but that was Emily, not anyone else.'

'What about that woman who died up North? Strangled. Did she upset you too? Did she reject you?'

If Bradley were any whiter, he'd have been in an advert for laundry detergent.

'I had nothing to do with that. They let me go. The police let me go. There wasn't any evidence.'

Interesting choice of words, thought Singh.

'You say that, but I think we all know what women are like.' Harris leaned forward. 'I've had my own share of troubles with them, let me tell you.'

'You're still trying to pin those murders on me, aren't you?'

Bradley shuddered as if a cold wind had blown through the tiny room with the bare walls. 'I'd never do something like that, you must believe me.'

'Then why was your blood found at the scene of Cynthia Cole's murder?'

Harris watched his suspect turn a fine shade of green. He hoped the bastard wasn't going to hurl. That would not be a good end to an otherwise satisfactory day. They had their man, it was still his case – no way the Commissioner could take it away to give to one of his shiny-suited, blue-eyed boys. All he needed to wrap it up was for this little worm to confess.

'It can't be – it must be a set-up. You guys are looking for a fall guy. I've never even heard of a Cynthia Cole.'

He was panicking, eyes red-rimmed, lips dry and cracked, pupils enlarged.

'The DNA doesn't lie, Martin.'

'Yeah, but people do ...' The bitterness in his voice was audible. 'I don't know her or that other, Fatima Daud.'

An impressive memory for the names of dead women, thought Singh. Suggestive perhaps? Or maybe he just read the newspapers assiduously.

'So you claim never to have met either of them?'

'Never.'

'What about Fatima Daud – you seem to have heard of her?'

'Well, she was ... in the papers, right?'

Was there a hesitation?

'Before the murders?'

'No, why would I know anything about her? Women aren't really interested in me.' Bradley was sullen.

'Exactly – women aren't interested in you. Why would they be? You're such a puny guy, pimply – who has pimples at your age? I bet they cross the road to avoid you. And that's why you're mad. That's why you kill them – walk away with a trophy. Finally, you win.'

'It's not like that. You're just making up stories ...'

'Nah, I couldn't do it – takes a perv to come up with something like chopping off people's hands. That's just sick. And that's why your blood was at the scene.'

Bradley opened his mouth, closed it again. Tried once more, this time the words came out in a whisper. 'I'm not the Hand Man, I tell you, I'm not. I really don't know any Cynthia Cole.'

Harris slapped a photo of Cole on the table, swivelled it round to Bradley, blown up, A4, smiling, a come-hither look in her eyes.

'She look familiar now?'

He placed another one next to it, Cynthia Cole, eyes shut, wounds dry, bloodless skin. 'Or how about this one – after your handiwork.'

Bradley's face began to quiver like blancmange. He pushed his chair back, stood up, swaying on his feet like a boxer being counted out.

Harris remained seated, impassive, but inside his heart was going like a tribal drum. Was this it? The recognition in Bradley's eyes had been determinative. There was no doubt at all that he knew Cynthia Cole.

'I ... I ... Oh my God! Oh my God.' And then he collapsed to his knees and began to howl, a bizarre, terrifying sound for a grown man.

'You saw?'

'Yes.'

'What's your conclusion?'

'He clearly knew the dead girl although not necessarily by name,' said Singh.

Harris stood up, scrunched the sheet he was holding into a ball and threw it into his bin. The inspector knew this was pure theatre and not the destruction of evidence as the written statement in his hand had been a photocopy.

Harris slammed his palms face down on the desk. 'This is precisely the story he would make up if he killed her.'

'Yes,' agreed Singh. 'It is also precisely the story that might explain the presence of DNA that is consistent with Bradley not being the killer.' He stood up, went over to the bin and recovered the statement, smoothing it out and looking at it again.

'Sorry,' said Harris.

Singh waved a stubby hand. He understood the other man's frustration. He'd been so sure he was on the verge of getting a confession. Instead, he had this long-winded but exculpatory statement.

'So he says that he met Cynthia Cole when he called a mobile number pasted in a phone booth on Tottenham Court Road.'

'She was a working woman who was engaged to be married, why would she moonlight as a prostitute?'

'She took him to a hotel – one of those places that you can rent for a few hours at a time. He'd brought some wine and a couple of glasses.'

'Did he think it was a date?'

'He was so nervous that he broke one of the glasses, cut his hand quite badly. She lent him a handkerchief from her bag to wrap it up.'

'There were no marks on him,' pointed out Harris. 'The docs gave him the once-over when we brought him in.'

'Ten days ago – they could easily have healed. Do the dates agree with what we know so far?'

Harris nodded reluctantly. 'Yes. He claims to have met her the evening of the morning we know she left home. She was killed that day or at most a couple of days after.'

'According to him, he was so embarrassed, having never used a prostitute before, that he emptied his wallet of his money – about thirty pounds – and left as soon as he could. She asked for the handkerchief back on his way out. He didn't see her again, never knew her name.'

'As far as I'm concerned, even if his story is true, it explains how he met her, selected her ... and then killed her.' Harris's mouth was set in a stubborn line. 'Nothing more.'

'What about Fatima?'

'What about her?'

'He seemed to hesitate when you asked him if he'd heard of her.'

'I didn't notice.'

'Anyway, you have nothing connecting him to that murder.'

'That's the one upside of serial killers,' said the other man, 'you only have to pin one on the guy, and the rest fall into place – just like dominoes.'

'So you're still sure you have the Hand Man?'

'I'm still sure I have him. I'm meeting the CPS later – if they're on-board, we'll press charges and tell the public what they want to hear.'

Not just the public but his bosses as well and all the demons in his past, thought Singh. Harris was a man who was desperate for a win. And he was prepared to cheat a little to achieve that much sought after victory.

'Aren't you going to look into his story at all? The telephone booth, the hotel – someone might have seen them. There must be CCTV.' The inspector would have given a fat arm or a fat leg to be in a position to bark out orders at underlings.

'We're on the job,' said Carmen, who had been leaning against a wall, watching the two male policemen with an objective interest that suggested she was a theatre critic watching a complex two-man play. 'We've asked for CCTV, we have officers interviewing hotel staff, anyone who might have seen them together.'

The point of Singh's turban bobbed up and down to signify his approval.

'And I'm going to interview one of her colleagues and friends right now,' she continued.

'Once I put killer and victim together, the tabloids will be clamouring for the death sentence to be reinstated.' Harris was almost rubbing his hands together.

'We have the death sentence in Singapore,' replied Singh, 'and I assure you that sending a man to his death, however heinous the crime, is overrated.'

'Have you ever been wrong?' asked Carmen.

'Sent an innocent man to the gallows? I hope not.'

'And if you discovered you had? What would you do?' Harris was almost manic, eyes staring, neck cords strained.

'I don't know,' said Singh. 'I really don't.'

The other man relaxed. His mood swings were starting to concern Singh – the case taking a greater toll than warranted for an experienced policeman.

'You don't have to worry – as we used to say in the old days, we have Bradley bang to rights.'

CHAPTER 13

Carmen was on her way to interview a friend of Cynthia Cole, Kate Chatsworth. Inspector Singh had invited himself along for the ride.

'You can't just come with me to interview witnesses,' she'd said as he cornered her on the way to the car park.

'Well then, I'll just have to hang around Harris while he wonders who leaked the information to the press . . .'

'You wouldn't tell?'

'I might.'

'So this is blackmail?' She smiled as she said it.

'Such an ugly word,' he complained. 'I prefer to think of it as an incentive for you to do the right thing.'

'Why do you want to come along anyway?'

'I'm worried your boss is developing a serious case of tunnel vision, insisting it's a serial killer, adamant it's Bradley.'

'You're in the same tunnel,' she said tartly. 'You're just facing the other direction.'

Now they sat in a small bedsit in Golders Green within walking distance of the nearest Northern Line station. It was decorated as if Kate was eleven: soft toys, floral wallpaper and a patchwork quilt on the unmade and unfolded futon. Kate herself was in a dressing gown, curled up in an armchair and stroking a cat. She was in her mid-thirties and had worked with Cynthia at the posh hairdresser's in Bond Street although she hadn't been there when Singh and Carmen had attempted to hunt her down at her workplace.

'It's the shock,' explained Kate. 'I couldn't go into work, could I? My hands are shaking the whole time.'

'We know that this has been a difficult time for you,' said Carmen automatically. 'But I'm sure you want to help us catch the person who did this terrible thing to Cynthia.'

'They say he's worse than Jack the Ripper,' hiccupped Kate.

What did that mean? wondered Singh.

'That's why we need your help,' replied Carmen.

'I don't know anything about it. Why would I? Besides, you've got him, innit? I saw it on the telly.'

'We have someone helping us with our inquiries,' said Carmen. 'We need to make sure we have an airtight case.'

Kate appeared to get this because she nodded her head vigorously and her bleached hair fell across her forehead. Maybe she watched *Law and Order*.

'So you and Cynthia were close?'

'I guess you could say that. We worked in the same place and we both liked a laugh.'

'Were you surprised when she came to stay with you?'

'Nah – it wasn't the first time, right? She just needed a place to kip for a few days. On account of having had a quarrel with her fiancé.'

'Did they quarrel often?' asked Singh.

Carmen glared at Singh, reminding him of his promise to be seen and not heard, like a Victorian child. Why had she ever thought he'd play that role with any conviction? He was too hairy for starters.

'All the time,' said Kate. 'He had a lot to put up with – our Cynthia wasn't the easiest, you know?' She seemed to belatedly remember that one shouldn't speak ill of the dead because she added hastily, 'Mind, she was much too good for him. He was such a stick-in-the-mud.'

'What do you mean that he had a lot to put up with?' asked Carmen.

'She liked to go out, have a drink, party a bit. But Nick preferred to stay at home and watch the footie on the telly – an Aston Villa fan, he is. Cynthia was always on at him to switch to Chelsea.'

'She was a Chelsea supporter?'

'She didn't give a hoot about any of them, but Chelsea are really successful, right? That Villa couldn't buy a win.' She shook her head. 'Don't know what she saw in Nick really, with his red face and red hands. And he never made any money.'

'Would that have bothered her?' asked Singh.

'For sure – she liked nice things did our Cynthia.' Kate was stroking one of her teddy bears now, the cat having slunk off.

'And the hairdressing job didn't pay much?'

'Course not – we weren't even allowed to keep the tips! Had to put the cash into a pool.'

A bit more money under the pillow and this young woman

would be complaining about taxes and immigration too, longing for the end of the socialist regime so women could keep their own tips.

'So do you know if she tried to supplement her income in any other way?' asked Carmen.

'Eh?'

'Did Cynthia, you know, try to earn a bit of money on the side?' asked Singh. Why was he having to translate for two English people?

'And so what if she did? It's a free country, right? Even if them Poles are stealing all the jobs.'

How free was it when women were afraid to go out? When the nation was constantly on high alert because of potential terrorist attacks? When so many people believed that 'them Poles' were out for their jobs.

'Who put you up to asking me all this?' asked Kate. 'Was it Monsieur Pierre?'

'Of course not.'

Singh and DI Carmen had already had the pleasure of meeting Monsieur Pierre on their visit to Kate's place of employment. He was a fake Frenchman from East London, camp as a day out at Glastonbury, eyes like agate, who'd professed profound sorrow and loss at the death of his 'best hair washer – the clients, they loved her'. But he'd washed his hands of any further knowledge of the dead girl – 'I always respect their privacy. It's the best way.'

'But she was earning a bit on the side?' Singh was persistent.

'Maybe. She needed it what with the wedding coming up and Nick not having any idea of the expense.'

'What did she *do* for the extra money?'

'It's none of your business.'

'We're not making any judgements, Kate. But we're trying to grasp what caused the killer to select Cynthia as a victim.'

'OMG! You mean . . . I told her it was dangerous. There's no telling about people these days. I told her but she wasn't one to listen!'

'What wouldn't she listen to?'

Instead of replying, Kate padded off to a drawer in her rabbit bedroom slippers, opened it, rummaged about until she found what she was looking for and handed it to Carmen.

The policewoman looked down at the white name card in her hand – 'Call if you wanna have a GOOD time!!' A mobile number was embossed and the rectangle was decorated with handcuffs.

She passed it to Singh who blinked, taken aback by the tawdry invite.

'Er . . how did she hand these out? At the hairdresser's?' he asked.

'Course not. I'd have liked to see Monsieur Pierre's face if she'd done that. She'd just leave them around the place, you know, phone booths and stuff.'

He was too sheltered in Singapore where phone booths were usually both operational and devoid of offers of entertainment involving forms of restraint.

The fat man caught Carmen's eye. Bradley's story was panning out.

'And was business good?'

'Brilliant. She was making a killing.'

The words hung in the air between them – the most inappropriate epitaph Singh had ever heard.

'Is that how he met her? Is that how the killer met her?' demanded Kate, her earlier sorrow giving way to excitement. It seemed that deep down, Victorian values dictated.

'It's a possibility that we have to consider.'

'She was going to stop, you know? Once she got married.'

Singh didn't know, didn't necessarily believe it and didn't really see how it mattered. Cynthia hadn't stopped in time and this wasn't a morality play.

'She just wanted to earn enough for a really nice white wedding. That's all.'

'Are you with us?'

'Yes.'

Hanif had no doubts about the course of action he was adopting. This was the beauty of doing the right thing by Allah. Once the decision was made, the path to follow became visible, easy, worn smooth by the footsteps of those who had led the way. Not paved with gold or good intentions but soaked in the blood of martyrs.

'This time is different,' warned the man who had called him on the number he had left in the Hotmail folder. His voice was muffled and Hanif guessed he was speaking through a handkerchief held over his mouth.

'I know. I read the plans.'

'Some of the others weren't comfortable with it.'

'At the end of the day, it is a question of the goal that we have in mind. The methods have to be tested by only two criteria: whether they meet the goal and whether they are feasible.'

'And what is your opinion?'

'I think your plan has the potential to be highly successful.'

This pleased the other man because he laughed out loud. 'You are right about that, Hanif.'

He didn't like it that the man knew who he was but not the reverse. But he also knew that this was the way it worked. Separate cells, limited information, on a need-to-know basis only.

'How many are involved?' he asked.

'One other and myself.'

'So when do we start?'

'Ahhh – that's where I have a surprise for you.'

'I don't like surprises.'

This was true and had been true since a birthday party when Hanif was eight. He'd pissed his pants when the other kids jumped out at him.

Fatima had rescued him; rushed him upstairs, hosed him down, found him a spare pair of shorts, talked him back downstairs with promises of presents.

And look what had happened to her. Birth to death – very few were privileged to choose the hour of their demise.

'You'll like this one.'

'What is it?'

'We've started. We have one already.'

'You've started? What about me?'

'This time, you're on the bench. But don't worry, you'll get a run out ... soon.'

'But I am ready now! I am the point of the sword.'

'Your turn will come.'

'It is better if I am with the first wave. That was my mission.'

'Your enthusiasm is a credit to Allah but you will have to wait.'

Before he could protest once more, the caller hung up.

Hanif stared at the phone, his eyes bleak and cold.

'It's all gone tits up.'

'What do you mean?'

'We're going to release Bradley tomorrow.'

'What? I thought you would have charged him by now.'

'He lawyered up ... and produced an alibi.'

'For which murder?'

'Fatima Daud.'

Singh wrapped his hands round the Costa Coffee paper cup, looking for warmth to soothe his arthritic fingers. The weather had turned on him as he hurried to the café to meet Harris. The sky was grey and the rain fell like cold pinpricks. Singh was reminded of the time he'd tried acupuncture for a stiff back. It was nippy too; a mild breeze fingered his neck.

Singh contemplated this new information while looking out the window. A brisk wind was reversing umbrellas and shifting debris like tumbleweed in the desert. This was more the weather he'd expected on his London trip – the sort he saw as he tried to watch the cricket on television only for the groundsmen at Lord's to roll out the covers.

'It looks solid too,' continued Harris.

'Any man who has an alibi for a crime is of immediate

suspicion to me,' retorted Singh. 'You need to check it like a dentist with a mortgage and a mistress.'

This drew a small smile from the other man, more a wry twist of the lips.

'He was in prison up North – it wasn't on his record because the girl he was accused of assaulting refused to testify but it's there all right.'

'That does sound airtight,' agreed Singh.

'Can you believe this guy? A conviction for attempted rape; picked up for two murders and another sexual assault, but I have to let him go.'

Singh felt his pain. There was nothing worse for a policeman than having a carefully constructed case come down like a house of cards. The inspector from Singapore wasn't happy about the turn of events either. He'd apparently wrestled an innocent man to the ground. That sounded like a civil suit to him. Would Superintendent Chen cough up damages?

'It doesn't mean he's not good for the second murder – that of Cynthia Cole,' suggested Singh.

'We're still treating this as a one-for-one offer. The bosses are adamant. And I think they're right.' Harris's blue eyes had clouded over just like the sky outside. 'But that's why I asked you to meet me, in case I'm wrong.'

'What do you want me to do?'

'You said you were still looking at Fatima's murder.'

'Yes.'

'Go all out – and keep me in the loop. I'll help where I can.'

'Shouldn't you be doing that?'

'I couldn't agree more, but we have manpower shortages, an irate and terrified public, questions being asked in Parliament.'

Singh nodded.

'That's not all.' He lowered his voice and glanced around to ensure there was no one within hearing distance, 'There's chatter that Islamists are planning something here as well – my colleagues in the security services just briefed us to keep our eyes peeled for trouble.'

'Like the Tube bombings?'

'Could be anything. We're a nation of sitting ducks.'

'I thought you had a public alert system to raise awareness if an attack was imminent?'

'The government doesn't dare raise danger levels in case it looks like some ham-fisted effort to sway the coming election.'

Politics – everything was politics. Life and death, terrorism and safety, all superseded by the desire of a few men to stay in elected office.

He remembered what his wife had told him. 'What about Hanif?' he asked. 'Any feedback?'

'Nothing useful – just a message from the security services that they have everything under control and we should stay away from him.'

'Stay away from Hanif? Why?'

'Who knows? Those guys just love the cloak and dagger stuff. Maybe they have an eye on him, hoping he'll lead them to the big guns.' He cracked his knuckles and it sounded like tree branches snapping in a storm. 'Or maybe they know nothing at all but just want to seem important.'

Singh remained quiet.

'I don't know how long I'm going to be on the case anyway,' added Harris. 'It's not going to look good when I release Bradley.'

'And if he's *actually* innocent – there's still a killer out there.'

Being a Londoner was a complicated affair, trying to steer between the dangers posed by terrorists and serial killers while going about one's daily business. Singh felt quite homesick for Singapore.

'Well, we haven't said that we've caught the Hand Man, only that we have someone in custody assisting with inquiries.'

Singh trained his turban on an abandoned paper at the next table. The headline in the *Daily Mail* read, HAND MAN BEHIND BARS, with an illustration of two hands, dripping blood, clutching prison bars.

'There's something else bothering me more and more,' said Singh. 'The interval of five years.'

'Too long?'

Singh nodded. 'This type of fetishist – the time lapse doesn't make sense.'

'So what's your explanation?'

'There are two possibilities excluding different murderers.'

'Which are?'

'The killer was prevented from carrying out more killings for some reason. Maybe he was in prison or abroad. If the latter, there might be some murders with a similar MO wherever he was ...'

'What's the other possibility?'

'That there are more bodies out there, as yet undiscovered or not yet linked to these murders.'

'What do you suggest?'

'Review every missing person file and every unsolved murder case for the last ten years involving a female between the ages of fifteen and forty.'

'There are more of those than you can imagine.'

Singh didn't want to imagine it. Wives, daughters, sisters.

'I'll do my best,' said Harris. 'We've already looked at the unsolved cases. No bodies without hands.'

'Widen the search? If the timeline is pre-Fatima, maybe no missing hands?'

'You mean it's a quirk the killer developed later?'

Singh opened his palms. It was a possibility. There were more things in heaven and earth than were dreamed of by overworked police forces.

'And cases where only parts of bodies were found ... for whatever reason.'

'All right, I'll do that. Anything else?'

'Missing persons ... ' said Singh.

Harris nodded his agreement. 'And what about Fatima?' he asked.

Singh briefed him quickly; the presence in the country of the fiancé from Pakistan, his meeting with Fatima despite his insistence that they'd never met.

'If we find out he's a hand fetishist, we might have grounds to arrest him,' said Harris.

'There's also the family. The father and brothers are quite conservative, she was bringing shame on them.'

'I can't believe they'd have killed her over it. Not her own family.'

'My wife is certain they did it. But that might be because she tends to have murderous thoughts about her own relatives ... and me.'

'How did we miss all this the first time round?'

'A conspiracy of silence by all concerned.' Singh wasn't

going to admit it but it seemed that community tensions had shut down the information flow.

Harris pinched the bridge of his nose. 'Anyone else?'

'The boyfriend and the best friend.'

'What?'

Singh explained the connection between Fatima Daud, Sara Kendrick and Jimmy Kendrick. He had to admit that it sounded like a cheesy soap opera plot.

'A love triangle, eh?'

'A painfully common reason for murder, I'm afraid. Poor Fatima Daud was not meant for happiness.'

Harris shook his head in disgust. 'Was the body even cold yet?'

'Not very,' said Singh. 'And Jimmy is quite a bit older than either girl, a successful lawyer living in some mansion in St John's Wood. He's quite the collector as well: women, art, cars.'

'Hands?'

'I guess that's the million dollar question.'

'If he has a mansion in St John's Wood, it's a ten million pound question.'

CHAPTER 14

Three brothers. Of whom he'd only met one, Dr Fauzi – antagonistic the first time, seeking help the second. Why? He said because Singh's visit had reopened old wounds, upset his mother who did not want to go to her grave without knowing what had happened to her beloved daughter and, most of all, because he was dismayed by the suggestion that Fatima had been the victim of a serial killer.

'Is that strange?' he asked his wife the next day as they walked to their appointment along Kensington High Street.

'No.'

'Why – why does it matter?'

'There's something very unholy about being murdered by a serial killer. Unclean. UnIslamic.'

'I don't see it.'

'That must be why they sent you here to advise on community policing.'

Dark brows, speckled with grey, drew together in irritation.

The rain had stopped, although a glance at the sky suggested this was just a temporary hiatus. He rubbed his hands together and, when that didn't work, he tucked them deep into the pockets of his trousers. His nose was cold; he couldn't feel his toes. Only his head was warm. The unexpected advantage of a turban, as effective as a hood. The policeman, doing his best imitation of a nervous turtle, tried to retract his neck into his tan suede overcoat that smelled of mothballs, had the stickiness of dead flesh and was lined with yellowing wool.

'I really don't see why it matters who did it.'

'Then you are in the wrong job.'

'It matters to society and the family that the killer is caught,' he said grouchily. 'But it doesn't matter to the *victim* who killed her.'

'It would matter to me.'

This caused him to pause in step and speech. He turned to face his wife. 'What does that mean?'

'If someone killed me, I wouldn't like it if it was a serial killer.'

'You'd rather it was someone you knew?'

'Of course.'

'Why?'

His wife was struggling to articulate her position; she reserved her natural eloquence only for criticism of him.

'If a stranger kills me, it has no meaning. I am not a person to him.'

Singh noted that all his wife's imaginary killers were male. It was a reasonable statistical approach.

'If you killed me . . .'

A startled glance from a pedestrian caused her to stop until he was past.

'If I killed you . . .' prompted Singh.

'At least I will know that I managed to provoke you.'

'I see.' And he did. His wife wanted the privilege of bringing her death upon herself if the fates required that she be murdered.

'I'm sure if I'm driven to kill you, it will be for something you did or said,' he said reassuringly.

She glared at him and stalked off ahead.

'This is the place,' she said, when he caught up with her, looking up at a tavern sign on a Tudor building that said the Fox and Anchor. 'Are you sure you don't want me to interview him too?'

He'd rather poke his eyes out with pins than have his wife interrupt him at regular intervals. 'He might recognise you from the restaurant,' he pointed out. 'And you might lose your cover.'

'That's true,' she agreed, after thinking the matter over.

'So better if I do this myself.'

'Just don't get distracted by the beer, that's all.'

And, on this admonitory note, she slipped into the Oddbins next door, an odd choice for a teetotaller. No doubt she'd assumed it was an outlet that sold bins of assorted sizes and colours rather than alcohol.

Singh was mildly surprised that Ibrahim, the younger brother of Fatima, had agreed to meet him and greatly surprised that he'd suggested a pub in Kensington. However, as Singh was not one to say no to beer on tap and he was curious to meet this rebellious Muslim, he agreed at once. Now he stood at the entrance, scanning the dim interior, wondering if he should have suggested that Ibrahim carry a copy of *Pride and Prejudice* and a rose.

'Are you Singh?'

He turned to see a young man who was both better looking and much taller than he'd expected. It was just as well he'd sent Mrs Singh away. This fellow looked like a Bollywood star, not any of the current ones with their too big hair and whitened skin but one of the old-timers – Raaj Kumar, the Indian James Bond.

Singh followed the man inside, noting that he seemed comfortable in a place that sold the devil's drink. As his eyes adjusted, he admired the ships in bottles that were tucked into every groove. A large anchor hung from a wall. The place had the welcoming smell of old beer, chips and cigarettes. Wooden chairs padded with green leather, polished old oak tables, flagstones underfoot, a bar running almost the entire length of the premises, subdued but sufficient lighting from ship lamps and a view through rectangle paned windows on to the busy street.

'What will you have?'

Singh eyed the long line of draught beer handles – Strongbow, London Pride, Guinness, Stella Artois. He was riven by unusual indecision.

'London Pride is a good ale,' suggested Ibrahim.

'London Pride then.'

A couple of moments later, glasses in hand, the men found a quiet corner in a booth with high backs and a table polished by generations of drinkers between them. The atmosphere was somewhat ruined for Singh by the plastic NO SMOKING signs everywhere.

233

'My brother Fauzi said you were looking into Fatima's death. How come?'

'I was part of a task force on police community relations – your sister's case came up.'

'Five years too late, isn't it?'

'That's why I'm trying to help.'

'But you don't even have crime in Singapore.'

Singapore's squeaky-clean reputation was undermining his own.

'It must have been a difficult time for your family,' said the inspector, valiantly trying to get back on point.

'You think?'

Singh ignored the sarcasm. 'What do you believe happened to Fatima?'

'They're saying there's a serial killer.'

'I don't mean now, I mean then. When it first happened.'

'I was only nineteen at the time ...' He was staring over Singh's left shoulder with an intensity that almost made the inspector turn around except that he knew Ibrahim was gazing into the past. 'Fatima was twenty-four.'

'The whole family was at war with Fatima when she died?'

'What nonsense is that?'

'The nonsense I heard from credible sources including members of your family.'

'She was not keen on the family arranged marriage. It was no big deal. She would have come round.'

'That's not what I heard.'

'From your credible sources?'

'She wouldn't have come round because she had an English boyfriend. White.'

'That's a lie!' He thumped the table, but the timing was awry. It was just as well that Bollywood didn't require acting ability, just a chiselled jaw and swivelling hips.

'You might not have known about it, but it was true nevertheless.'

Was he prepared to admit he was out of the loop to maintain his story?

'It wasn't serious. Some rich guy sending her flowers is all.'

'It's been known to work before.'

Singh alias Casanova. It was just as well Mrs Singh had not come along. She'd have been rolling around the aisles.

'Fatima was just going through a rebellious phase.'

'You mean she'd have grown out of it?'

'Of course.'

'Why are you so sure?'

'Because I grew out of mine.'

'But Fatima never had the chance, did she?'

'I guess not.'

'Was that because someone in the family doubted that she'd "grow out of it"?' Was there anything in the world more annoying than stubby fingers tracing inverted commas in the air?

'What are you trying to say?'

'That your father or one of your brothers might have seen the dishonour to the family as permanent.'

'Oh! That's your angle is it? Stone Age Muslims kill sister to save family honour? I can read the *Daily Mail* headline now.'

'Look, I'm not saying that's what happened. Nothing annoys me more than being stereotyped.'

This was true. Singh couldn't stand it when everyone

assumed that all Sikhs were tall. He had less to say about the presumption that he enjoyed his drink. 'But I need to ask the questions, eliminate the possibilities. If the police had done it five years ago, maybe we'd know who killed your sister.'

'But that wouldn't bring her back, would it? So what's the bloody use?'

'Don't you want to know who did it? Don't you want justice?'

For some reason that Singh couldn't fathom, this brought a small smile to Ibrahim's lips. 'Yes, you could say that. I do want justice.'

'Were you close, Fatima and you?'

'Yes.'

'And your brothers?'

'Fauzi was a bit older. Poor Hanif was probably her favourite.'

Hanif, the brother he hadn't met, who'd been in Syria but was back now in the land of his birth.

'Why "poor Hanif"?'

'No particular reason.'

'Is he the black sheep of the family?'

'Middle child syndrome, I guess. He's always been a bit quiet, low in confidence, dropped out of school early, the religious one in the family.'

'Was he the most upset at Fatima – if he was the religious one?'

'Stop trying to twist my words – that's not what I meant at all! Anyway, I was religious once too – it's a phase. He's just a bit slow growing out of it, that's all.'

'I hear Hanif has been helping out at the family restaurant.'

'You're very well informed.'

'I guess you need the help – business has not been good?'

'Everyone's a bloody expert now, eh? Just so you know – and you can tell this to Fauzi too – business is fine. Has been for the last two months after a rough patch before that.'

'How come?'

'What can this possibly have to do with Fatima?'

'You never know . . .'

'More customers is all.'

So whatever his relationship with Raj, it wasn't something he was keen to divulge.

'So help me – tell me what you know about Fatima's death.'

'You want my opinion? I'll tell you. It was the bloody lawyer.'

'Jimmy Kendrick?'

'Is that his name? I never knew it. I just knew he was a bastard.'

'Why do you believe it was him?'

'Because Fatima was coming round, she told me so herself just before . . . she died.'

'She told you that she was going to marry the fiancé from Pakistan?'

'She told me that family must come first, that the lawyer had been nothing more than an infatuation.'

'That was a sudden change of heart surely?' The lines on Singh's forehead were as straight as crop furrows.

'She had her reasons.'

'And what were those?'

Ibrahim hesitated and then shrugged to indicate that he couldn't see the harm in telling. 'She found out that the lawyer had been having it on with her best friend, Sara her name was. Nothing better than a slut.'

237

'Fatima told you that?'

'Yes. It was the night before she was killed. I went up to talk to her, try and persuade her to see sense. She was crying, face down on the pillow, banging her fists on the bed like a small child. I thought at first it was about Shaheed, the fiancé, that she was still determined not to marry him. But then she told me about Sara and the boyfriend.'

'The night before she was killed?'

'Yes, that's what I said.'

'Did you inform the rest of the family of her change of heart?'

Ibrahim's mouth had already formed a 'no' when he stopped, took a deep breath and said, ''Course I did, it was the first thing I did.'

Singh drained his glass, not saying a word, waiting for the other man to continue.

'And so none of us had any reason to kill her, right?'

'I guess not,' said the policeman. 'But why would this lawyer have killed her?'

'How do I know? Maybe he was the jealous type.'

'But he was the one playing around. Not her.'

Singh had disliked Jimmy Kendrick when it transpired that he'd moved on to the next thing even before his girlfriend's body was cold. It seemed that he'd been too generous. He'd been playing around *before* she was killed.

What had Shakespeare said? Kill all the lawyers?

'It would have made more sense if Jimmy was killed.'

'Here's hoping,' said Ibrahim.

'But I still don't see it – there's no reason for a wealthy successful man to murder the victims of his philandering ways.'

238

'Maybe there was more . . .'

'Like what?'

'Like I'm not going to do your job for you.'

'But why didn't you accuse Jimmy then – during the initial investigation?'

'I guess none of us wanted to ruin Fatima's reputation.'

'And having a white boyfriend would have done that?'

'In our community? Of course.'

Singh stuck out his pink bottom lip. So much unhappiness for so many people because people couldn't live and let live.

'Anyway, it wasn't the lawyer or anyone she knew, right? It was this Hand Man fellow. A real sicko by the sounds of it.'

'You're sure of that?'

The other man nodded emphatically. 'No one else would have done that thing with the hands. It's not normal, is it?'

'Not very,' agreed Singh, feeling his palms itch. His mother would have said that the sensation meant he was about to come into money. But she'd lived and died in a gentler era where the murderous collectors of body parts were not so prevalent.

'My sister was just unlucky, that's all. It happens . . .'

The words were flippant but the sorrow in the brown eyes was real.

Retirement did not suit Jackson McMaster. As he trudged through the undergrowth, whacking the heads of bits of foliage with a stick he'd picked up along the way, he longed for the days when he'd wake up in the morning, don a suit and catch the train to work. He'd been a good boss and run a successful business, put two kids through university and maintained a good relationship – albeit one distinguished by routine and affection rather than excitement and passion – with his wife of forty years.

And this was his reward. To walk the dog through Epping Forest every morning. Purgatory for a man who did not like dogs or nature or walks, especially after heavy rains.

It was his wife who had brought the dog home. 'Isn't he the sweetest thing? You'll be able to take him for walks, get some fresh air, exercise, it will be wonderful for you, love.'

Did she not know him at all? Or maybe she was just desperate to get him out of the house. She had her routine, chores, friends, charity work, bridge. And he was – there was no polite way to put it – in the way.

'What shall we call him?'

In the end they'd settled on Rover although in his mind and out of earshot, he referred to the dog as 'that damned mutt'. That Damned Mutt.

Where was that Damned Mutt anyway? He'd wandered off the minute Jackson had let him off the leash. There was no way he could lose the dog, his wife would never forgive him. And as much as he disliked the creature with his flappy ears, lolling tongue and waving feathery tail, he didn't want anything bad to happen to him.

'Rover! Where are you, boy? Heel!'

That was the height of optimism – Rover did not heel or lie down or roll over or anything like that.

'Rover!'

Was that barking he could hear? The sun had disappeared behind a cloud, the air was damp with a nasty chill in it, thin mist was rising off the ground like some ghostly visitation; he needed to get the dog, trudge home, make himself a hot cup of tea and make some plans for the rest of his life. He'd find himself a proper hobby. Trainspotting?

'Rover, come here right NOW!'

Suddenly, the mutt bounced into view, leaping around him and yelping with excitement.

'All right, boy, I'm pleased to see you too.'

Reassured of his affection, the mutt took off like a bullet into the forest again. Jackson left the path and hurried after the dog. He'd hire a dog walker, that's what he'd do. Get the dog, go home; change his life.

The sun appeared suddenly and the day improved immediately. The leaves glistened with dew, diamonds on a green velvet gown. The sun lit up the mist and turned it golden; Jackson felt as if he had the Midas touch. To prove his point the Damned Mutt reappeared, dropped a stick at his feet, wagged his tail so hard that his entire body shook.

'All right, Mutt. Just this once.'

He picked up the stick and threw it with all his might. The dog yelped and turned to race after it. He followed at a slower pace.

The mutt had found the river and was splashing about along the edge. What's worse than a dog? A wet dog. What's worse than a wet dog? A wet dog poking its nose in a great mass of rubbish – leaves and brush and twigs as well as plastic bottles and beer cans.

'Rover!'

To his surprise, the animal immediately turned his head towards him, barked once, picked up the stick and bounded towards him.

He dropped the stick at his feet, but Jackson was having

none of it. He clipped the leash on the mutt, but the dog pulled and whined.

Irritated past bearing, Jackson grabbed the dog's collar and then the stick. He raised his hand to throw it as far as he could.

And realised – almost in slow motion, visual stimuli passing the message to his brain, his brain rejecting it outright, once, twice, three times – what he had in his hand. He dropped it, sat down suddenly on a flat rock.

Rover fetched once more.

This time he placed his booty gently at Jackson's feet, sat down on his haunches, and whined softly.

Jackson stared at it, felt sick.

It was a human femur.

Mrs Singh watched her husband enter the pub with the younger brother of Fatima. The minute the inspector and Ibrahim were safely within, she escaped the alcohol shop where she had sought refuge. Such a misleading name, 'Oddbins', what were they thinking?

She loitered on the street for a while but the inclement weather disheartened her. The grey skies merged with the grey buildings and grey pavements; it felt as if she was standing in the middle of a damp cloud.

Mrs Singh wandered further down the street and was tempted by a gift stall erected on the pavement. They had a lovely selection of knick-knacks: salt and pepper shakers in the shape of Tower Bridge, ceramic bulldogs, tea towels emblazoned with the Union Jack – fortunately Scotland hadn't seceded or the souvenir sellers would have had a lot of wasted stock.

The proprietor was an elderly Sikh man whose beard hung down like a bird's nest fern. His turban was a termite mound and he wore round glasses that were smudged into opacity.

'Discount for you, sister. High*est* quality souvenirs.'

The snow globe with a Beefeater battling the elements was tempting. Reluctantly, she decided that gathering collectibles was probably a mistake in the middle of an investigation. What if she was called upon to do something?

Ibrahim stepped out of the pub. He stood for a moment, looked up and down the street as if considering his options or getting his bearings. He retrieved his phone from a pocket and glanced at the screen. Mrs Singh developed an interest in a tea towel featuring London Bridge. The non-appearance of her husband led Mrs Singh to deduce that he'd decided to have one for the road.

It was all very well being a cerebral copper, but this was a dereliction of duty.

'Half price for you, sister.'

She was still holding the tea towel.

She thrust it at the shopkeeper as Ibrahim walked away with a determined stride. What if he was going to admire his secret stash of hands?

Her jaw tightened. Once again, the photo from the front cover of the file flashed before her eyes. The girl haunted her sleep and now her waking hours. Fatima Daud, someone's daughter if not her own, deserved her every effort.

'I'm sorry,' she said to the proprietor of the gift stand. 'I have to go – police business. Top secret.'

Mrs Singh set off in hot pursuit.

CHAPTER 15

Inspector Singh, as befitted a man with a beer and a murder mystery, had forgotten about his wife. He contemplated the young man who had just left. Ibrahim had a chip on his shoulder, a smart mouth and a seemingly genuine affection for his dead sister. But was he also her killer?

The policeman gulped down his beer and then wiped the foam away from his moustache with the back of his hand. The brother's recommendation had been sound; the ale was rich and smooth.

He rang the number Shaheed had given him and the ex-fiancé picked up immediately.

'This is Singh.'

'Yes?'

'I know you met Fatima – you lied to me, lied to Regina.'

The silence at the other end went on for so long, Singh thought the other man had hung up.

And then Shaheed said, 'Will you tell her?'

'It depends on what you tell me.'

'What do you want to know?'

The inspector listened as Shaheed repeated a story that agreed on the major points with Sara's version. He'd met Fatima in a last ditch attempt to persuade her to marry him just two days before she'd been killed. She'd been polite but determined in her refusal. He'd begged, cried, promised her rainbows, to no avail.

'I think there was someone else ... In fact, I know there was someone else; she told me.'

'So why didn't you tell me the truth?'

'I was afraid – afraid of losing Regina, losing Emma.'

'I see.'

'If she finds out I didn't tell her ... about meeting Fatima, didn't tell her everything ... she will leave me, take Emma, I'm sure of it.'

'Did she say anything else? Anything that might shed light on her murder?'

'Nothing! I swear it, nothing.'

Singh hung up, feeling exhausted. He had no idea whether to believe Shaheed, the serial liar, any more.

Fatima Daud had been the centre of a maelstrom of emotions before she'd died that day. The brothers, the fiancé, the lawyer boyfriend, the boss. But had any of those feelings sharpened into anger sufficient to kill? And then – the worst of it – the bit that caused the bile to rise in his throat, had any of them seen fit to desecrate the body? And if so, why?

No wonder Harris was adamant that Cynthia and Fatima had been killed by a stranger with a grievance against women, but not these women in particular.

His phone rang and he reached for it, still lost in thought. 'Inspector Singh? It's Regina de Klerk.'

The last person he wanted to speak to given that he'd just discovered her husband had lied to both of them.

'I needed to talk to you – about Martin Bradley.'

He struggled to assimilate what she'd said.

'They've arrested him for the murders, I just heard.'

'Yes, they picked him up for questioning about the murder of Cynthia Cole.'

'I know him. He works at the Commonwealth Office. He's a clerk, a general dogsbody.'

Small world. But so what? Didn't they say that if one walked down Oxford Street in London, one would definitely meet an acquaintance? Not him, because he would never walk down Oxford Street.

'You don't understand,' continued Regina. 'The thing is, he knew about the Fatima Daud case, because he worked on the files with me. He helped me choose the cold cases.'

The inspector sat up straight.

'We discussed all the details – even the thing about the hands.'

Singh's own hands had turned to ice.

No wonder Bradley had hesitated for a scintilla of time when Harris had asked him if he knew of Fatima Daud.

'And there's more – he's a real weirdo. He was following me – I saw him outside my flat once, even though he lives south of the river. And a few days ago, he cornered me round the corner from the office and acted like he and I had a relationship, that I was going to leave Shaheed for him.'

Her voice was hysterical and Singh couldn't blame her.

'He even mentioned Emma by name.'

'What did you do?'

'Nothing! I just told him he was imagining things, to stay away from me. But I never thought . . . I never guessed . . . that he was really dangerous. I just thought he was a bit sad, you know?'

At first, fired up by the chase, Mrs Singh padded after Ibrahim with enthusiasm. She followed him along Kensington High Street and down the grimy flight of steps to the High St Kensington Tube Station. Ibrahim headed towards the westbound District Line platform.

It was early afternoon and the platforms were largely deserted. Ibrahim leaped on-board the first train with the athleticism of youth. Mrs Singh minded the gap as she had been advised. She sat on the cleanest of the seats in a row facing the windows. Ibrahim slumped into a double seat and put his crossed legs up on the opposite chair. The policeman's wife winced. The hygiene standards in this country were appalling. She couldn't stand the gum stains adhering to every surface – thank God it was banned in Singapore. Forgetting for a moment that she was supposed to be tailing Ibrahim incognito, she looked at his feet pointedly and glared at him.

He grinned back and she felt the force of his personality, which, combined with his looks, was likely to render him as troublesome as a fox in a hen house in families with impressionable young women. She hoped the restaurant recovered. He was a matchmaker's dream but Asian families were not so foolish as to place any importance on looks when unaccompanied by discernible monetary value.

If Mr Singh had been present, he would have informed his wife that she was echoing Mrs Bennet's mantra on marriageable gentlemen, but he wasn't so she remained in comfortable ignorance of her Regency values.

Lost in thought, she almost failed to react when Ibrahim hopped up and out at Earl's Court. She belatedly followed suit and, for a moment, on the platform, was convinced she had lost him. But then she saw the lithe figure, already some way ahead. Earl's Court Station was a massive cavern of steel struts and glass panels. It looked very old but then so did everything else in London. She liked the sense of history but was suspicious that the authorities built in an old-fashioned style to fool tourists.

He'd better be on the way to his stash of body parts. Her feet were aching too much for this to be a wild goose chase.

In her mind, Mrs Singh grumbled, *Why should Ibrahim kill his sister?*

Why indeed?

Might as well chase a wild chicken. At least if you catch it, you can curry it for me.

'Of all the brothers of Fatima, you were the one I was most curious to meet.'

'Why? They told you I was the black sheep?'

'There was a suggestion that you did not see eye to eye with the rest,' Singh admitted.

Hanif snorted and tugged on his beard. 'To agree with my brothers would be a betrayal of everything I believe in.'

'That isn't a bit of an exaggeration?'

'They only care about worldly things.'

The policeman raised an eyebrow.

'My oldest brother is interested in status, being a senior member of our community like our father was before him. He wants to be invited to every wedding, deliver all the babies, hold the hands of the dying.'

'And Ibrahim? What are his vices?'

'Wine, women and song.'

'You object?'

'He was a better man than that, once upon a time.'

'And you? You have no interest in worldly things?'

As if he had to ask. The other man would look less pious if he were dressed in sackcloth and ashes.

'I believe in the man, in the soul, not the trappings.'

Singh made a mental note to trim his beard and buy a new shirt; he didn't want to be mistaken for a religious extremist or have people try to fathom the contours of his soul. They sat at a small table, knees almost touching – was that weird? A latte for Singh and a black coffee for Hanif sat between them, largely untouched.

'What about Fatima?' he asked.

'What about her?'

'Where did she fit on this family spectrum?'

Singh watched while Hanif grappled with his answer. He looked around and noted that the Mayfair Starbucks had an unusual clientele. The surrounding area was a haven for oil-rich Arabs and the coffee joint could have been in Saudi Arabia with its robed men and women draped in black.

At last, Hanif said, 'She was very young.'

He made it sound exculpatory. Singh had heard habitual criminals use the same tone when they said, 'I was drunk – I didn't know what I was doing.'

'Too young to understand . . . what exactly?'

'That life is hard. That people betray you. That love matters, but not as much as family. And family matters, but not as much as God.'

Was this fellow a killer or a poet? Or both? He was much more interesting than your run-of-the-mill murder suspect.

'Did you choose this Starbucks because it makes you feel comfortable?'

Hanif looked around with an air of bemusement. 'Because of the Muslims here, you mean?'

Singh nodded. 'Fatima would not have felt welcome here,' he added.

'*I* do not feel welcome here,' growled Hanif. 'Look at these people, cloaked in their religion, but underneath it is Armani and diamonds. They are hypocrites, reverent at home, partying in the West.'

'So why are we here?'

'Because I have another appointment around the corner.'

Singh looking sheepish, tried again. 'What do you think of the Hand Man?'

'That he is lost.'

'So are the hands,' said Singh and then regretted it when real pain crossed the other man's face. His sister might have been a victim. This was no time to react with hostility to the overt spirituality on display.

'In a way it lets you off the hook, doesn't it?'

'What do you mean by that?'

250

Hanif's eyes were so dark, irises and pupils the same colour, impossible to read his thoughts.

'It means that the family are no longer suspects.'

'Were we suspects before?'

'I think you know the answer to that.'

'None of us would have laid a finger on Fatima. She was the glue that held the family together. Look at what has happened to us since ...'

The man had a point. 'But she was acting against the family's wishes.'

'With that lawyer, you mean? He was a worthless human being.'

'How would you know that?'

'I went to see him.'

'To scare him off?'

'What would you like me to say? Yes? And, when that didn't work, I murdered my sister?'

'I'm looking for the truth.'

Singh's quiet tone was more effective than the other man's rising anger.

'I went to see if he truly loved my sister.'

'And did he?'

'Kendrick loves trophies, not people.'

'Your brother thinks he killed Fatima.'

'I don't see why he would have done that.'

'He's married to Fatima's best friend now.'

The clenched fist suggested that the devout exterior was cracking.

'It's a mystery what my sister ever saw in him.'

Singh tried to imagine Kendrick five years ago, slimmer,

suave, successful, moneyed. His wife assured him that these traits, absent in his own person, were attractive to women. Maybe she was right.

'How did they meet?'

'He was her employer's lawyer – they met there, I think.'

'At Raj Real Estate?'

Hanif raised his coffee to his lips. 'You certainly have been busy.'

'What's your opinion of Raj?'

'That he is every kind of crook . . . but not a murderer.'

'That's what Fatima thought too – that he was a crook, I mean. And now he has dealings with your brother?'

'I don't know anything about that.'

'But he doesn't pay to eat at your family restaurant?'

'My brother's lack of business sense is not a crime.'

Ibrahim boarded the Piccadilly Line towards Heathrow.

What if he was leaving the country? Was she to follow him to the departure gates and wave goodbye, time and money wasted?

Maybe Ibrahim was going on a weekend away with some woman. That would be shocking indeed as he was unmarried. But surely Cousin Goody would have told her if such a relationship existed? That sort of thing would be impossible to keep quiet in a small community like Southall.

She saw through the window that Ibrahim was seated with his back to her. She rang Goody and gave her a quick update, unable to complete the story as her phone battery died. A shame. Now might have been a good time to tell her husband where she was with a particular emphasis on how she was doing his job for him. There was no point being an intrepid sleuth if there was no audience. Mrs Singh wrapped her scarf around her head like an elderly woman and sidled down towards the opposite end of the carriage. She picked up a newspaper that had been left on the seat and read the football news. Chelsea was basically a small team, just like Stoke apparently. It seemed that this was a bad thing from the tone of the article.

As the journey grew long and Ibrahim made no move, Mrs Singh, lulled by the swaying of the train, dozed off. Her last bleary thought was to wonder whether her husband had been able to drag himself away from the Fox and Anchor.

Thanks to Sara Kendrick, helpful if puzzled, he knew where to find Jimmy that afternoon. Singh took a black cab and felt a genuine frisson of excitement when he was dropped off outside the building with the famous statue of justice, blindfolded and with scales and a sword in each hand.

The Old Bailey.

Home of the most extraordinary trials in history – from Dr Crippen to the Kray brothers, from the Yorkshire Ripper to Lord Haw-Haw.

Would the Hand Man get his day in court too?

Singh's investigative efforts took a knock when it transpired that it was not possible to just stroll into the building and hunt down a barrister. Instead, he found himself lining up to enter the various public galleries through a back channel that smelled of cigarettes and piss.

'Which trial?'

'Money laundering,' said Singh, as briefed. 'With Jimmy Kendrick.'

'Is he the defendant?'

'The lawyer.'

'Through there,' barked the policeman, his eyes already on a collection of youth wearing thick gold chains and leather Nike shoes. They were pushing and shoving each other as an argument broke out. It seemed a peculiar choice to appear in court wearing the proceeds of crime – surely that was a red flag to the police? But the coppers didn't leap at the chance to arrest them. Maybe, policing was different in the UK.

Singh found himself in the upper tier of a narrow gallery. His seat creaked and earned him a glare from the court clerk. Kendrick, gowned, wigged and larger than life was holding forth, one hand on the wooden podium, another stabbing the air with a pen. The two accused sat in the dock, leaning forward, hands together. One was of Indian origin and the other white. The former was balding, the latter tattooed up to his sleeves. Neither looked like a master criminal. How had they found the money to employ Kendrick?

Listening intently, he deduced that the two were accused of using their car-wash business as a money-laundering operation. Apparently, the place had been suspiciously profitable, made too much money. Singh shifted uncomfortably in his seat. Where had he heard that phrase before?

'M'lud, should my clients be penalised for their entrepreneurial spirit?'

'According to the prosecution, they'd have had to wash a hundred cars a day to make that kind of money!' The judge, contrary to the usual stereotype, was awake, alert and attentive.

'And they did, M'lud.'

'On their own?'

'As they testified, M'lud, with the help of students and part-timers.'

'Whom they paid in cash and about whom they kept no records?'

'These are businessmen, not accountants, M'lud.'

They looked like petty criminals to Singh.

The men had family present or at least there was an elderly Indian woman weeping noisily into a handkerchief. To his surprise, he spotted Raj of Raj Real Estate, sitting a few seats to the left of the mother, the comb-over and hooked nose an unmistakable combination. What was he doing here? Was the Indian defendant a relative?

Singh remembered why the lawyer's words had sounded familiar. Sara Kendrick had mentioned that Fatima had been puzzled, when she went through the accounts, because Raj Real Estate also made 'too much money'.

Certainly, his little agency didn't look that flush. Was it a coincidence? And hadn't DI Carmen told him that Raj's empire included a car wash? Maybe it was this one, now at the centre of a money-laundering trial. It would explain his presence, at least.

There was a sudden shuffling around him as everyone in court stood. Singh lurched to his feet hurriedly, no point being found in contempt of court. Apparently, the judge had decided he needed a break and was making an exit, perhaps to set up his own car-wash business. The inspector worked his way down and was pleased to find himself outdoors again. The court had been stuffy, the heating turned up too high; the droning voices soporific.

He walked away from the entrance and spotted Kendrick having a tête-à-tête with Raj. Both men were smoking and absorbed in their conversation.

He could only hear snatches of speech, fragments of phrases. 'Not much chance' ... 'bloody fools' ... 'careless' from Kendrick. If the Indian defendant was related to Raj, the lawyer was not mincing his words. And then a sudden change in the wind and pitch and a full sentence from Raj, 'As long as no one knows where the money is from, it doesn't matter.'

And the response: 'I've got that in hand. There's nothing to worry about.'

Kendrick turned as he spoke. Singh knew there was no way of avoiding him so he grasped the bull by the horns. He stepped forward and said loudly, 'Mr Kendrick, might I have a word?'

The lawyer looked nonplussed. 'What are you doing here?'

'Looking for you, of course.'

'How did you know where I was?'

'Where else would a barrister be except at the Old Bailey?'

'Inspector Singh?' This was Raj, belatedly joining in the conversation.

'You know him?' demanded Kendrick.

'He was looking into Fatima's murder.'

'How do you know each other?' asked Singh, eyeing the odd couple.

'Mr Kendrick handles all my affairs,' said Raj.

'And you have "an affair" in there?'

'A minor matter.'

They hadn't seen him in the public gallery.

'How do you know each other?'

'It was Raj here who introduced me to Fatima all those years ago. I was his lawyer and she helped me with some documentation for a matter involving Raj Real Estate.'

'Certainly that was the case – only to help, mind you. Nothing more than that!' He prodded Singh in the stomach and winked. The fat man considered killing him on the spot, going into the Old Bailey and accepting his punishment like a man.

'For which I am always grateful, of course,' said Kendrick, philanderer.

Singh considered making it a multiple killing.

'Poor Fatima,' added Raj, face lugubrious. 'She was like a daughter to me.'

'It seems your "daughter" wasn't happy with the state of your accounts,' snapped Singh.

'What are you trying to say?' Raj took a step forward. Kendrick hadn't moved but Singh sensed that the man was suddenly humming like a high-tension wire.

'That Fatima found irregularities – you were making too much money,' he replied.

'What nonsense! How can you make *too much* money?'

'I can think of many ways – chief of them – money laundering.'

A direct hit.

'How dare you? If you repeat one word of this slander, you'll hear from my lawyers.'

'Which lawyer? Your errand boy here? The one who was two-timing your so-called daughter?'

'You're treading on thin ice, Singh.'

'I had nothing to do with Fatima's death. Do you hear me?'

Raj was off balance, unlike Kendrick, possibly a consequence of having a less nuanced comprehension of the rules of evidence. In other words, Kendrick knew Singh had squat.

'I took a call,' continued Raj. 'I made a mistake sending her to the house. That's all.'

A dawning recollection caused Singh to pause, to grasp at the shape of the crime, hovering on the edge of his imagination. Once, when he was young, he'd found a loose thread in a shawl his mother was knitting. Even as her needles clicked, he'd pulled and pulled, watching the garment unravel before his eyes. He hadn't sat down for a week but he had learned to look for that same loose thread in murder investigations.

'Do you understand me?' Raj's lips were bloodless but covered in spittle.

The ring of his phone sounded like a bell tolling. It took a few moments to penetrate the inspector's black mood.

He was glad to have an excuse to walk away from the two men, both planting imaginary daggers between his shoulder blades.

'We might have another one.' Singh recognised Harris's gruff tones immediately.

The inspector closed his eyes – images formed against the dark screen of his heavy lids, women without hands and, in his imagination, without tongues to speak, to blame, to beg.

'I'll send a car for you . . .'

Epping Forest. It sounded familiar. Or was he thinking of Sherwood Forest? Or Nottingham Forest? Come to think of it, wasn't the last a football club? That was the problem with London, with England. It featured so much in his reading, in his history lessons, in his father's propaganda, that he couldn't disentangle the past from the present, fiction from cold, hard brutal fact.

Jack the Ripper was real, but Robin Hood wasn't. The Moors Murders had happened but Camelot was a dream of chivalry. What about the Scarlet Pimpernel? Singh had no idea. Macbeth was surely a creature of dark imagination but Richard III was present and accounted for in the annals of history and had apparently died in a car park. Queen Elizabeth I had 'the heart and stomach of a king' – Singh had the latter.

But had anyone done 'a far, far better thing' outside the pages of a book? And why was he being assertive about the line between fact and fiction? After all, tall tales were based on kernels of truth. There had been a legendary figure called Arthur in the fifth or sixth century but he had not pulled a sword from a stone.

The inspector stood on the pavement, waited for the car, tried not to get ahead of himself. Kendrick and Raj had disappeared back into the Old Bailey. Singh was convinced that Raj was fronting a money-laundering operation and had been since Fatima's days.

He texted DI Carmen with clumsy fingers. Maybe she could look into it – she'd said that Raj was well known to the police. Was it for money laundering? And did his manor extend beyond Raj Real Estate to include a car-wash set-up? Was Kendrick involved too?

Maybe Fatima had got wind of it, quarrelled with Raj, confided in her brother. Had Raj killed her?

But where did that leave Cynthia Cole and this third body that Harris had just called about?

A police car drew up and he climbed in the back. He had no idea why Harris wanted him at the scene. But he understood the inclination. The Englishman needed someone from outside. A sounding board. A security blanket. A friend. The inspector was accustomed to doing the same. He smiled when he remembered Chhean in Cambodia – a squat woman with a keen mind who had never fully embraced her role. Come to think of it, neither had Bronwyn in Bali. The women in his life were not inclined to the role of subordinate. Including his own wife.

Singh's heart sank, as heavy as a guilty conscience.

Where was his wife?

He'd forgotten all about her and now he was racing to a crime scene while she might still be looking for a way out of Oddbins. He reached for his phone; he really needed to call her if he ever wanted a hot dinner again. He tried, her phone was switched off or the battery was dead.

The WPC driving said, 'We're here, sir.'

Singh abandoned his mobile and his wife. Duty called.

A crime scene had its own internal dynamic.

Singh walked slowly forward, taking it in. The light was fading. The cold air brushed his cheeks like the clammy fingers of a dead lover. The police cars gleamed in the half-light, their reflective strips shining as the sun should have done. An ambulance was parked to one side, doors open, two men sitting in the back, legs dangling out, accustomed to death and accustomed to waiting. Crime scene tape cordoned off the entrance to a path into the forest. The darkness beyond the fringe of car lights and temporary halogen lamps was profound.

He spotted DI Carmen and waved. She came over, managed a smile although her heart wasn't in it.

'You'd better get suited up if you want to come through,' she said.

He followed her instructions and was soon ready, in white overalls and covered shoes. The path was lit by a constable with a torch and he stayed in the beam, watched where he placed his feet. The path was uneven, winding, definitely the one less travelled.

The inspector from Singapore, who did most of his investigating in cities, where crime scenes were back alleys and gutters, luxury apartments and run-down flats, found the location unnerving. The stillness, the sense of creatures in the bush – what wildlife did they have in England? If he glimpsed the eye shine of some predator, he was going to flee.

Carmen led the way down a slope, picking her way carefully between the slicks of mud and exposed roots. Singh did his best to avoid scooting after her on his backside. In the distance, next to a body of water, the area was lit like a bright day. As Singh drew closer, he spotted Harris talking to a man crouched on the ground.

'Singh, you made it.'

'What have you got?'

'Skeletal remains.'

'How long have they been here?'

'Impossible to determine,' grumbled the crouched man.

'This is Dr Marlow,' said Harris.

A grunt acknowledged the introduction. Singh warmed to him. A man of few words, just like him.

'Some fellow walking his dog found the remains,' explained

Harris. 'Apparently the dog "fetched" a femur instead of a stick. He went to investigate and found the rest of the body wedged in the roots of this tree.'

'Any clues to identity?'

'Female, youngish. Some shreds of clothing, teeth are intact.'

'Definitely murder?'

'There are some nicks to the ribs that look like they were made by something sharp. And blunt instrument trauma to the head.'

The inspector looked around. 'Is this the kind of place that a body could remain undiscovered for long?'

At night, with the darkness hovering, it was easy to imagine a victim undiscovered for aeons. But they were only a short way from London and the body had been found by a man walking his dog.

'Usually, I'd say "no",' said Harris. 'But in this case, it looks like the body was trapped underwater – whether by luck or judgement on the part of the killer, I don't know. The body was wrapped in tarpaulin, that's what kept the remains intact.'

'So how come it surfaced?'

'The rains must have dislodged the body, but then it was caught in this small eddy.' Harris shone a torch at a collection of brush and garbage wedged against tree roots encroaching into the water.

'The tarpaulin's come undone. I doubt we'd have found so much of the frame intact in a few days . . . pieces could have washed up anywhere.'

'So she could have gone into the water anywhere upstream?' asked Singh.

Harris nodded. 'I'll have a search party on the job at day-break but I doubt we'll find anything.'

Singh doubted that they'd find anything either. But that was police work. You still had to look and hope and waste manpower and man hours and tax-payer dollars because society, and the victim, demanded that no stone was left unturned in the hunt for a murderer. And sometimes, unexpectedly, something was found. And that made it, and every unsuccessful search that had gone before, worthwhile.

'So why are you sure it's connected to the other victims?' he asked.

'Show him, Doc.'

The pathologist struggled to his feet and Singh could hear his knees creak with the effort. He moved to one side so Singh got his first full view of the collection of bones. The light from the torch played across the skull; eye sockets empty, a cavity where the soft nose tissue had been and the teeth, herbivorous, clamped shut. The skull beneath the skin was hardly human.

Harris moved the light down the skeletal remains. The bones were washed clean from long immersion in water and Singh saw the nicks that Marlow had mentioned.

'Could it have been animal damage?' he asked, gesturing at the nicks.

'Maybe,' said Marlow.

'But not this,' added Harris as his torch traced the humerus and then the radius and ulna. He repeated the action on the other arm.

Where the hands should have been, there was nothing.

Dr Marlow squatted down and held up the truncated wrist so that Singh could see for himself the clean flat edge.

'A chopping wound with a heavy blade,' he said.

'Just like the others,' said Harris. 'You were right – there were more.'

Singh, for once in his life, would have much preferred to be completely and utterly wrong.

The video went viral within half an hour.

A man dressed in black standing with his back to a wall draped in an ISIS flag. His face was wrapped in black cloth. It was difficult to judge his build but he looked to be tall and gave the impression of relative youth, something in the posture or the swagger. He held a long blade of some sort.

On his knees, with his hands bound behind him, was a Caucasian man dressed in a bright orange jumpsuit. He was blindfolded, but, as the video unfolded, the man holding the machete removed the blindfold and said, 'This is Roland Thomas. Roland has a few words to say to you all.' The captor's voice had all the cadences of London, capital of the world.

The prisoner held up a newspaper, it was the *Evening Standard* from the previous day. He began to speak, his words almost inaudible, shaking with fear, but then growing in strength. It was obvious that he had prepared what he was going to say or been instructed on the contents. The camera focused on his face, most noticeable for its sheer ordinariness – thin brown hair, a day's growth on his chin, pale blue eyes. Only, the pulse in his throat and the constant swallowing suggested anything outside the norm.

'I am Roland Thomas. I have a wife and two children whom I love very much.' He paused, tears running down his cheeks, creating tracks in the grime and there was a brief muttering off camera. Roland nodded as if understanding the instructions and continued.

'I live on Madras Road, Ilford. Yesterday, as I was walking home from work, two men grabbed me and bundled me into the back of a van. They brought me to this place; I don't know where it is – somewhere in London. They said that I am a warning to the British government that they can strike anywhere and at anytime. None of us – none of you – is safe.'

The camera angle widened to encompass both men again. Machete man kicked the kneeling prisoner in the middle of the back. He dropped the newspaper, fell forward on his knees, head bowed.

His captor stepped forward, lashed out with the blade.

He turned to face the camera.

'We will continue to seize infidels and execute them. We are everywhere among you. You are not safe and neither are your womenfolk nor your children. We will only stop when the British government ceases to wage war on our Muslim brothers around the world.'

He waited for his words to sink it with his audience and then said, 'The *next* infidel – Mary Jane Houseman – will be executed within forty-eight hours.'

The camera zoomed in on a photo of a middle-aged woman with brown hair, glasses slightly askew reflecting the camera flash.

The screen faded to black.

CHAPTER 16

Mrs Singh followed Ibrahim down a winding side road. At first, there had been other pedestrians but as she drew further away from Hounslow East Station, the streets were largely deserted. A few cars passed, dusty and dented. One blared thumping music out of open windows. A rush of delivery vans forced her off the road and on to the grass verge where she stood gingerly, waiting for the convoy to pass.

She continued in the same direction although Ibrahim was no longer visible and she guessed he'd taken the side street in the distance. Mrs Singh was hot and tired, her lips were parched and cracked and her low back ached. The only thing she wanted to do was get back to the hotel, have a hot shower and put her feet up. Instead, she marched on, feet throbbing inside her previously comfortable shoes.

The side road was a dead end. It finished at a heavily padlocked high mesh gate. It was an abandoned industrial estate, she decided, peering through the fence, various square buildings with dark windows stood within. Ibrahim must have gone in here, but how? The rusty locks didn't look like they'd been undone in years. She looked back in the direction she'd come. Time to give up? But what if this was where Ibrahim stashed the dismembered hands?

She took her phone out and remembered with disgust that the battery was dead. There was no way of calling Singh and asking for advice. She knew what it would be anyway.

Get out of there now. What the hell do you think you're doing?

Why should she listen to her husband's opinion for the first time in her life? The inspector's wife followed a dry path of flattened grass along the outside of the fence and was rewarded by the discovery of a neat hole cut in the mesh, big enough for a person to squeeze through, the sharp cut ends bent back.

It was a pity it was still light. This sort of breaking and entering was best done in darkness.

Mrs Singh stepped through the makeshift entrance and followed a potholed track towards the scattered buildings. A burnt-out truck rested on hubcaps, twisted metal was piled in heaps and a sharp chemical smell lingered. Mrs Singh reached the main building and reluctantly wiped away the caked dust from a window with an elbow. She placed one eye against the peephole and stared in – the place was in darkness except for a square rectangle at the far end. An open door leading to a room with the lights switched on. No doubt where Ibrahim was lurking. She'd seen enough. It was time to get back to her husband and report her derring-do. She would adopt a matter-of-fact tone, she decided. It would be all the more impressive for such nonchalance.

There was nothing more she could do. They'd need dozens of men and sniffer dogs to find the hands in such a place. But she, Mrs Singh, had led them to Ibrahim's lair. She might even get some recognition for her efforts.

> *Pussy cat, pussy cat, where have you been?*
> *I've been to London to see the Queen.*
> *Pussy cat, pussy cat, what did you there?*
> *I received a medal from the Queen.*

She retreated slowly, eyes still on the window, smiling. A few feet away, she turned.

And found herself face to face with Ibrahim.

'Who the hell are you and why are you following me?'

Inspector Singh rang his wife but the call went straight through to voicemail. He left a message – not trying to keep the exasperation out of his voice. He knew he was in hot soup for abandoning her outside a pub in the middle of London but that was no reason for her to be childish, refusing to pick up his calls. He'd tried four or five times now, keen to tell her about the third body, finally putting an end to any notion that Fatima had been murdered by someone she knew. A lot of work wasted on his part but that was the way of murder investigations.

A particular pity when he had solved the crime in his head – used his little grey cells to build a working hypothesis – before Harris called. Just as well he'd kept his conclusions to himself or he'd look a right fool now.

'Wife done a disappearing act?' asked Harris.

'Looks like it.'

'Mine too – went for a yoga lesson, never came back.'

Was that likely? Singh didn't think so. On the other hand, his wife had been acting very peculiarly since getting to London. Since when did she take an interest in his cases or wear trousers?

'Three bodies.' Harris, leaning back against the faux leather of the car's back seat, had used up his quota of sympathy for Singh's marital troubles. There was only one thing of interest to him.

The inspector nodded. He understood the single-mindedness. Indeed, he shared it, which was why he was in trouble with his spouse in the first place.

'No way of knowing yet whether this was prior to or after Fatima.'

'You'll have to find out who she was before we can know that,' said Singh. 'The forensics aren't going to be accurate, not after immersion for that length of time.'

'We'll find out who she is,' said Harris. 'Sooner rather than later.'

'Why the confidence?'

'Based on the missing persons list we've gone through with a fine tooth comb at your suggestion. I'd say there's maybe four or five possible candidates ... And this girl had a good set of teeth with some expensive work done to make it better – we should be able to find a dental record match.'

'What's the situation with Bradley?'

'We let him go.'

'Even after what I told you?' Singh had called in Regina's information.

'That he was familiar with Fatima's file?'

'It might have been a copycat killing of the second victim. After all, we know Bradley's a weirdo with a history of violence towards women.'

'You're right, but we had to press charges or let him go and I wasn't ready to do that.' Looking at Singh's face, a picture of doubt, he added, 'Anyway, we know it wasn't him now – not with *three* bodies with the same MO.'

'I suppose so.'

He texted Regina, warned her that Bradley was out. It seemed prudent although he doubted the man would be at work anytime soon.

They were back in central London now and the street lights reflected off puddles on the dark road. The sun had given up on the day a few hours earlier and it was a dark night, no gleam of moon or stars under the heavy sky. Headlights from oncoming traffic dazzled him intermittently. Each point of light was surrounded by a hazy circular glow and Singh had to blink hard to focus. The weather had driven pedestrians indoors and the streets were more deserted than usual.

'Quiet evening,' said Singh, nodding in the direction of the shopfronts. 'Fear of the Hand Man?'

The last time he'd seen something similar had been during the SARS outbreak in Singapore. Humans were a gregarious species until fear overwhelmed them. Then they bolted for safe places, fell out of love with their fellow man.

A fear of strangers, whether killers or disease carriers, would define human interaction until such a time as a capture or cure was effected by the authorities, and then the people would come out into the light, blinking, wary, until the next time.

'More likely the extremists,' said Harris, pressing his fingers against his eyes. 'There's plenty to keep London folk indoors tonight, home with their families.'

'It didn't make any difference before.' Singh had been impressed by this exhibition of the Blitz spirit, Londoners going about their business despite the terror threat. Singaporeans would have been stocking up on provisions for the apocalypse.

'You haven't heard?'

'About what?'

'A few jihadists picked some poor bastard – a father of two – off the streets and beheaded him. Recorded the whole thing and put it on the Internet.'

'Here?'

'Yes, right here in Londonistan.'

Singh hadn't seen a newspaper since that morning and had not been near a television. Viral videos did not tend to attract the attention of a Luddite from Singapore.

'When?' he asked.

'The video was recorded yesterday; they had a newspaper front page. *Evening Standard*. But only released this morning.'

'Jesus.'

'Wrong God,' said Harris.

If Singh had his way, all religions would be banned.

'That's not the worst of it.'

There was worse? 'What could be worse?'

'They've named their next victim and the family has confirmed that she's missing, has been since yesterday. She went down to the supermarket, walked from her home near Wimbledon Common, didn't come back. The family made a police report right away.'

271

'Which was ignored ...'

'Yes,' said Harris, 'because she's an adult who might have just decided on a break. There was nothing to suggest anything untoward.'

'Local jihadists?'

'British accents,' replied Harris.

They drew up outside the station and Harris gestured to the driver to carry on into the car park. Singh sympathised – the press were three deep on the pavement outside the station.

'This is where they're running the investigation,' said Harris.

Singh remembered his earlier tour – terrorism matters were handled by the Met from Paddington Green. It would make the business of finding the Hand Man that much harder; resources were going to be scarce and cops distracted by this latest atrocity as they desperately tried to identify the killers, from their accents, from their clothes, from voice recognition spyware, or pinpoint the location from any features on the video. They'd be rounding up suspects, leaning on informants, speaking to the spy agencies of other countries.

A race against the clock to save this woman, the official definition of an innocent, except that there was no such thing any more, not in the eyes of men in suicide vests, not in the eyes of Western forces using drones to drop bombs on wedding parties. Everyone was a combatant.

'Who is she?'

'Mary Jane Houseman.'

Why had he asked? What could he do?

As if reading his mind, Harris said, '*We've* just got to focus on finding our guy.'

Singh felt a sense of futility so great he was overwhelmed. He could no more find 'our guy' than the terrorists.

The fact of the matter was that he couldn't even find his wife.

Ibrahim dragged her into the abandoned warehouse, pushed her along ahead of him until she was in a small room at the back. The windows were covered but faint light crept in through a dislodged board and broken pane. He shoved her to the ground, grabbed a piece of twine and bound her hands and feet.

'Are you quite mad? Why are you doing this?'

'Who are you? I've seen you before.'

His brow tightened as he racked his brain, trying to place her.

'Let me go.'

'At the restaurant. You were at the restaurant. And then again on the train.'

'I don't know what you're talking about.'

Mrs Singh had no idea what to do. Her thoughts were churning, as was her stomach. The chemical smell in the air was making her light-headed. Or maybe it was fear. She had no idea what to say, what to admit, what to deny. Through her confusion, she managed a frisson of irritation at her husband. This was his fault, hanging around pubs while she did his dirty work.

'You don't look like a cop.'

'I am not a policewoman, what a ridiculous thing to suggest.'

The policeman's wife was genuinely offended. It was not a

job that would be considered acceptable for a Sikh woman, consorting with criminals and people without a proper education.

Mrs Singh regained her composure.

Even if Ibrahim was the killer of Fatima and the rest, she hardly fitted the profile of his victims. Most likely he was up to his neck in some nefarious activity; drugs or house-breaking, but he would be a fool to harm her, to commit any more serious crime. From her reading of the newspapers, this country was lenient with criminals unless and until they actually committed grievous bodily harm – or worse.

'Why were you following me?'

'I wasn't. I was lost. And I spotted you in the distance. I thought you might be able to help me find my way.'

'Are you a tourist?' demanded Ibrahim.

'Yes, from Singapore.'

'Another lackey of the American imperialists.'

'What's that supposed to mean?'

'That you might have a role to play, after all.'

Mrs Singh had no idea what he was talking about, but she didn't like the general tenor. The tension had gone out of Ibrahim. He seemed pleased, as if he'd come to some conclusion to which she was not privy. And, it didn't look like he'd decided to escort her to the nearest train station with an apology for the misunderstanding.

'If you give me my phone, I will call my husband to pick me up. I won't even mention you.'

'I tossed it,' said Ibrahim and the policeman's wife felt her heart sink down to her toes. 'Battery was dead anyway. Does anyone know where you are?' he continued. 'Where you were going?' She thought he was going to kick her, where she sat, propped up against the filthy wall, and she flinched.

'Of course,' she said. 'Everyone. They'll be here soon so you better let me go.'

Ibrahim taped her mouth, going round and round viciously until the pressure on her mouth and lips made her feel faint, nauseous. Mrs Singh tried to breathe slowly through her nose, knowing that she might choke to death if she threw up, the contents of her stomach forced into her lungs.

She was dragged to her feet and made to hobble to another room, this one unlocked with a key by Ibrahim. He gave her a sharp shove in the back and she fell to the ground, winded. She heard the door slam, the key turn – noted these facts somewhere at the back of her mind. The immediate present was spent coming to terms with the darkness, the pain in her knees where she had fallen and the gravel under her cheek.

They gave Martin Bradley back his things – wallet, watch and coat – told him to stay out of mischief and let him go. He was surprised. Even though he knew that they didn't have enough to pin the killings on him. Another woman, another misunderstanding, but at least his brief incarceration had provided a useful outcome, a watertight alibi for Fatima Daud's murder. And if he hadn't killed Daud, he couldn't be the Hand Man. So they had let him go.

Thank God.

But the reality was that he *deserved* any punishment meted out because he'd shown such weakness in picking up a prostitute like Cynthia Cole, betrayed the sanctity of his feelings for Regina – how could he have done that? He'd been tempted by a cheap calling card in a phone booth, the modern equivalent of the apple in the Garden of Eden. It had almost cost him everything.

And so he'd have expected to rot in jail; separated from his love, unable to protect her even though he knew that the fates had her in their sights.

His love. Regina.

Who, just before his arrest, had rejected him and in such a way as to flay the skin off his back with her cruelty.

I love my husband and daughter.

The words rolled around in his head like marbles, pinging off each other, hurting him, confusing him.

How could that be? He'd watched them – she and that Pakistani man who didn't even have a job, spent his day hanging out at jobcentres.

The tension, the distance, the quiet.

There was no love there. Not even liking. Maybe once upon a time, in a fairy tale from the past, there had been affection but it had atrophied into mutual indifference punctuated by fear when Regina had thought that her own husband might have murdered Fatima Daud.

And who was to say he hadn't done it? Not him, that was for sure.

I don't even know you.

Why was he reliving the conversation with Regina in his head? Using her words as a form of self-flagellation.

If he had any self-respect, he'd walk away. He'd offered her everything – his life, his love, his protection – offered to treat the child as his own, even though she could never be his,

276

never be *thought* of as his because of her dusky skin and dark eyes. What more could he do?

A part of him, a growing part, wanted revenge. Such humiliation could not be borne without a response.

But mostly, he still wanted what was best for her. And what was best for her hadn't changed. It was to leave her husband and come with him, to him, to be with him. He'd seen her face when she read Shaheed's name in the file on Fatima Daud. He'd watched her blanch and then rush away, like a wounded animal trying to find a quiet place. It hadn't taken him long, going through the papers she had left on her desk, to see what had upset her.

The man she had married had previously been engaged to a woman who had turned up dead – murdered, and in such a way. At the time, Bradley had seen it as a lucky break, an opportunity to show Regina that her husband, the man that she had trusted, might be involved in a heinous crime. But instead of fleeing into his arms, she'd involved some absurd inspector from Singapore, trying to get to the bottom of things.

And instead of arresting Shaheed, it was Bradley who had spent a couple of nights in jail accused of all manner of atrocities towards multiple women. What sort of person did they think he was?

The police weren't going to protect Regina, whether from her husband or all the other madmen out there.

So it was up to him.

Martin kept his distance as he followed Regina to her home and watched her enter from across the road.

The lights were on behind the curtains of her small flat.

277

Indistinct figures moved within like a shadow puppet play. He waited and watched as he had done most evenings for months. He desperately wanted to hear what they were saying to each other, this couple married in name only. Had she told her husband about him? How had Shaheed reacted? Was Regina in any danger?

The thought caused his blood to run cold. Had he put his love in harm's way?

Martin hurried across the street, his coat flapping about his ankles as if he was being impeded by a flock of birds. He wasn't sure what he was going to do, just knew he had to be closer. Close enough to protect her, save her, fend off the irate husband, rescue the child if necessary. A driver honked angrily as Martin reached the opposite pavement.

The path of true love never ran smooth.

Inspector Singh realised as he lay awake that night that he had never previously been called upon to worry about his wife.

He had worried about her opinions, where they conflicted with his own; he had worried about her actions, where it involved him in activities he disliked such as weddings and funerals. He had worried briefly about her absences – shopping trips, visits to relatives, marketing – but only in so far as it affected his meals being served on time and piping hot.

He had never worried about *her* – her safety, her whereabouts or her health. And now he was doing all three.

He didn't change out of his clothes, didn't unwind his turban – right now, it was the only thing stopping his head exploding. In all their married years, Mrs Singh had always returned promptly, criticism and food at the ready.

He had no personal experience dealing with her unexplained absence. But the policeman in him could think of a thousand possible reasons and none of them were good. Had she been in an accident? A victim of a crime? And how bad was it that she hadn't called him?

At four in the morning, he couldn't stand it any more; he called her oldest sister in Singapore. There were two sisters, but the older one pulled the strings and was the highest repository of family information.

'What do you mean you don't know where she is?'

'I left her around midday in the middle of London and she hasn't come back to the hotel.'

'What time is it there?'

'Four in the morning.'

'Something must have happened. Something bad.'

Never ask a Sikh woman for reassurance. They were all wired to imagine the worst. He should have known that from his own wife.

'Have you tried her mobile?'

'What do you think, that I called you first? Of course I've tried her mobile, but her phone battery must be dead. It goes straight to voicemail.'

'What about the hospitals and the police?'

'This is London – they don't get excited until people have been missing for a while.'

'By then it will be too late. She's probably been in an accident. Lost her memory. Needs a blood transfusion and they can't find her blood type.'

'She's O positive – the most common type.'

Singh mentally pulled himself together. He wasn't going to

find his wife by being sucked into a discussion of worst-case scenarios with her sister.

'Did she call you? Say anything?' he asked.

'I didn't speak to her yesterday. Before that she said she was shopping and helping you with an investigation because you had no idea what you were doing and always she has to step in to stop you making a fool of yourself.'

He could almost hear his wife speaking. He wished he could actually hear her. He'd even put up with the critique of his detective skills.

'Could it be something to do with your case?'

'My case?'

'Yes, did you expose her to any of the London criminals?'

'It was a cold case, the girl's been dead for five years.'

'Once a criminal, always a criminal.'

Was it possible? Singh couldn't think of a single way that the Fatima case could have landed his wife in trouble.

'I don't see how it can have anything to do with the Fatima murder. No one we were investigating had anything to hide – it was some serial killer. They found a third body yesterday.'

The silence at the other end reeked of doubt but for now the sister kept her powder dry.

'I don't know what to do,' he said.

'I'll call around. Find out who spoke to her last, when and what it was about. Also where she was at the time.'

'All right.' He was reassured. The family machinery that he disdained was kicking into action.

'What will you do?'

'I'll try and get the police to take an interest.'

*

'I don't know where she is, you have to help me find her.'

DCI Harris stared at him, struggling to find the right words. 'Look, Singh. She's probably gone on a jaunt with some girlfriends. Forgot to tell you, is all.'

Singh placed his fingers together, a prayerful pose from a man who didn't believe in God. How to explain that Sikh wives did not go 'on a jaunt'? That being missing for more than two hours was the equivalent to being lost at sea for Mrs Singh.

'I assure you that she would not be missing unless something . . . has happened.'

'Besides, you didn't always see eye to eye . . .'

'That's normal!'

' . . .so she's probably gone off to teach you a lesson, eh?' The jocular tone was forced. A man whose wife had left him for a yoga instructor did not provide marital advice willingly or easily.

'I'm telling you something has happened to my wife!'

Harris looked across at DI Carmen, his expression pleading for intervention. She obliged, placing a comforting hand on the inspector's arm. 'I'm equally sure that there's nothing wrong.'

'Her phone is dead but you can track it right?'

'That's not straightforward. We need a court order and wouldn't get it as things stand. There's just no evidence that anything has happened to her. And that's why you really don't have to worry.'

'So there's nothing you can do?'

'Not for a few days at least.'

Singh sat down heavily. Was it possible that Mrs Singh had just gone walkabout? Was she teaching him a lesson like these two cops were implying? If so, he was learning it well. He could visualise her as he'd last seen her, glaring at him as he walked into the pub to meet Ibrahim, warning him not to be distracted by the devil's drink, slipping into Oddbins.

'She's been investigating Fatima's murder on the side,' he said. 'Gossiping to the relatives in the area, dining at Khan's, the family restaurant. Could it be related?'

Harris shook his head. 'The murder of Fatima has nothing to do with the family or anyone else connected with her.'

'How can you be so sure?'

'I was just going down to the briefing room when you came in. Come with me. It will take your mind off things.'

'There've been developments?'

'Yes – we've identified the third victim.'

Singh followed him meekly, not knowing what else to do, where else to go.

When she'd calmed down and the pounding of the pulse in her ears no longer drowned out everything else, Mrs Singh pushed herself into a sitting position against a wall. The room was in almost total darkness but, as her eyes adjusted, she thought she could make out a prone figure a few feet away. That was almost the most frightening thing yet until she realised that the still creature was a prisoner too, not the enemy.

She listened hard.

Soft breathing.

At least the person in there with her was not dead. It was impossible to tell if her cellmate was male or female, conscious or not.

She made some sounds through her gag, muffled grunts –

like Singh after a couple of beers – but there was no response from the other form.

She would have tried to pinch herself awake, convince herself that this was a bad dream caused by too many samosas with her cousin, but her hands were tied with a piece of twine. She struggled against this bond for some time, rubbed her wrists raw so that she could feel the pain, enough to make her eyes water, like a carpet burn. But it was no use. This was no dream and her bonds were tight.

She stopped struggling and drifted between sleep and unconsciousness, a no-man's-land of the mind.

Eventually, another noise attracted her attention, repetitive, muffled. It took her a few moments to remember where she was, to process once more that she was a prisoner.

Mrs Singh eventually decided that it was the sound of muted sobbing.

A woman was in there with her.

Who was she? Why was she there?

Mrs Singh could not even begin to guess.

Martin slept intermittently in the stairwell. He woke every hour, rose to his feet on stiff knees and returned to the door that separated him from his beloved. But all was quiet within. He watched the dust motes dance in the half-light as the sun rose. He stretched and felt his back click.

He heard stirrings within; a child crying, a man's voice, the even tone of morning radio. The stab of jealousy was so intense that all his other pains faded into the background. He warned himself to get a grip. He was no use to anyone, no use to Regina, if he wasn't in control of his emotions.

But it was hard.

Would she tell Shaheed that she was leaving him that morning? How would he react?

When he heard the front door, he ran down the stairs, dashed into the coffee shop next door and watched. Regina emerged a couple of minutes later, dressed for work: smart linen suit, mustard silk blouse, a scarf in a floral pattern and those familiar knee-high boots. Martin's heart swelled with pride as he watched the sun reflect off her golden head. He took a step back into the shadows so that she would not catch a glimpse of him. He must look a sight after a night spent in a dusty stairwell. He ran his hand over his chin – he probably looked like a criminal, maybe even a serial killer like that Hand Man. There was nothing to be gained by scaring Regina. He chuckled; it wouldn't be a good way to start their life together.

The team was smaller, but had the same air of fatigue and determination that Singh had seen so many times before, cops on the verge of a breakthrough or a breakdown, anyone's guess which would occur first. Watching Harris from a front seat, the inspector thought it was going to be a close run thing.

'We've identified the third victim.'

'That was quick,' said a policeman.

'Yes, we put on the afterburners and the pool of possibilities was small.'

Harris stuck a photo of an athletic woman wearing a number on her vest on the whiteboard.

'Annette Winston, twenty-four years old, went missing five

years ago. She was reported as having not returned from a jog exactly a week after Fatima's body was found. There was a huge manhunt at the time but without a body, it was a dead end – until now.'

'Are we sure it's the same killer?' asked Carmen.

'The wounds to the hands, age of the victim, timing, all suggest a link,' said Harris.

'So he didn't wait five years before killing again after all,' said Singh.

'No, but there is still the long gap between the second and the third victims,' pointed out the first speaker who smelled, to Singh, like a pub. Cigarettes and stale alcohol.

'Is there any other link between the three victims? Aside from having stumbled across a man with a fetish for hands?' asked Singh.

'None at all, I'm afraid. I can say that with certainty with regard to Fatima and Cynthia Cole and there's nothing to suggest so far that the third victim had any connection to either of them.'

Three women with nothing in common except the worst of bad luck.

No wonder Harris had ruled out a personal connection in Fatima's killing despite Singh's legwork and the host of possibilities amongst her family and connections.

'It doesn't look like a lack of inclination so there are only two possibilities – there are more undiscovered bodies out there or he took a break for some reason,' said Carmen.

'So that's your question then,' said Singh. 'What do serial killers do for a break?'

'Have a KitKat?' asked Harris but this cultural reference

point was lost on Singh who stared at the DCI in puzzlement and then returned to the contemplation of his missing wife.

When Goody, the second cousin, called him, Singh was on his way to the spot he had last seen his wife. He took the call outside Oddbins, staring at his reflection in the window, remembering his wife doing the same.

'She called me yesterday,' said Goody.

'What did she say?'

'That you were in a pub.'

If he found his wife safe and sound, he would give up drinking, decided Singh. And smoking. And put in for a promotion. And attend family weddings and funerals without complaint. And lose some weight.

'Did she say where she was going, what she was doing? Anything?'

'You know we were assisting you in investigating Fatima Daud's murder?'

'Yes.'

'She was following a suspect.'

'What??'

'When I spoke to her, she was on a train, hot on the trail.'

'Which suspect, for God's sake?'

'She didn't mention.'

Singh stared at the crates of wine nestled amongst plastic grapes, trying his best to grasp what the silly woman was saying. 'Can you remember *exactly* what she said, the words?'

'Maybe not exactly,' said Goody cautiously. 'She called and said that she was on the trail of a suspect because she always has to do your dirty work while you hang around drinking instead of doing your job.' There was a pause, whether to let the import of what she'd said sink in or to spend a few seconds in further recall. 'And then she said that she hoped he didn't go all the way to Heathrow.'

At least, the so-called suspect was male. He'd eliminated half the inhabitants of London now.

'Didn't you ask her who it was?'

'I did, and I think she was about to answer but then the phone went dead. No reception on the train, I guess. Or battery dead.'

Singh hung up and considered what he'd been told. His wife, last seen by him on pretty much this exact spot, had decided to follow a suspect. A suspect in the Fatima killing unless his wife was also investigating other murders on the sly which seemed unlikely. He took out a photo of Mrs Singh, emailed to Harris by his sister-in-law and printed out at his request.

His phone beeped. It was DI Carmen responding to his earlier query: 'On Raj: definitely money laundering. Long suspected. Nothing proven so far.'

He could barely remember why he'd asked her that. So what if Raj was money laundering, if his lawyer was a scumbag, if Ibrahim had missed his calling in Bollywood? None of it was relevant to the matters at hand.

Three dead women.

A hostage.

His missing wife.

He walked a few yards down the street and came upon a Sikh manning a pavement booth selling souvenirs. Inspector Singh went up to him immediately. He knew full well that his wife would not have been able to pass by a countryman selling the sort of tat she collected by the truckloads.

'Have you seen this woman?'

The elderly gentleman peered at the picture, took off his glasses, wiped them with the end of his shirt, put them back on and looked again.

'Why do you ask, brother?'

'Because she is my wife.'

'And are you often looking for your wife in this manner?'

'Usually she is looking for me.'

'That is more customary.'

'This reverse in our situations makes me concerned about her welfare.'

The old man nodded thoughtfully. 'She was here yesterday, browsing these extremely high quality souvenirs at reasonable prices.'

'And?'

'And before she could decide what to purchase – she had her eye on a tea towel – she set off in hot pursuit of a young man.'

'Did she say anything?'

'Only that she was on top secret police business.'

There was no question at all that they were talking about his wife.

'I of course did not doubt the sister for one second despite the extreme handsomeness of the young man she was following.'

Ibrahim.

He should have guessed.

Singh had a fairly clear idea what had happened now. His

wife had seen Ibrahim leave the pub and waited a few moments for Singh to follow suit. When he didn't appear, she had decided, through a combination of boredom and curiosity, or just to impress the old Sikh at the souvenir stall, to follow Fatima's brother.

He had led her to a train if Goody's evidence was credible. Singh trotted down the street in the direction the souvenir seller had pointed until he reached the High Street Kensington Station. He stared at the Tube map at the entrance. She had feared that the trip might take her to the airport according to the cousin – which meant, if he was interpreting all the coloured lines correctly, that she had ended up on the southbound Piccadilly Line to Heathrow.

Singh flagged a taxi. With this information, the police could trace her. Using CCTV cameras, it would be possible to see where and when she had disembarked, whether she was still following Ibrahim.

He needed to get Harris on board.

'I almost can't drive for the worry, innit?'

'I beg your pardon?'

The cabbie stared at him through the rear-view mirror. 'It's today that they're going to do that other woman, right. Behead her.'

Singh caught on – his wife's disappearance had temporarily pushed all other thoughts from his head. 'Yes,' he agreed. 'That's what they said. But I'm confident the police will find her before anything happens.'

'That'd be a first.'

It didn't matter where you were in the world; the supposed ineptitude of the police was a universally held belief.

'They haven't even caught that Hand Man fellow, he's probably hacking his way through London even now. And the terrorists are snatching us from our beds. It just doesn't bear thinking about.'

'These are difficult times,' agreed Singh.

'I told the missus, stay at home, keep the kids away from school, lock the doors.'

'I'm sure they will be safe,' said Singh, wishing he could say the same thing about his wife.

Harris, when he found him, was uncooperative.

'Nothing has changed, Singh.'

'But we have a starting point, we can track her movements.'

Harris had his hands on his hips, looming over the policeman from Singapore. 'But we still have no evidence of anything untoward happening. So she decided to follow Ibrahim. So what? Even if that were true, there's no evidence that he had anything to do with her disappearance. Why would he?'

'He's a murder suspect!'

'Well, he isn't, is he? We know we're looking for a serial killer, a psychopath, who's murdered three women. Not the family of Fatima. So even if your wife followed him, there's no reason on earth why he should have harmed her.'

A vein on Singh's forehead throbbed.

'I can hardly demand CCTV footage from more than a dozen stations just because your wife might have disembarked at one of them.' Harris was more conciliatory now. 'Who'd go through them? We're incredibly short of manpower with the hunt for the Hand Man and the terrorists all happening at the same time.'

Singh nodded slowly. He was being a fool, seeking help from the police.

He was a loner, a one-man show. He didn't trust the authorities (except himself, of course, but he didn't identify himself with those in power and never had). It didn't matter whether it was Superintendent Chen, the Beijing police or Scotland Yard.

His wife was missing and it was up to him to find her.

CHAPTER 17

'Where's Ibrahim?' demanded the policeman, forcing himself to loosen his grip on the phone before he damaged it.

'I don't know,' she said. 'He's not at home, maybe at the restaurant?'

'I tried there first, he hasn't come in today.'

'Oh . . .'

'It's urgent. I must find him. What about your husband? Will he know?'

'Fauzi has gone to work at the clinic but I doubt he knows where Ibrahim has gone. They are not on good terms at present.'

'What about Hanif?'

'I don't know where he is either.'

Singh thumped the table with his fist, frustration spilling over. 'Dammit, I have to find Ibrahim, do you understand?'

'Why?' she asked. 'Is it about Fatima?'

'I don't know. I don't think so. Maybe. My wife has disappeared. And the last thing she did was follow Ibrahim when he left our meeting in Central London yesterday.'

'You think Ibrahim did something to your wife?'

The sister-in-law's incredulous tone was like a pail of cold water to the face.

'I realise it sounds far-fetched, but he might have seen her. She might have said something stupid to him. Accused him of Fatima's murder. Maybe he got angry.'

'Why in the world would your wife do such a thing?'

'She was helping me with the investigation.'

'Helping you?' A docile wife was puzzled at the independence of other women. 'Why?'

'I don't know exactly,' he answered. 'Only that she felt great sympathy for Fatima – she said she was like the daughter she never had.'

The silence at the other end was difficult to read.

'Please, help me,' he said.

'You and your wife are good people,' she whispered. 'Ibrahim didn't come back yesterday. His bed wasn't slept in last night.'

Singh rang off and stared at the wall with unseeing eyes.

His wife had disappeared. Ibrahim had disappeared.

And the trail had gone cold.

'Eat,' said Ibrahim, tossing sandwich packets and a bottle of juice into the room.

He used a penknife to free Mrs Singh's hands and then the other woman's. Not waiting to see if they obeyed him, he shut the door and she could hear the key turn in the lock. Clawing

293

at her mouth restraint, ignoring the sandwiches except to note that they were 'reduced for quick sale', Mrs Singh looked around the room for some means of escape.

She wasn't going to be so lucky. It wasn't a room so much as a store; a small, rectangular space with a cement floor, completely bare and with one narrow window, too high to reach and boarded up anyway. She tried the door gently. It was locked and heavy enough to be soundproof. Not that it made much difference considering their lonely spot in the middle of the abandoned factory space. The bindings finally came away from her mouth, scraping away skin, and she gasped for a lungful of air. Stale and dusty, it tasted like nectar.

She turned to the other prisoner who was sitting up and watching her but had made no attempt to free her mouth. Mrs Singh scrambled over and, using her fingernails, worked to loosen her gag.

'I'm Mrs Singh,' she said. 'That mad man, his name is Ibrahim, kidnapped me. I have no idea what he's trying to do or why he has us here.'

The bindings came loose. The woman was in a much worse state than Mrs Singh. Her lips were cracked and bleeding, her pupils dilated with shock and fear. She was shivering, whether from cold or fright, it was hard to say. Mrs Singh took one of her hands and rubbed it gently, trying to warm the fingers, almost as cold as the hands of the dead.

'I will speak to his family about this behaviour when we get out. It is completely unacceptable to kidnap us and imprison us in this way.'

She held the juice to the woman's lips, wincing in sympathy as the acidic liquid hurt her chapped mouth.

'I don't know who they are, what they want,' whispered the other woman. 'They grabbed me – left me here for days.'

No wonder she was in such bad shape.

Mrs Singh put an arm around her shoulder. 'Don't worry,' she said. 'My husband is a policeman so I'm sure he will find us soon. He's probably on his way here right now.'

'That's good.' A weak smile.

'What's your name?' asked the policeman's wife.

'Mary Jane,' she whispered.

Inspector Singh just couldn't get his head around it.

Why would Ibrahim, however annoyed he was that Mrs Singh was following him or suspected him of murder, harm her? Why not yell at her, ban her from his restaurant and send her on her way? He could even have called the police and accused her of harassment.

The fact of the matter was that Ibrahim had not killed Fatima. And neither for that matter had the other brothers or the lawyer or Raj or Shaheed or any of the otherwise highly viable suspects.

A serial killer of young women, a fetishist who collected hands, had murdered them one by one and Singh had no more idea who had done it than any London taxi driver. Even his suggestion to Harris that Martin Bradley might have been the copycat killer of the second victim – since he had prior information on the Fatima Daud death from his work with Regina de Klerk – seemed a lot less likely with three deaths.

And yet, the evidence suggested that Ibrahim was responsible in some way for his wife's disappearance. Otherwise, he was required to believe in coincidence, the refuge of lazy policemen and believers in divine intervention.

'How often have I said to you that when you have eliminated the impossible, whatever remains, however improbable, must be the truth?'

Was Sherlock Holmes right?

And if so, what was the most improbable element of this current situation?

That Ibrahim had killed the three women for some as yet unfathomable reason?

Fine. He would work on that basis.

'My husband is a policeman. You're making a terrible mistake. If you let me go now I will ask him to be lenient with you.'

Mrs Singh, half a sandwich later, was refuelled for defiance.

'I don't care if your husband is the Queen of England,' said Ibrahim. He bound her hands again.

'And I know who you are as well.'

'What do you mean?'

'Ibrahim, brother of Fauzi, Fatima and Hanif.'

He stepped back as if he'd been slapped. 'How do you know that? What have you done?'

Ibrahim's eyes were bloodshot; he shifted his stance like a boxer. Mrs Singh would not have been surprised to discover that he was high on some drug. It was typical of criminals that they should look for courage in a pill or a bottle.

'I haven't done anything!'

Ibrahim pulled a flick knife from his pocket, released the

blade and pointed it at Mrs Singh. 'Tell me what you know and how or I'll cut you right here, right now, do you understand me?'

Anger overwhelmed fear in the policeman's wife.

'My husband is Inspector Singh . . . I think you know him.'

'That fat fool I met yesterday at the pub?'

'He was investigating your sister's murder. Trying to find closure for the family. And this is how you reward him? By kidnapping his wife? You should be ashamed of yourself.'

Ibrahim pinched the bridge of his nose as if he was trying to ward off a headache. 'But I still don't understand what this has to do with you? Why are you here?'

'I followed you,' said Mrs Singh, throwing caution to the winds. 'After you met my husband, I followed you here.'

'Why?'

'I thought you might be going to wherever you hid the *hands*.'

'You thought *I* killed my sister – and the others?'

'It seems a most likely conclusion based on your present conduct.'

'I didn't! Why would I do something like that? You must be mad.'

Why would a man knee-deep in a double kidnapping and wielding a switchblade at her throat bother with protestations of innocence? The criminal mind was unfathomable to Mrs Singh.

'What has it got to do with you anyway?' demanded Ibrahim.

'I was helping my husband. I regularly assist him on his cases. Without me, many of them would remain unsolved.'

297

'He's going to have to solve *your* murder without help,' said Ibrahim.

'If that is the case, he will certainly do so. He has the best solve rate in the entire Singapore police department. You are no match for him.'

This assertion seemed to calm Ibrahim. 'If I was on my own, you might be right, Mrs Policeman, but I have the hordes of the righteous at my back.'

It was not Mrs Singh's way to let a mere man have the last word. She looked over his shoulder and then at him. 'Hordes? You look quite alone to me.'

'I need to see you.'

Singh had grabbed the phone when it rang, expecting news, fearing bad news. Instead, it was Regina de Klerk. He could barely concentrate on what she was saying, struggling to convert her words into comprehensible speech. She was somewhere outdoors; he could hear car horns.

'Why?'

'You said they've released Martin Bradley?'

'Yes.'

'Jesus.'

Regina didn't know about the disappearance of Mrs Singh, of course. Her attention was still on the murders and her own tangential involvement. And she was right to be afraid now that Bradley had been released even if he had nothing to do with the murders. The thin, twitchy man was only a slight nudge away from madness.

'I have some information, or at least my husband has some information. I think you need to have it.'

'About the murders?'

'About Fatima's murder. It's important.'

'All right, so tell me.'

'I can't tell you over the phone. We need to see you. Shaheed doesn't trust anyone.'

He was about to refuse, to tell her to go to the police directly, to wash his hands of Fatima and the others, when he had a sudden insight.

A plan arrived, fully formed in his mind. His wife's last and best hope.

'Where are you?'

'On the way to the office.'

'All right,' said the inspector. 'I'll meet you at St James's Park Station.'

Again the call came on his disposable number, the number he had left on the communal Hotmail account 'Drafts' folder.

'This is Choudary from the mosque. You remember me?'

'Of course.'

Hanif's mind was racing, putting two and two together, wishing that he'd recognised this man's involvement earlier. He'd seen him as a useful conduit to let the fraternity know that he was back from Syria and ready for action on the home front, hence his hints when they'd met at Friday prayers. But he had not suspected Choudary of directly participating in any exercise, seeing his age and social status as impediments to the sacrifices required by Allah.

He could have kicked himself for being such a fool.

'You were told you that you were on the bench, that your turn would come.'

He remembered that Choudary had eyes like a lizard, heavy lidded, rarely blinking. It was impossible to read his thoughts, to guess what it was he was thinking. Now he knew. He had investigated Hanif after their meeting, been satisfied with his antecedents, arranged for an intermediary to prime him and was now prepared to reveal his own involvement.

'Yes,' said Hanif. 'I am ready to be called upon to do Allah's will.'

'That is good because there's room for one more,' said Choudary.

'This operation is *yours*?'

'Yes. Didn't you guess?'

'There was no way of knowing.'

'Impressed?'

'Very.'

'Ready to participate?'

'Yes. As I said before, I should have been involved right from the beginning. This is why I returned to this country.'

'I'll send you the address in the usual way. Your availability has proved timely.'

'Why now? What's happened? Has something gone wrong?'

It was the sensible question to ask. Contrary to the widely held belief, being a fighter for God did not equate with being a fool and Choudary would not expect him to be without questions.

'Nothing that you need concern yourself about, I assure you.'

'I'm a soldier.'

The warning in Hanif's voice was clear; there was no way he was walking into a failed operation.

'It is prudent to increase the manpower, that's all,' said Choudary, condescending to explain. 'We have one more guest than was anticipated so an extra pair of hands to ensure their comfort is necessary.'

That was strange. Reading between the lines, it sounded like they had an extra hostage, which was either good planning or very bad depending on how it had come about.

'It will be a privilege to join your battle.'

'And you will be at the front lines, just as you desired.'

Hanif was exultant. 'Then my martyrdom will be a just reward.'

There were no taxis to be had for love or money. The inspector spotted the red and blue 'Underground' sign. Why emphasise that the trains were underground, like coffins?

He crossed the road and ignored the array of free newspapers screaming of terrorists and serial killers.

In the station, he abandoned the effort to use the automated ticket machine and queued up at the counter, controlling the desire to shove people out of the way. A large West Indian woman said, 'Where you going, love?'

'St James's Park.'

'It's the westbound Circle Line you'll be needing then.'

Singh handed over some money and the woman offered him a ticket and a glint of gold teeth in exchange.

The station was so crowded that he was borne towards the trains without the need for any conscious effort on his part. The crowd dispersed once he reached the platform.

Harris called. 'Any news on your wife?'

'Ibrahim didn't come back last night.'

'You still think they crossed paths?'

'It seems the most likely explanation.'

'But why would he do her any harm?'

Singh hung up – this was no time to bring up Sherlock Holmes and 'improbable' solutions.

He spotted an electronic sign that assured him the train would be arriving in five minutes, followed apparently by three more a minute apart. What was it they said about buses? You waited for ages and then three came along at once? Well, apparently it was true also of trains.

Did the London transport system not realise he had lost his wife?

'We have good service on all lines.'

The inspector felt a sudden, powerful headache developing. His throat was dry and his back bowed with the pressure of not knowing. He ran his tongue over the cracks in his lips and thought he could taste blood and salt.

He would see Regina. She knew something; had information from Shaheed, about Fatima's murder

Singh couldn't even guess what it might be about, didn't really care. All he wanted was some information that would indicate that Ibrahim had murdered his sister. If he had that, Harris would have no choice but to throw the whole might of the Met behind the effort to find his wife.

And he knew in his gut, a pain as sharp as a tumour, that time was running out for Mrs Singh.

Thomas Gordon had been a train driver for thirty years. London had changed a lot in those years but not so much underground. Systems had been updated, platforms modernised, escalators installed, disabled access improved. But in his habitat, the dark tunnels, the pipes, the soot, the wires, had hardly altered.

He was given the all-clear from the control room to proceed, drew out slowly and then increased speed, listening for instructions, one hand on the driving lever, keeping an eye out for signals information.

Thomas pushed his glasses further up his nose and smoothed his hair with one hand. Passengers didn't get much more than a glimpse of him as he pulled into a station but he was proud of his job and wanted that fleeting image to be of a neat man in his blue uniform, a credit to London Underground.

'We have good service on all Circle Line trains.'

Thomas was pleased to be able to say it with a straight face. It didn't take much to delay a train: a faulty signal, a suspicious package, a breakdown, a medical emergency on board, busy platforms, a football match, some idiot pulling the 'emergency stop' lever next to the double doors on a dare or for a lark.

'Don't tempt fate now, laddie,' he muttered.

He eased the train round a corner and could see the glow of a platform in the distance, a sharp contrast to the velvet blackness of the tunnels. He wondered whether other drivers were as superstitious as he was. He'd bet they were – it was inevitable down there, miles under the surface, alone with their thoughts and the darkness.

The faces on the platform turned to him, eyes wide, mouths hanging open slightly, ears cocked; that combination of relief that a train had arrived, concern that they wouldn't be able to squeeze aboard and a more primal fear of the huge clanking screeching beast hurtling towards them.

'This is the eastbound Circle Line stopping at Westminster, Embankment, Temple, Blackfriars . . .' he said into the speaker.

'The next station is St James's Park.'

They were waiting for him on the platform.

As the commuters hopped on the train from which he had just disembarked, the place cleared until it was just the three of them standing on the grey cement, a few yards away from the edge marked with the yellow paint and the superfluous advice to 'mind the gap'.

'Shall we go to the office? I'll make coffee.'

'I haven't time,' said Singh. 'Just tell me what you know, please.'

If Regina was surprised by his abruptness, she didn't mention it.

'Why did they release Bradley?' asked Shaheed. 'My wife told me that he's a complete weirdo *and* he was obsessively interested in Fatima's murder file.'

'The information hasn't been released to the public yet, but they've found a third body, so they're sure it's a serial killer now. And Bradley has an alibi for Fatima's killing; he was in jail at the time suspected of another crime.'

'For what?'

'Indecent assault.'

Regina shuddered.

'That just goes to show how dangerous he is,' said Shaheed.

'Yes,' agreed Singh. 'If he approaches you again, Regina, I would call the police immediately.'

'Definitely,' she said.

'So why did you ask to meet me? What do you know?'

'I told you when we spoke on the phone that I had lied,' said Shaheed, staring at the ground between his feet. 'I *did* meet Fatima, a couple of days before she was killed.'

'I know,' said Singh.

'I've told Regina now. I'm sorry. I was just desperate to stay out of trouble at the time.'

'Why the change of heart?'

'He must be caught. Whoever did this, killed Fatima, killed these other women – must be caught. There cannot be secrets.'

Singh thought he understood. The arrest and release of Martin Bradley had brought home to Shaheed that there were no bystanders in life; either one was on the side of the angels or complicit with the devil. And standing on the side-lines might lead to hurt, not only to his wife or daughter but other women just like them. Women like Singh's own wife.

'What did she say?'

'When I met Fatima, marriage was the last thing on her mind.'

'Marriage to you?'

'That's right. I didn't understand at first; asked her whether there was someone else; why she was not interested in me when the families were keen and so was I.'

Regina slipped an arm through his and hugged him close. Apparently, their relationship was back on an even keel. In a parallel universe, where his wife was waiting for him at the hotel to show him her absurd purchases, he might have given a damn.

'She said there was someone, a lawyer she had met through work.'

Jimmy Kendrick.

'That she loved him and could never marry me or anyone else.'

So this was before poor Fatima had found out about Sara.

'But she was very upset – there were tears in her eyes, I remember. And she kept wiping them away.'

'Why would that be? Did she fear being forced to marry you despite her reluctance?'

'I asked her that, explained I was still keen and this white lawyer guy would never fit in, never be accepted by her family.' Shaheed hung his head. 'I'm afraid I put her under quite a lot of pressure. I was desperate not to go back to Pakistan.'

This corroborated what Sara had said. But when was this going to lead anywhere? He had a wife to find. Singh was struggling not to grab the man by the collar and scream at him to hurry.

'She said no; she would never agree to an arranged marriage, she was upset about something else. It was her friend Sara who asked her what it was then, why she was in such a state.'

'And?'

'She told Sara – I think she'd almost forgotten I was there – she suspected her boss was using the real estate agency to launder money for all sorts of nasty people: terrorists, people smugglers, the works.'

'How did she find out?'

'She'd been working on the company accounts, and she said she just followed the money.'

Too much money. He knew it already.

'What was she going to do about it?'

'She was afraid that the boyfriend was implicated as well.'

'She thought Kendrick was money laundering?'

'No, not at all. I got the sense she trusted him completely. Sara chipped in and said he would never do anything illegal, he was a good man.'

'I bet she did,' muttered Singh.

'But Fatima was worried he'd been too trusting of Raj and might be implicated in the schemes even though he was innocent.'

'Did she have proof?'

'Not exactly, but she said any good accountant would be able to ferret out the money trail.'

'What was she going to do?'

'She wasn't sure. She wanted to go to the police. I got the sense she was really upset about the sources of the dirty money, but she was afraid for the boyfriend.'

'Had she told Jimmy Kendrick about her suspicions?'

'I don't think so – she was worried about how he'd take it, his whole career was about to go up in flames. She was afraid he might do something rash.'

'What was Sara's opinion?'

'Sara wanted her to keep her trap shut. Keep the lawyer out of trouble.'

'What about you?'

'I said it didn't involve me so I had no opinion.'

Was that a cock crowing in the distance?

'I was still upset that my plans with Fatima had come to nothing.'

'She must have said more. Think dammit. Did she say something that might have implicated a family member in the mess as well?'

He was his own worst ideal of a policeman now, demanding answers that fitted with his desired outcomes, not following the evidence so much as channelling it.

Shaheed shook his head.

'If Raj had found out about her suspicions, he'd have a clear motive for murder.'

'Yes.'

'But you didn't tell the police about it when she was killed.'

'I didn't want to get involved. The police didn't even know I was in the country. Besides, it didn't sound like Fatima was going to risk her boyfriend's fate by going to the police so how would Raj have found out?'

'I guess she really loved the lawyer.' Regina's voice was tentative, a woman who no longer believed in uncomplicated relationships, trying to understand covering up a major crime.

'Kendrick was two-timing her with Sara.' A blast of cold air from the tunnel made the hairs on Singh's neck stand on end.

'The train approaching Platform Two is the eastbound Circle Line, terminating at Tower Hill. Passengers needing the Northern Line or the Bakerloo Line should change at Embankment.'

'Has the second one ... occurred?' asked Hanif.

'Not yet. A small delay caused by events outside our control. The same reason that we have called on you to join our fight at this time.'

'Wait then.'

'Why?'

'Because I'll do it myself.'

Choudary chuckled. 'Your devotion to the cause does you credit.'

'I did not become the right-hand man of Omar Al Shishani by waiting for others to do what was right and just.'

The name-dropping worked. Choudary drew in a sharp breath and said, 'May Allah protect him . . . and you.'

'So you will wait till I am ready to be the point of the sword?'

'Time is short and delay is always dangerous.'

'Yes, but I feel strongly that this role was intended by Allah for me and me alone. And who are we to gainsay the will of God?'

'It shall be as you wish.'

'Good.'

'However, you must hurry then so that there is no further delay. As you know, the time to strike is when a nation and its people are on the verge of general panic.'

'Indeed.'

Was his cold tone sufficient to remind this bureaucrat of the difference between a general hiding behind his desk and a soldier in the field?

'There is one more thing you should know,' said Choudary.

'And what is that?'

'A piece of information that will fill you and all your kin with great pride.'

*

Two front lights, searing in their brightness, appeared in the black hole. It was easy to believe that this was a wormhole to another dimension, full of dark matter that defied the laws of the universe, but not, unfortunately, the rules of evidence, which were immutable.

What was the most important thing that Shaheed had told him?

That Raj was up to his neck in dirty business? He knew that.

That Fatima believed Kendrick was an innocent party, caught up in the crooked wiles of the real estate man? That seemed to Singh to be highly unlikely. If he was to adopt his wife's style of criminal analysis, a man who would two-time his girlfriend with her best friend was surely capable of other nefarious behaviour including money laundering for terrorists and child traffickers.

But the key point made by Shaheed was that she had not *told* either man.

Might she have accused either one of them when she discovered that Kendrick was cheating on her? Yes, but he had no proof. She'd certainly never gone to the police or there would be some record of it.

And there was not a shred of evidence of Ibrahim's involvement. He'd been clutching at straws. Sherlock Holmes was an idiot.

His wife's information came to mind.

Too much money.

Khan's was mysteriously profitable again and Raj didn't pay for his food when he dined there. Ibrahim had come to some arrangement with the dodgy real estate man. But that had only happened recently, as a consequence of the restaurant's money troubles.

Maybe Sherlock Holmes wasn't an idiot after all.

There was no evidence of any connection from back in the day, before Fatima's death. But his wife's evidence did tie Ibrahim to Raj and to the money laundering – which was a start. But was his wife at the finish line?

He reached for the phone. A real policeman went where the evidence led, even if it was not in his preferred direction.

In the distance, he heard the rumble of a train.

Hanif flung a few necessities into a bag – spare T-shirt, toothbrush, Swiss Army Knife. He wished he had a better weapon; an AK47 would suit him down to the ground, maybe a few grenades or a mortar. He'd never been a Boy Scout but desert living had taught him the value of being prepared and right now he felt as prepared as a goldfish, discovering the world afresh every six seconds.

He was still reeling from Choudary's information; his careful plans strewn across his immediate future like bomb debris. Part of him still didn't believe it, but he had to find out. There could be no intermediaries now. He'd been told to go to the rendezvous point as quickly as possible. Suffice to say, he'd get there faster if he could, so fast that maybe he would be able to reverse the flow of time until he was in at the beginning, able to dig channels to determine the direction of history.

'Where are you going?'

His sister-in-law was at the door, fresh bedding in her arms.

'I might be away for a while, Mariam. Please inform Mother and Fauzi.'

He assumed she would go away, leave him in peace, this docile, dutiful wife of his oldest brother, so different in every way from Fatima, his beloved sister.

If he were ever fortunate enough to wed, which type of woman would he choose, one like Fatima or one like Mariam? It was difficult to know; there were strengths in both. He reminded himself that the Prophet's wife had been a woman of strong character. In any event, as matters stood, marriage probably wasn't a realistic option.

Mariam defied his expectations, stepped in the door, almost as if she had the temerity to block his exit. 'Are you going back?'

He knew she meant Syria. What else could she mean? He hadn't been sure whether she was aware of his foreign adventures. The police hadn't come looking for him so she knew how to keep her mouth shut. Whether this was from family loyalty or sympathy to his cause, there was no way to tell.

'Are you going back there?' she repeated, dropping the sheets on the floor at her feet.

'No,' he said. 'I'm not.'

She looked relieved. 'That's good – whatever they say at the mosques, that is not a true jihad. Those men are just killers of women and children, destroyers of innocence. Evil.'

He was not going to debate theology with her.

As if she suspected that he might need more convincing, she added, 'They are no better than the murderer of Fatima.'

That hurt. He considered responding and then put the thought away; this was not the time or the place. Instead, he zipped his bag, slung it over a shoulder.

'Do you know where Ibrahim has gone?'

The change of subject caused him to blink, to look at her suspiciously. What did she know?

'Shouldn't he be at the restaurant?'

Did he sound at all normal? He didn't think so; his voice was half an octave higher than normal.

She didn't seem to notice, her worries focused elsewhere. 'He's not there.'

'Ibrahim follows his own drummer,' said Hanif. 'No one knows where it will lead him.'

'Nowhere good,' retorted Mariam.

'Why do you say that of our much beloved brother? Do you know something about him? Something I should know too as his elder?'

'Only that he is moody and stubborn and does not know what he wants or why he wants it.'

That was a conundrum that he would have to solve very quickly if his family was not to fragment any further. He closed his eyes – a vision of his mother shattering into a million fragments of glass made him weak at the knees.

'What is the matter, Hanif? You are pale.' She put out a hand but did not touch him.

'Nothing, nothing. Ibrahim's probably just up to some mischief somewhere – had his head turned by a beautiful woman. Do you need him for anything?'

'That policeman was asking – Singh. He called earlier when you were out.'

'Oh.'

'I don't know why but he seems to think that Ibrahim is involved in the disappearance of his wife.'

'His wife?'

'Mrs Singh.'

'Why would he think something like that? That's just ridiculous.'

'I have no idea. But Ibrahim didn't come home last night; his bed wasn't slept in. And he's not picking up his phone.'

Martin had a feeling of intense panic; he could feel his heartbeat in his fingertips; it left him light-headed. He stood behind a vending machine, clutching the lapels of his own trench coat, twenty yards away from the three people on the platform who consumed all his attention. He'd seen Shaheed hurry after Regina, catch up with her, their heads together in intense conversation. But he'd not expected this. He couldn't believe that Regina was standing arm in arm with Shaheed, so close that you couldn't slide a playing card between them. And wasn't that the fat Sikh who had tripped him up and then held him until the police arrived the day he was arrested for the murders?

Was this a conspiracy against him?

Was Regina involved in setting him up in the first place? Was that how the police had found him?

He felt cold fingers drum up and down his spine.

How could these three, his two worst enemies and the woman he loved, be together?

As he watched, the Sikh man, shoulders slumped as if he'd been dealt a body blow, turned and walked away.

A train drew in, slowing down, screeching like a suicide of cats as the wheel flanges scraped against the outer rails of the curve.

The attention of the remaining two was on each other.

Martin inched closer, straining his ears to hear what they were saying against the noise of the approaching train.

'I'm so sorry, for the lies, for the cowardice, but the most important thing of all is that you know I love you.'

She returned Shaheed's embrace, and Martin could see that she was smiling and tearing at the same time. 'I love you too,' she said.

'No!' he howled. 'Regina, what are you saying?'

'Martin. Why are you here?' She moved closer to her husband and he put an arm around her protectively.

'Saving you – from him!' He pointed a finger at Shaheed. 'You can't go back to him.'

'I never left him ... he's my husband!'

'Look, man. I don't know who you are and what's going on but you need to get away from me and my wife, right now. Do you understand? Or I'm going to call the police.'

'Like you did before, Regina?'

'What do you mean?'

'It was you who set me up. I know it; I saw you talking to that policeman. It was you.'

Singh heard the raised voices. He turned back.

Was that Martin Bradley? It looked like him: thin; that flapping trench coat a few sizes too big.

A tinny voice echoed through the loudspeakers, 'Mind the gap. Mind the gap.'

He hurried towards them, breaking into a trot, not sure why, not sure what he feared.

Even as he closed in on them, he saw Martin launch himself.

Not at Shaheed, the hated husband, but at Regina.

Even as Regina was propelled towards the edge, Shaheed flung himself at the other man.

They grappled violently for a few brief moments; or an eternity if you were running as fast as your clogged lungs and heavy legs would allow.

Singh arrived just as Regina teetered backwards. He grabbed one flailing hand and yanked her forwards, towards him.

Even as he did so, both men went over the ledge.

In an instant, they were lost under the wheels of the behemoth. The screams were cut off so suddenly that the surrounding cacophony sounded like silence.

The train came to a violent, sudden stop and for a moment it appeared that the carriages must balk at the abruptness and concertina forward. The passengers within, packed tightly, shifted forward and then back, helpless in the face of the changing momentum.

Thomas knew.

Even as the train ground to a juddering halt, he knew that the two men had gone under. He didn't pause to think. He leaped out of the cab, shouting for help, blowing the emergency whistle to summon the station manager. He was vaguely aware that people were shouting, running towards the train. He ignored them, didn't look under the wheels of his train, just ran to the end of the platform. There was only one thing to do and that was cut the juice. He reached the end, found the circuit breaker on the tunnel wall and pinched the copper wires together. If by some chance they had survived, were still alive, turning off the electricity was their only hope.

She was crying and shaking, trying to get to the edge, held back by Singh, afraid of what she might do. He peered down; there was nothing to see. Both men were under the train. Singh's teeth chattered as if he was trapped in a blizzard. He couldn't seem to focus, his vision blurred with shock.

Strangers sobbed, faces drained of colour.

A few had their mobiles out, vultures around a kill.

The inspector held on to Regina, unable to think of what else to do.

'What happened?'

'Martin Bradley turned up – accused me of betraying him. He was so mixed up. I tried to explain that I wasn't leaving my husband, it was all just a mistake, a misunderstanding on his part.'

He had seen what happened next.

'He just leaped at me; pushed me towards the tracks. Shaheed tried to stop him. And then ... they both went over. I was falling too – before you grabbed me.'

She didn't seem to remember what Bradley has been shouting at her, to her, about her – maybe she'd been too distracted by events. But Singh did. Bradley's words were seared in his brain.

The station manager and London Transport Police officers arrived. Blue uniforms, official caps, badges, reflective strips on their jackets. The emergency services would be tens of minutes away.

The public tannoy crackled and an unemotional voice said,

317

'There has been an incident on the Circle Line, Platform Two. The eastbound Circle Line platform is closed. All train services at St James's Park are currently suspended.'

The inspector left Regina with an officer and made for the front of the train, pushing his way through the gathering crowd. He'd never yet come across a calamity that did not draw spectators as certainly as a corpse drew flies.

Despite his anxiety to discover their fate, Singh found his footsteps slowing. A large man was down on the tracks, shining a torch under the carriages. He wore a blue uniform and Singh guessed he was the train driver.

He jumped into the well and almost tripped over a track.

'Hey! Get out of here!'

Singh regained his balance. 'I'm a policeman,' he said.

The train driver said, 'I see one.'

He handed the torch to Singh and crawled forward on his belly under the train.

Singh, on his hands and knees, followed the beam with his gaze. He swallowed hard. He could see a figure, not that far under, between the wheels in the deep alcove running down the middle of the tracks. The arms were outstretched, crucifixion style. The hand nearest to him was palm up, fingers slightly curled as if the person was begging for help. Singh's breath caught in his throat.

The driver flat on his belly, legs sticking out, reached forward as far as he could. He felt for a pulse.

'Nothing,' he said. 'He's gone.'

'Jesus,' said Singh, but it was not a prayer. 'What about the other?'

'I can't see him. He must be deeper. There's no way he'd have made it.'

The beam wavered in Singh's hand, lighting up random pits of darkness.

'We'll have to move, reverse, the train. It's the only way to get them out.'

The inspector shifted the light from hand to hand, wiped his sweaty palms on his trousers. He could feel the rough ground like sandpaper against his knees.

How to leave them lying there?

His eyes turned to the outstretched hand, maybe no more than ten feet away. He saw the fingers clench into a fist.

'He's alive,' shouted Singh. 'One of them is alive!'

But which of them?

CHAPTER 18

'But how could he survive?' asked Harris.

Singh, back at the station, drinking strong sweet coffee and needing something much stronger, said, 'Suicide pit.'

'What?'

'The ditch between the rails, jumpers – and those who get pushed – are wedged in there. The train passes overhead. They survive – sometimes.'

'Shaheed is a lucky man.'

'Luckier than Martin Bradley anyway.'

Regina's husband had suffered relatively minor injuries: cuts, scrapes, bruises, a broken collarbone and minor concussion.

Martin Bradley had lost a leg, sliced away by the wheels with the precision of a butcher. He'd bled to death before the emergency services could reach him.

But, for once, the fates had spared the innocent – Regina's husband and Emma's father was still alive.

Would the fates intervene one more time for his wife?

'A cock-up from start to finish,' said Harris. 'I suppose we should be grateful that Bradley wasn't the Hand Man or he'd have dodged his day of reckoning in court and we'd look like real fools letting him go to attack another woman.'

Martin Bradley's last words were ringing in Singh's ears, but he kept them to himself. This was not a long-term solution. Someone else might have heard, Regina or Shaheed might remember, but for now, he was buying time.

'Any progress on finding the killer?' he asked.

'None. We're no wiser now than we were five years ago when Fatima was killed, last week when Cynthia was found or in the last twenty-four hours since the discovery of the third body. This entire investigation is at a dead end.'

'I know who did it,' said Singh. 'I know who killed all three women.'

He had their undivided attention.

'Fatima was killed five years ago.'

Singh marshalled his thoughts, knowing that the way he presented his information now would go a long way towards determining how soon they found his wife.

'Yes,' said Harris, drumming his fingers on the table.

'The second victim, Annette Winston, was killed a few days after, but the body remained hidden, more likely by accident than by design. Correct?'

'Yes, so?'

'Bear with me. The third victim of this so-called serial killer, Cynthia Cole, was found just a few days after I started looking at the Fatima case again.'

'That's right.'

'And, in between, we have nothing, no other victims.'

'You said yourself there might be more out there or he was incapacitated for one reason or another.'

'I did,' said Singh, 'but I was wrong.'

Harris listened without interrupting as the inspector explained his thinking.

'And you're sure it must be Ibrahim?' he asked, his voice betraying his uncertainty. But he'd listened and he hadn't rejected Singh's theory, carefully modified for circumstances, outright. Which counted as a victory.

'But if you're right, surely any of Fatima's brothers or the other suspects might be responsible.'

This would have been a good time to mention everything else he knew, but Singh remained uncharacteristically and unprofessionally silent. Who would have thought that he'd find himself in London actively perverting or attempting to pervert the course of justice? Only Superintendent Chen would have imagined him capable of such calumny.

Instead, he said, 'Until such time as my wife puts in an appearance, Ibrahim *has* to be the number one suspect. It's the *only* explanation that accounts for the disappearance of both him and my wife.'

'Which means we need to find him ASAP.'

'Which you can best do by tracking my wife's movements from the time she boarded the train at High St Kensington Station.'

'What's your opinion of Singh's theory?' asked Harris, looking at DI Carmen, who had remained silent and expressionless during Singh's exposition.

'It's possible.'

'Probable?'

'No – but it's not like we have much else to go on.'

Her eyes met Singh's before she continued. 'I think a long shot is better than no shot at all and we should throw everything we have at seeing whether our good friend here is right.'

Harris hesitated for one long moment – while Singh did his best to look confident – then grabbed his phone and barked instructions.

'All the CCTV footage from the stations between High Street Kensington and Heathrow and I want it yesterday.'

Singh nodded his acquiescence as he listened.

Harris hung up and turned to DI Carmen. 'Send a few men to Southall; see what you can find out from friends and family. Maybe the bastard has some bolt-hole along the route.'

Singh felt weak with relief. He had the Met focused on his wife, bringing their full resources to bear to the hunt.

It was his best hope.

His last hope.

'Anything else, Singh?'

'We're on the right track. I'm sure of it.'

There would be hell to pay when Harris discovered he'd been misleading them for his own purposes, but he'd cross that bridge when he came to it. The only thing that mattered was finding Mrs Singh.

'It's done – we'll find her.'

'Let's say you find the station where she disembarked, with or without Ibrahim, then what?'

'We blanket the area with search parties, look for possible hiding places, patrol the streets – we'll find her – and him. Don't you worry about it.'

Singh didn't doubt it. Harris was grim, dedicated, enraged

by the murders of the women, the desecration of their bodies. Ibrahim would soon be apprehended and then they would find out whether and why he had abducted Mrs Singh.

The 'why' was still a mystery as there was no way, in Singh's opinion, notwithstanding what he'd said to Harris and Carmen, that Ibrahim had killed his sister or any of the other women.

But Ibrahim was somehow responsible for the disappearance of his wife.

And Singh would have pinned the Kennedy assassination on Ibrahim if he thought it would speed up the manhunt.

The only real question, the only real worry as far as the inspector was concerned, was whether they would find him in time to save Mrs Singh.

Ibrahim's eyes were bloodshot and his hands were unsteady. He'd brought the women a couple of shrunken apples and a plastic cup of water; if it had been glass Mrs Singh would have smashed it and attacked this mad man with a shard.

'Getting worried?' she asked. 'My husband will arrive with the British police at any moment now.'

She couldn't resist needling him even though it was a dangerous game to play. But her experience of managing Singh had taught her that men were easiest to manipulate when they were off balance. The way to achieve that was to annoy them with regular frequency.

'I thought you had an army of confederates? I suppose once they knew that my husband was the famous Inspector Singh, they fled.'

Her fellow captive was making faces at her, urging her to be more circumspect in her dealings with their captor.

Ibrahim's eyes glittered and Mrs Singh felt a frisson of doubt, but she persevered manfully. 'I wouldn't be surprised if the police have surrounded this place. You'll soon be under arrest.'

'Don't get your hopes up.'

'Why not?'

'Because by the time the police or your husband get here, it will be too late for you and your quiet friend over there.'

Harris and Singh sat in the canteen and waited for news. Both mobiles were on the table. Singh's beeped regularly, messages from Mrs Singh's family demanding updates. He ignored them all. He had nothing to tell them and he didn't want to hear their accusations and insinuations. He knew very well it was his fault that Mrs Singh had disappeared; the only thing that wasn't clear was whether he was directly responsible because he'd involved her in a dangerous situation or answerable in a more cosmic sense.

'Anything from Southall?' asked Singh.

'Nothing useful. Ibrahim has disappeared into thin air and so for that matter has the other brother, Hanif.'

Singh wrinkled his nose. Was that relevant? It was difficult to see why it mattered that Hanif was gone unless he had some insights into Ibrahim's whereabouts. Most likely, he'd gone back to Syria, poet and warrior. And fool.

'The restaurant hasn't opened today in their absence and the eldest brother is irate.'

Typical drama for any family originating from the Indian sub-continent except that there was so much more here than met the eye.

'No secret bolt-hole somewhere on the way to Heathrow?'

'Nothing so far.'

The inspector sighed. The television was playing in a corner of the canteen and he saw news of the impending death of Mary Jane Houseman. Three dead women, but the live one dominated the news.

'Should have been online by now,' said Harris.

'What?'

'The second beheading. They're behind schedule. The video should have been online by now.'

'That's good news, right?' Singh concentrated on the talking heads on the TV.

'It is possible that this indicates a change of plan on the part of the terrorists . . . '

' . . . or, in a best case scenario, some falling out within the ranks.'

'Look, unless and until Mary Jane Houseman is free and safe, we have to assume the worst.'

Singh wouldn't do that; he wouldn't follow the advice of this so-called expert. He refused to assume the worst even if he did not yet have Mrs Singh free and safe.

'Did you kill your sister?'

'Of course not! What kind of pervert do you think I am?'

The denial rang true. Which left Mrs Singh more in the dark than ever. Ibrahim had retied their hands after the unsatisfactory meal of rotting apples but had not re-gagged them. Instead, he sat inside the door and picked at his fingernails with a small blade. He was clearly waiting for something but it was difficult to fathom what it might be. A day's stubble,

326

lank hair and gaunt cheeks had altered his Bollywood appearance somewhat; from Shashi Kapoor in an early film to Shah Rukh Khan in a later one.

'My husband didn't really think it was you either.'

'I'm grateful, of course.'

'So, if this is not about Fatima, why are we here?'

'You really want to know?'

He pointed at her with his blade as he asked the question and she remembered that she'd been taught it was rude to point, even with a finger. Her upbringing had not incorporated information on the etiquette of knives.

'Yes, I want to know.'

He laughed and Mrs Singh had a nasty suspicion that the joke was on her.

'Don't you worry; you're going to find out soon enough. He pointed at Mrs Singh's companion. 'And so will she.'

Harris and Singh watched the staccato black and white images in silence, digitally recorded by station cameras. The inspector didn't know whether to laugh or cry as he watched his wife's antics. She had been easy to spot on CCTV, a middle-aged Indian woman in comfortable shoes behaving surreptitiously. She would have been easy to spot by Ibrahim as well, her methods more appropriate for tracking animals than human suspects of crime.

The experts had traced her quickly from High Street Kensington through Earl's Court and then to Hounslow East. They scrutinised her movements until she disembarked and followed Ibrahim out of the station and into the wilderness where Big Brother wasn't watching any more.

'I've sent every spare man to the area,' said Harris. 'Although I'll be frank and tell you that's not a huge number because they're all hunting terrorists. At moments like this, Homicide and Serious Crime comes second to the anti-terror squads.'

Frustrating but not surprising.

'Anything from the trains?'

'No cameras on board.'

DI Carmen walked in, looking harassed and tired. 'We've been going through a list of Ibrahim's acquaintances as provided by his nearest and dearest. Looking for red flags.'

'Anything?'

'Nothing.'

Another dead end.

'Any connection in his past to the Hounslow area?'

'We're doing our best, Singh.'

He nodded. He could see they were. This was professional police work of the highest order performed by dedicated, intelligent officers.

But it wasn't enough.

'I'm going to Hounslow,' said Singh.

'There's nothing you can do there.'

The inspector shrugged. His eyes were sticky with fatigue, he stank like a polecat; his nerves were jangling like bells. 'What can I do here?'

Harris considered it for a moment and then nodded. 'All right. Who knows – you might spot something. You've been ahead of us all along.'

If only he knew, thought Singh. If only he knew.

'Is it too much to ask that DI Carmen drop me off?'

'Sure, if the boss doesn't mind,' said Carmen and Singh smiled his thanks. This was a good woman. Just like his wife. He hoped she wouldn't disappear too.

Harris nodded his head as well. 'I guess we only need one of us sitting on our hands here hoping for a breakthrough.'

When Singh stepped outside, it was late evening. He'd been in a cocoon where weather patterns, daylight hours, meal times had ceased to have meaning. Just waiting for news, any news, as long as it wasn't bad. He didn't think he could face bad news.

The last light of day was dim and reluctant. A drizzle had darkened all surfaces except where car lights and street lamps reflected off the wetness. London was a city on edge; the people were wrathful, stalked by violence, prone to mob aggression and sudden riots.

DI Carmen drew up in a police car and he jumped in.

'I'm in a rush,' he told her.

'I know.'

The police vehicle raced down the narrow roads, lights on but no siren, skidding on cobblestones as it took corners like a racing car.

Singh leaned back and tried to organise his thoughts.

The past was not linear, he was sure of that. In philosophical moments, he saw it as a rope of separate strands, and one slipped from one thread to another as they ran close or touched. Each thread was an option; each change was a choice. The more complicated the family, the politics, the country, the thicker the rope, the more numerous the choices, the more certain the mistakes.

Was there another strand where he was at home in Singapore, waiting for his wife to put dinner on the table, sniffing hungrily as the smells wafted in from the kitchen? Did he have a daughter who loved him? Or a feckless, no-good son?

What was the matter with him? Focus on finding her, he instructed himself in the sort of tone Mrs Singh might have used. Worry about the offspring in a parallel universe later.

'You got my message earlier that Raj has been suspected of money laundering?' asked Carmen. 'Most recently through a car-wash operation in which he's a shareholder.'

'Good work,' said Singh.

'Why did you want to know?'

Should he tell her? Could he trust her?

He beat around the bush. 'This dodgy relationship between Raj and Ibrahim in relation to Khan's – I'd bet that was money laundering as well.'

'We should find out soon enough – my men have instructions and a warrant to seize all the restaurant records.'

'I wouldn't be in the least surprised if it's dirty money from Islamic Front and such like.'

'That would be a breakthrough,' she said. 'The unlimited source of funding for these terror attacks is a huge headache or so I'm told by the security services.'

'But probably not in time for that poor woman.'

'No,' agreed Carmen, the tightened grip and white knuckles on the steering wheel the only overt sign of her rage.

They drove in silence for a while and then she said, suddenly, apparently apropos of nothing, which Singh knew well from his own wife's habits meant that she'd been chewing on her accusation for sometime, 'There's something you're not telling us.'

He glanced at her profile – noticed that she looked tired,

fine lines making her skin look like old parchment. Her eyes were on the road but her attention was on him.

'What do you mean?'

'What do you know that you're not telling Harris – or me?'

'I have no idea what you're talking about.'

'I've heard your theory – you make a convincing case that it is Fatima's murder that is the key . . .'

'Thank you. I do my best.'

'I even think you might be right about the three murders and why they are all linked.'

The inspector from Singapore remained silent, watching the signboards flash past. They were almost at their destination; he'd soon be out of the interrogation hot seat.

'But I don't think it was Ibrahim.'

'If it wasn't Ibrahim, why did he abduct my wife?'

She glanced at him, sympathetic yet persistent. 'I don't think you think it was Ibrahim who killed Fatima and the others *either*.'

'Nonsense. Why would I lie to the cops?'

'For this – for this manhunt for Mrs Singh.'

His shoulders were rounded with defeat but his words were not. 'Your enhanced interrogation methods will not make me talk.'

'Enhanced interrogation methods?' She was temporarily distracted.

'You're shouting,' he explained.

'Ah . . .'

She pulled up outside the Hounslow East station and pointed out the Underground sign.

He stared at the building with the sloping blue roof,

opened the door and swivelled to plant his feet on the ground.

'If you don't tell me what you know, a murderer may get away.' She addressed his broad back but he heard her loud and clear. 'Surely, you don't want that? And I'm sure Mrs Singh wouldn't either.'

His wife.

She, who was in trouble because she'd decided to stick her nose into a murder investigation for the first time in her life.

Because the young Fatima had struck a chord with the older childless woman.

Because his wife had wanted the dead girl avenged.

And here he was – a rotund roadblock between Mrs Singh and what might end up being her last wish on earth, that Fatima receive justice. His eyes grew moist and he hated himself with a passion in that instant.

He looked back at DI Carmen. 'Can I trust you?' His voice cracked.

'Yes.'

He told her.

Hanif rode the trains. A taxi might have been quicker; he had the cash, but it would have left a trail that others might follow, the breadcrumbs of memory. He was still trying to think, find a way through, but his instincts for anonymity were sound and he trusted them even in times of mental turmoil. He'd left his phone behind; had the new one with a temporary SIM card; those who needed him could still get him. But not family.

A message. 'Still nothing?'

He texted back. 'Nothing.'

The first fork in the road, the first choice, the first lie.

He thought of Fatima again. Why was she in his thoughts so much? Was it because the end was almost upon him? He'd be pleased to see her again, in the afterlife. The afterlife, a place of rest and reward, and questions answered.

What would Fatima want him to do?

He would use that as his guiding principle, he decided. In uncharted waters, that would be his lodestar.

Half an hour later, Singh had walked five hundred yards down almost every street leading off from Kingsley Road and recognised the futility of his task. Why wasn't there any proper urban planning in this town? It was impossible to find a pattern in such organic growth and impossible to know where Ibrahim might be, or his wife. He could be holed up in the upper floor of one of those old, run-down double storey houses where even the windows were misshapen; in a flat behind a locked door in the vomit-coloured concrete block in the distance; even in one of the more attractive homes near the scratchy park a few hundred yards from the station.

Singh was panicking. He knew it from his elevated heart rate, the dry eyes; the quickstep as he went back towards the station. He was almost running because he was running out of ideas. It came down to the fact that he had no idea why Ibrahim would have – he didn't even know what word to use – kidnapped/attacked/assaulted his wife.

Could he be completely wrong? Had his wife just wandered off into the sunset, finally too fed up of him to hang around? But then she would surely have told her family, who would have been quick to crow. He would not have been long in the dark. Harris had checked the hospitals and police stations; there were no new Jane Does, dead or alive.

Stick to the facts, he told himself. You know she followed Ibrahim; you know she left the train at this station. The few shops – an Indian butcher and a travel agent with a poster of the Taj Mahal in the front window – suggested that it was an area of London popular with ethnic minorities so Ibrahim might have been familiar with it.

The inspector rang Mariam.

'Any news of Ibrahim?'

'No. The police were here asking as well; they searched his room. A woman sergeant was in charge. She was kind, but she would not tell me anything. Why are you all looking for him? What has he done?'

'We don't know yet – maybe nothing.'

'Did he kill Fatima?'

'That's almost the only thing I'm sure he hasn't done,' said Singh. 'Do you know if Ibrahim has any connection to the Hounslow area of London?'

'I don't think so – I will ask my husband.'

'Thank you.'

'Hanif was here for a short while as well. I asked him whether he knew what was going on. He doesn't know where Ibrahim is either.'

'I appreciate your help on this, Mariam.'

'Is there any news of your wife?'

Was everyone going to ask him that? 'No.'

'My husband rang and said that the police have taken all the documents away from the restaurant too.'

334

Carmen walking the walk; there should be enough there to implicate Ibrahim in Raj's money-laundering scheme, albeit belatedly. Too much money was not a good thing for anyone if not earned through hard work, lottery tickets or betting on a horse.

Had Hanif known or suspected? Had he been involved? He'd struck Singh as a profoundly honest man – on the other hand, he might have acceded to such a scam if it allowed for the availability of funds for terrorists on UK soil. All things being equal, the fellow was still a zealot recently returned from holy war.

More importantly, was there any conceivable way the money laundering was related to the disappearance of his wife? Singh's extensive experience as a criminal investigator informed him that he was clutching at straws. On the other hand, he had nothing else to clutch at. Right now, he'd clutch at imaginary straws held by his imaginary friends.

'Where's Hanif now?' he asked. Perhaps the middle brother needed to answer that question directly.

'He said he would be away for a while; he packed some things into a rucksack.'

'Where was he going?'

A hesitation. 'He wouldn't say.'

'Back to Syria?'

If Mariam was surprised that he knew of Hanif's previous sojourn, she didn't reveal it.

'He said not.'

'Did you believe him?'

Should he inform Harris so he could warn the security services or were they all too busy chasing down Mary Jane Houseman and her captors?

'Did you believe him when he said he wasn't going to Syria?' he asked again.

'I'm not sure.'

The policeman hung up, sat down at a small metal table with a plastic top just outside an Internet café, ordered a drink and rang Harris next.

'You were right; I'm wasting my time here. Any developments at your end?'

The sigh was audible down the line. 'Nothing much. Hanif was on a terror watch list.'

'The family thinks that he might be on his way back to Syria.' He explained what Mariam had said.

'I don't know what the security services are playing at,' snapped Harris. 'We warned them and they've done nothing to stop him. I'll call them again – it may not be too late to pick him up at one of the airports.'

'Hands full, I suppose.'

Hands. Missing hands.

His wife's hands. Cooking, cleaning, gardening, pointing an accusing finger at him. If she were still alive, she'd have expected him to find her by now. She'd been right all along. He was a disappointment, a failure. A man un-promoted, unsung and now ineffectual.

'Singh? Are you still there?'

The inspector rang off without further words; there was nothing to say. He stared blankly across the road.

And saw Hanif emerge from the main entrance of Hounslow East station.

He almost put up his hand and waved and then thought twice.

There was something odd about the man. He looked both ways as he came out of the station and then made a sharp right turn. He was walking at an even pace but quicker than a man at leisure. Singh threw a five pound note down on the table and set off after him, his brain churning as he went.

There was no such thing as coincidence in an investigation. Storms were not caused by the flapping of a butterfly's wings on the other side of the planet. And Hanif had not turned up here because he fancied a lamb chop from the Indian butcher. He was here for his brother. He had to be. Which meant that he was on his way to Mrs Singh.

The inspector fell into step behind, trying to figure out what was going on.

Fortunately, night had fallen and clouds obscured any moonlight that might have made a Sikh stalker visible. He skirted the pools of yellow light from the street lamps and kept the other man in sight.

Singh's phone beeped and vibrated in the same instant; he almost flung it into a ditch. Hanif did not turn. Perhaps that most common of noises was not sufficient to alert him to trouble. With a clumsy thumb, Singh switched the phone to silent and read the text.

'Ibrahim was made redundant from a meat-packing factory when it shut down three years ago. On Myrtle Street.' The message was from Mariam.

Hanif made an abrupt right turn down a narrow lane. Singh counted to ten in his head and then headed for the junction. The white sign with black lettering affixed to a corner house read MYRTLE STREET. He peered around the bend and was just in time to spot Hanif march down a road marked PRIVATE.

For the first time, Singh spotted the rucksack on his back. He'd told Mariam he'd be away for a while.

But not to Syria.

To Hounslow East. To join his brother, Ibrahim.

The pieces of the puzzle were falling into place. But it was not a picture he'd been expecting.

He typed this latest information to Harris with clumsy thumbs.

The phone vibrated in response but silently this time – a reply from Harris: 'Stay back. We're on our way.'

If only that was an option, thought Singh.

He might already be too late.

'Come with me.'

Mrs Singh contemplated her options. Ibrahim had abandoned the switchblade in favour of a machete. He beckoned the women, who exchanged glances. Their hands were bound but feet and mouths were free. Ibrahim had not bothered with the full restraints after their last meal break. He was getting lazy, or cocky. Or tired.

Two of them.

One of him.

The door behind him was slightly ajar. If they made a dash for it simultaneously, one of them would likely get through. The other would feel the edge of that vicious-looking blade.

And then?

He'd chase after the escapee. Would either of them make

it to a public area before he caught up? Mrs Singh considered the way she'd come in, squeezing through the hole in the fence after following the path around the building, at the end of the private through road. That had been during the day. She'd lost track of time, but she knew from the small window that night had fallen. A young man might succeed. A middle-aged woman with bound hands and arthritic joints wouldn't. And neither from the look of her would her companion. There was no escape.

She rose to her feet slowly and Mary Jane followed suit, following her lead.

'Where are we going?' she asked.

'To a better place,' he said.

Singh did not know it but he was retracing his wife's footsteps.

Hanif had disappeared, but Singh was sure he was somewhere within the compound, ring-fenced, the dark silhouettes of buildings faintly visible against the velvet sky. He wished he dared switch on his phone, the faint light would be useful, but it was too much of a risk.

Instead, he shuffled forward, one hand on the fence, another in front of him defensively. As he rounded the corner, a glow against the night sky warned him that one of the buildings was inhabited.

He felt the gap in the fence before he saw it, squeezed through and wondered whether his wife had done the same two days earlier. Such out of character behaviour for her and all because she'd felt a bond with the dead girl. If he found her safe and sound, would he have to turn down all investigations involving young women of Indian or Pakistani origin to avoid this sort of thing happening again?

His phone vibrated once more. Singh reached into his pocket, hurrying across the yard towards the obscurity of the sheds. He didn't like to be in the open, even when cloaked in night. As he glanced down at the message, his foot caught on something and he fell forward with the grace and impact of a ton of bricks. The phone flew from his hand, text unseen, and disappeared into the blackness.

The inspector scrambled forward on his knees, rummaging in a pile of debris – boxes and coils of wire. The dark was now absolute.

It was gone. Who needed it anyway? Who was he going to call? Nine-nine-nine? It was most likely the police who were texting him in the first place.

Singh got back to his feet, holding a hand to his side. He'd landed on something sharp, could feel the wetness of blood. There wasn't much pain, but he feared that was shock, not the shallowness of the wound.

There wasn't much he could do about it. There was no turning back now.

He had taken gingerly two steps forward when an immense blow landed on the back of his head.

His last thought, as pinpricks of light exploded in his vision, was of his wife.

CHAPTER 19

At first, he was only conscious of his throbbing head. And then Singh became aware that he was in a brightly lit room. The windows and one wall were draped in black cloth covered in Arabic writing. He was half sitting, half lying against a wall and his hands and feet were bound in tape.

A man in a black ninja-style outfit, face and head wrapped in black cloth, eyes and mouth showing, stood against the backdrop. He was tall and slim but there were no other clues to his identity. Was it Hanif? Too tall and thin, surely? The man's body language suggested that he was feeling the strain of being the most wanted man in Britain, but he held the blade in a loose grip, ready to carry on.

A woman knelt by his feet.

She spoke and her words were simple. 'I am Mary Jane Houseman. They have asked me to warn you that this fate may befall anyone – that you should all be afraid of the wrath of God. I don't believe that. These are mad men, nothing more.'

She received a cuff to the back of the head for her rebellion. To Singh that was almost worse than the fate about to befall her. This was not a man on a mission for his god, however misguided, just a thug high on the power of violence.

'Check the recording; if it's good we can do the final take.'

Singh turned his head slowly, feeling the pain exploding like starbursts, desperate not to black out again.

Another man stood ten yards away, recording events with an iPad. Singh didn't recognise him, but he looked innocuous, like a dentist, or a hedge fund manager. He was not dressed in jihadi chic so his role was limited to behind-the-camera work. Did that make him the boss?

'I need the spare iPad,' he said. 'This one is out of battery. I'll just be a couple of minutes and then we'll get this show on the road.'

He walked towards the door with the calm of a man trying to organise a family photo, not record an execution.

'Stop it, do you hear me, stop it!'

Who was screaming at the mad men? Did he or she have no sense of self-preservation? He turned to look at a creature in the shadows. The inspector felt a sharp pain in his chest shooting down his arm and into his jaw.

It was his wife.

'Shut her up, will you? She'll ruin the sound recording.'

Another man emerged from the shadows in response to this instruction.

It was Hanif.

'As you wish, Choudary,' he said and the man called Choudary nodded his head and left the room.

'Be silent, please,' said Hanif. 'Or I'm going to have to tape your mouth.'

The inspector's head was spinning like a carousel. How hard had they hit him? Or was he merely confused that terrorists said 'please'?

'I won't shut up. Your sister would be ashamed of you. How can you even consider doing such a thing to that poor woman?' continued Mrs Singh.

'There's nothing you can do for her.' Hanif's voice was almost gentle.

His wife was trussed up like a Christmas turkey and propped against the opposite wall. Taken in by the original tableau being enacted for a World Wide Web audience, Singh had not even seen her at first.

'You don't understand the suffering of our people.'

Singh realised that the man holding the blade was Ibrahim despite the head and face covering. He recognised the voice, the stance, the gleaming eyes.

'Is that you, Ibrahim. This is a long way from a pub, isn't it?'

'Ahhh ... so the famous Inspector Singh has regained his powers of deduction.'

'I wouldn't say that – I bought your whole Bollywood act.'

'Don't kick yourself, everyone did.'

'My wife is right, you know. Fatima would be ashamed of what her brothers are doing here today.'

'This is our jihad,' he said, swinging the machete in a lazy arc. 'Is that not so, my brother?'

'Hanif, I know this is not who you are,' said Singh.

Ibrahim laughed, false and snide. 'You know my brother better than I do, Singh?'

'He does.'

They all turned to stare at Hanif, his two quiet words louder than the shouts of angry men.

'Ibrahim, you must listen to me.' Hanif spoke urgently, his voice still low, his eyes on the door through which Choudary had left.

'What is it? What are you saying?'

'That this is wrong; that we should stop. We must not kill this woman, these people.'

'What? Are you a martyr or a coward?'

'Neither. I am your brother trying to save you from the greatest sin – the murder of innocents.'

The bump on his head was making Singh slow, or maybe it was the loss of blood from the wound to his stomach. He couldn't understand what was going on.

'Fatima was an innocent!' It was Mrs Singh again. 'How can you do to others what was done to your family?'

'This is different.'

'Brother, I swear to you, it is not.'

Ibrahim left his post, marched up to his brother and was now toe to toe with him. The blade was loose in his hand but Singh had no doubt that he was ready and willing to wield it.

But why was Hanif questioning Ibrahim? Wasn't this the Syrian jihadi? Why the change of heart?

'How is it different?' demanded Mrs Singh.

He needed to have a word with his wife about arguing with terrorists.

'Because all Westerners are complicit in the murder of Muslim women and children in Gaza, Pakistan, Syria, Iraq and therefore revenge against any individual is justified.'

'That is not true,' said Hanif.

'Are you mad? Why did you go to fight in the first place if that is how you feel?'

Singh tensed. The pitch of Ibrahim's voice indicated that he was losing control, and quickly.

'I realised my error when I was there,' said Hanif, his voice as calm as a deep pond. 'You cannot fight injustice by adding to it.'

'Then why in Allah's name are you here?'

'To save you, you fool. Your life and, if that is not possible, your soul. I had no idea that you could be involved in something like this.'

'Because I don't have a long beard to my waist? Because I have a drink sometimes? You are a fool, Hanif. The trappings do not make the man, only what is in his heart.'

'Allah does not want this, Ibrahim. I swear it.'

'When Choudary told me you were the new man, sent to smooth our path towards Allah's grace, my heart sang, I forgot all that was wrong between us and remembered that we were brothers. Brothers by blood and brothers-in-arms.'

'Ibrahim, listen to me! Choudary will be back any second now. We have to end this now. We have to set these people free, escape ourselves.'

'You are a disgrace,' said Ibrahim and spat on the floor. He turned on his heel and walked towards the still kneeling woman, machete swinging in his hand.

How the inspector wished Hanif had come armed with something other than insufficiently persuasive words. How long would it take Harris to get here? What was the delay? Singh needed to buy time.

'I know who killed your sister.' His voice was weak, barely audible. He said again, 'I know who killed your sister.'

He had their attention.

'Who did it?' demanded Ibrahim. 'Who killed Fatima?'

'Not just your sister, but another woman as well.'

'The one from last week?' Hanif asked the question.

'No, another body was found. But the victim was killed around a week after your sister.'

'Tell me who did it,' demanded Ibrahim, 'so that I can avenge my sister when I am done with God's work today.'

'The solution to every difficulty is not murder,' snapped Hanif.

Singh adjusted his position. His head was clear now despite the pain, but that didn't make the situation any more tenable. He knew without looking at her that his wife was watching him, hoping no doubt that he had a plan.

'Who did it?' demanded Ibrahim.

'Don't you know? Can't you guess?'

'Just tell us!'

'Raj.'

'Raj – her boss?' Mrs Singh was still participating as if this was some sort of slightly fraught dinner party.

'I don't believe you,' said Ibrahim, white-faced.

'Why would he do something like that?' asked Hanif.

'Fatima discovered that Raj Real Estate was a front for a money-laundering operation. She believed that Kendrick, her boyfriend, might be wrongly implicated in Raj's crimes.'

'Kendrick? Innocent? He was born steeped in original sin,' said Hanif.

'I couldn't agree more,' said Singh.

'She warned Kendrick?'

'No, but her best friend Sara, whom she told, did.'

'Sara – the one who was having an affair on the side with him?'

The policeman nodded. 'I spoke to her earlier today and she confirmed it. She was and is convinced of his innocence. Unfortunately, the lawyer was knee-deep in the scheme. Kendrick feared Fatima would go to the police so Raj faked a call from the non-existent Mrs Hamid and sent her to an empty house. Kendrick was waiting.'

Even in this moment of his impending death, Singh was smug. 'Raj never takes calls from clients, you see. He's too big and important – in his own eyes – for that. When I heard that he claimed to take the call from the so-called Mrs Hamid, I was suspicious already. I just couldn't work out a motive or a chain of events until more recently.'

'No, it's not possible! I don't believe you.'

'Because you're now working with Raj to use Khan's to launder money?'

Ibrahim's expression was unfathomable because of his face wrap but his shifting stance suggested guilt.

'You are almost irredeemably stupid, brother.'

'Shut your trap, why don't you?'

'Why would you do that? Why would you get involved in such a crooked scheme?'

'We needed the money – the restaurant was going bust. I'd been using a lot of the cash flow to work on … on this sort of thing, this sort of plan.'

'I thought you might have a gambling habit.'

'Your low opinion of me has never been justified, Hanif.'

347

'I wouldn't say that, brother.'

What was this? Circle time?

'And it is money from Iraq and Syria that we are bringing into the country – at the same time as saving the business, I am doing God's work.'

'Your god requires you to launder money? Manna from heaven isn't what it used to be, eh?' Singh was determined to keep Ibrahim off balance.

'You went into business with the men who killed our beloved sister. The pain in my heart knows no bounds.'

Ibrahim was sobbing now. 'I will punish them, I promise. I will avenge Fatima.'

How long would it take Harris and gang to get to him? Might they be, even now, surrounding the building? Or was he alone with two women, one reformed but unarmed jihadi and a madman with a gun and a blade?

'My husband is wrong, of course.'

Even now, in such a situation, with minutes left in their lives, their marriage, their very existence, his wife was prepared to contradict him?

'Of course I'm right,' insisted Singh.

'Why would Raj or Kendrick attack *other* women and cut off their hands too if it was just to keep their dirty little secret?'

The brothers' eyes flicked between the husband and wife team as if they were playing a long tennis rally.

'That's right,' said Hanif. 'It doesn't explain the other women. Only Fatima.'

'That is the genius and the cruelty.'

Harris and Carmen had disbelieved his theory too until

348

they'd seen that it was plausible if one allowed for a pit of darkness in the human soul.

'They did it to ensure that suspicion didn't fall on them. They disguised Fatima's killing as a violent, unhinged affair and then killed another woman, randomly selected, a week later to suggest a pattern to the police, send them on a wild goose chase.'

The police had been sceptical when Singh had propounded his theory and then they'd come around. But the inspector had misled them as to the identity of the killer, pointing the finger at Ibrahim, just to find his wife. And it had worked – sort of – if being in her company and getting killed at the same time was some sort of achievement.

'Why the hands?' asked Mrs Singh.

'Why not the hands? A hit of madness, a dash of religious extremism; perfect for their purpose.'

He was glad that he'd told DI Carmen the whole truth, sent her to look for evidence. If they didn't make it out of there, he didn't want to think the two men would escape.

'But you said the third body was just discovered?' asked Hanif.

'Best laid plans,' agreed Singh. 'The weather and a river conspired to hide the remains for five years until a recent storm. And, as it happened, they'd overestimated the investigative abilities of the police – they never came close to solving Fatima's murder, never suspected either Raj or Kendrick. There was no need for red herrings.'

'But what about the woman killed last week?'

'A copycat killing,' said Singh. 'That was a copycat killing.'

*

Choudary returned, holding another electronic device in his hand. Singh had bought some time, Hanif had tried to persuade his brother to abandon his plan – neither had been sufficient.

'Are we ready? There is no more time to waste.'

So this was the mastermind behind the operation. From his manner and accent, he was posher than the Indian newscasters but not as posh as the Queen.

'We must get the video online as soon as possible to maintain credibility,' he continued. 'It was due yesterday.'

The twenty-first century, where jihadist operations were run like businesses. Twenty-four-seven.

'I will do it,' said Hanif. 'It is what I said; why I asked for a delay in the killing of that woman.' He nodded dismissively in the direction of Mary Jane Houseman.

'I remember your enthusiasm for the cause,' said Choudary. 'Very well, I have no objection.'

Ibrahim was staring at his brother open-mouthed. 'But you said . . .'

'But nothing, brother. We are in this together. I was just testing your resolve and you have proven a loyal servant to the cause.'

Hanif grabbed a piece of black cloth from the table and wrapped his face and head. The inspector watched him. Had he decided to save himself, live to fight another day? There was no way out for any of them, the odds were against them, and Hanif had already made it clear he didn't have a taste for martyrdom. Or perhaps Hanif really *had* been testing his brother.

It could even be that in some convoluted holy way he was

trying to take the sin of murder away from his flesh and blood by committing the act himself.

Mrs Singh had fallen silent. Was she aware that she was about to witness an act of profound brutality? And that she was most likely next? All things considered, that was not something the policeman from Singapore felt able to witness, the death of his wife. Maybe one day it would have been all right, in her old age, as he sat by her bed and held her hand while she drifted away, but not here, not like this.

Unfortunately, as far as he could see, there was only one way to avoid that outcome.

'I should be the first,' said the inspector.

'What are you saying?' screeched his wife.

'I should be the first. It is fitting. I am the man.'

CHAPTER 20

'Very well,' said Hanif, before either of the others could dispute the suggestion. 'It shall be as you say.'

He ran up to Mary Jane Houseman, dragged her to her feet roughly and pushed her away from the front. She stumbled and fell and lay where she had fallen. There was no more fight in her, not even any relief at this briefest of respites.

Hanif walked across to his brother and held out his hand for the machete. Ibrahim withdrew the gun from his belt and said *sotto voce*, 'In case you have *another* change of heart.'

His brother didn't blink, merely waited until the blade handle had been slapped into his palm.

'I need to carry out the purification rituals,' Hanif said, turning to Choudary.

'There is no time. Allah will forgive you.'

Hanif shrugged, crouched down by Singh, slashed the bonds around his ankles and hands and then yanked him to his feet. The world spun and then righted itself. The other man pushed him forward and the inspector took a few unsteady steps.

He was almost out of time. His wife watched him, as silent as she had ever been in their marriage, and he saw that there were tears spilling down her cheeks. She did not protest any more. Perhaps she recognised the inevitability. Mary Houseman mouthed 'thank you', which was sweet but premature. As things stood, he'd extended her life by about ten minutes at most. Ibrahim remained alert, wary, unconvinced by his brother, suspicious of his loyalties, gun steady in his hand.

Where was Harris?

There was a certain irony, thought Singh dismally, that in the company of all these would-be martyrs, he was going to be the first to die, the Sydney Carton of the story. He cast a last look at his wife and winked; had she spotted the Dickensian air to this ending?

Another shove in the back from Hanif, a few more steps forward. Could he walk any slower? At any moment, Ibrahim was going to leap forward, grab the machete and have a go at him. How were they going to pick up his head by his hair and brandish it for the world to see online when he wore a turban?

Where was bloody Harris?

Singh remembered the closing lines of *A Tale of Two Cities*. 'It is a far, far better thing that I do, than I have ever done; it is a far, far better rest that I go to than I have ever known.'

He was between Ibrahim and Hanif now, between a blade and a gun, a rock and a hard place. The moment of his supreme sacrifice was nigh.

'Bollocks to Dickens,' muttered Singh and went for the gun.

CHAPTER 21

Chaos ensued.

He didn't reach Ibrahim's gun in time. The shot reverberated through the room like a tidal wave. Inspector Singh felt his ear sting, but it was as distant as an out-of-body experience. He crashed into the youngest brother and they both hit the floor hard.

Another shot rang out. This time he felt nothing.

The gun skittered across the floor.

Another shot.

Hanif fell to the ground next to him. He'd taken a bullet meant for Singh.

In that instant, the policeman realised that Choudary was armed too and a competent shot. He should have guessed; these guys always had their training camp experience to fall back on.

On the other hand, what difference did it make? It was not like he had a plan B.

Ibrahim, scrambling across the floor, had reached his gun; he grabbed it, whirled around and trained it on Singh.

In that moment he wasted smiling at his inevitable victory, Singh rolled to one side, grabbed the blade that Hanif had dropped and slashed backwards, a reverse sweep shot that would have graced Lord's.

Even as he registered that both the gun and the gun hand were now separated from Ibrahim, blood spurting from his wrist like water from a burst water main, a third shot rang out and the cement floor fragmented next to him; sharp pinpricks of pain on his face suggested he'd been showered with fine debris.

Close.

The inspector raised himself on an elbow and noted that Choudary's hands were steady. That was the problem with these godly types; they were so damned self-righteous that the usual shakes didn't affect them. Singh knew Choudary would not miss a second time.

Ibrahim moaned and staggered to his feet, staring at his truncated forearm in horror.

Singh met his wife's eyes and shrugged. It had been worth a try.

At least he'd gone down fighting, not on his knees before these cowards, mouthing prepared scripts.

And then the cavalry arrived.

Windows were smashed simultaneously. The door kicked in with force. Flash bangs first, through the openings. The sound was deafening, the light blinded Singh immediately. But he knew what it was, guessed who it was, so he dropped flat to avoid any crossfire and hoped his wife and Mary Jane would have the sense to do the same.

Many hours later, his ear was patched, his stomach patched, his head patched, hospital food had been eaten with reluctance and his wife was asleep in a chair by his hospital bed. He drifted in and out of sleep, either the shock or the medication taking a toll.

He was awake though when DCI Harris and DI Carmen walked in, both smiling.

Singh pressed a button on the control panel of the bed and waited until he was raised to a sitting position. It was all he felt he had the strength to do. He was hurting in parts he didn't know he had.

'What took you so long?' he demanded.

'Now or then?'

'Then! I almost got my head cut off, for God's sake.'

'London traffic – you should be used to it by now,' said Harris.

'We did get there in the nick of time,' pointed out Carmen.

'Yes, you did and I'm very grateful.'

'It was quite straightforward as far as these operations go. Ibrahim was too badly injured to understand what was going on when the stun grenades were lobbed in. All the hostages were on the ground, so there was no real danger to any of you.'

'Choudary?'

'Choudary had no inclination to see his own blood spilled; he didn't fire a shot. I hear he's hiring expensive lawyers as we speak.'

'I assume there's at least one expensive lawyer in London who's not available to take the brief?'

DI Carmen laughed.

'So it was Raj and Kendrick?' asked Harris. 'Not Ibrahim like you insisted.'

'Sorry,' he muttered. 'I needed to find my wife and it was the only way to persuade you to hunt down Ibrahim.'

'Just as well,' said Harris. He wasn't going to hold a grudge. Not when he was taking most of the credit for having solved a string of murders as well as a foiled terrorist plot.

'DI Carmen told you the rest?' asked the inspector.

'Yes, we've arrested them both.'

'And they're lawyering up too?'

'I've got them in separate cells and offered the first one to talk a deal to be tried as an accomplice rather than the main man. They're both singing like canaries, blaming the other.'

'Well done,' said Singh. 'What about Cynthia Cole?'

'We found the severed hands in a locker at Victoria Station. The key was in Martin Bradley's pocket when he went under the train. You were right; it was a copycat killing. How did you know?'

'The little grey cells?' Singh's fake Belgian accent caused both police personnel to wince.

'A more detailed explanation?'

'I thought it might be because Bradley was familiar with the Fatima case through working with Regina. And he was a man obviously on edge. I knew it for certain when he attacked Regina. He shouted, "I'm going to kill you, just like I did her. No one betrays me, no one!"'

'What a loon.'

'I can't help feeling sorry for him. Unrequited love, unfulfilled lust, a cold case for inspiration . . . he just wanted to be happy.'

His wife stirred in her chair but didn't wake.

'Is she all right?' asked Carmen.

'She will be,' said Singh. He hoped it was true. He had great faith in the resilience of his wife, but he'd certainly tested it to the fullest.

'Hanif?'

'He was gone by the time we tried to resuscitate, shot by Choudary in the original melee.'

So this London tale had required a martyr after all. He sighed for Hanif, but also for the other young men looking for meaning in all the wrong places. 'He saved all of us,' he said. 'He was a true hero.'

'Yes, when he came back from Syria under express instructions to wage war on the homeland, he contacted our secret services immediately and promised to tell them what he found out. They've been in touch with him all along. That's why they told us nobodies at Homicide to keep our distance.'

'But why did he not tell them about this plot then?' asked Carmen. 'Did he have second thoughts about helping the authorities?'

'Only because he discovered Ibrahim was involved. Hanif felt that he had to try and save him,' said Singh. 'I guess he thought it was too much of a betrayal to inform on his own flesh and blood, not without trying to pull Ibrahim back from the precipice anyway.'

'A wasted effort,' said Harris.

'Yes,' agreed Singh, replaying the conversations in his head, Hanif begging Ibrahim to abandon their plan.

'Ibrahim will spend the rest of his days rotting in jail.'

'I hope he finds time for regret,' said Carmen and he knew from the twist to her mouth that she was thinking of Fatima and Hanif, more evidence of a world in which the good guys finished last . . . or dead.

Singh stuck a fat finger on the control panel, lowered his bed once more. He needed to be alone with his thoughts. The two coppers took the hint, shook his hand and turned to leave.

'I almost forgot,' said Harris. 'Here's your phone. It was found at the site.'

Singh switched it on and read the final text from Harris: 'Hanif on the side of the angels.'

'How did you know? When did you find out?'

'I called the anti-terror boys once more to tell them that Hanif might be on his way to Syria again – this time they came clean.'

'Did you see the message in time?' Carmen asked Singh.

He shook his head. 'Dropped the bloody phone just before. It didn't matter. I knew anyway.'

Hanif had been on the side of the angels, and flights of angels would sing him to his rest.

Of that Singh was certain.

EPILOGUE

They stopped at the old man's stall on the way to Heathrow. His turban was gargantuan but his smile, when he saw them, was genuine.

'I see that you have located your wife,' he said.

'Thanks to you,' said Singh.

'I am always happy to be of assistance to a brother in trouble. A wife belongs at her husband's side, not chasing after good-looking young men.'

Mrs Singh picked up a tea towel that read, 'My husband went to London and all I got was this lousy tea towel.'

That and a few mental scars to last a lifetime, thought the inspector.

But Mrs Singh was made of sterner stuff. She cast it aside in favour of a snow globe featuring Westminster Abbey.

The purveyor of tat leaned forward on his stool. 'Wise choice, sister. And only the best price for you, of course.'

'I'll take it,' said Mrs Singh, smiling.